THE STEPSON

JANE RENSHAW

INKUBATOR
BOOKS

Published by Inkubator Books
www.inkubatorbooks.com

ISBN (Paperback): 978-1-915275-00-4
ISBN (eBook): 978-1-915275-01-1

Jane Renshaw has asserted her right to be identified as the author of this work.

THE STEPSON is a work of fiction. People, places, events, and situations are the product of the author's imagination. Any resemblance to actual persons, living or dead is entirely coincidental.

PROLOGUE

CAROL - NOVEMBER 1997

Later, in her statement to the police, Carol Jardine would say she had no inkling, as she swung her car off the little country road and onto the drive, that anything was wrong.

Then Nick leaned forward from the back seat and said, 'That's weird – why aren't there any lights on?'

Sunnyside was in darkness, the only illumination provided by the car headlights as they swept the short avenue of trees that led up the slope to the house. It was November, so the trees were pale grey and skeletal. Carol hated this time of year, when you turned round and suddenly all the trees had lost their leaves and the fields had been ploughed and autumn was tipping fast into winter, short dank days and long dark nights.

There was nothing necessarily sinister about the lack of lights.

'Maybe they've had to pop out,' she suggested as she pressed her foot to the accelerator.

'Could have been a power cut,' her son Andy, Nick's best friend, contributed from the back seat.

But the houses they'd just passed on the road had been cheerily aglow.

And if Duncan and Maggie had just popped out, why hadn't they left lights on for Nick, knowing that, by the time Carol brought him back from their day out in Edinburgh, the sun would long have left the sky?

Sunnyside – such a ridiculous name for this hulking mass of a Victorian monstrosity that turned not its grand frontage but its higgledy-piggledy rear end to the world, the jutting one-storey wings that housed the old kitchen and the pantry and the warren of little rooms that would once have been the dairy and the laundry room and the scullery. Usually the three kitchen windows would have been lit up, casting a warm yellow glow out into the night. And not just the kitchen windows. Maggie never bothered to turn off the lights when she left a room, so there were usually bright windows all over the place, as if poor Duncan were made of money – which from Maggie's point of view, of course, he was.

But tonight, nothing.

No lights at all.

'Were they planning on going out?' she asked Nick as she edged the car round the side of the house to the huge front door. 'Maybe they've been delayed?'

'No.' She could hear the tension, now, in his voice. 'They weren't going anywhere, as far as I know. And there's the car. If they've gone out, they must have gone on foot. And they wouldn't, would they, in the dark? Not with Isla?'

Almost before she'd brought the car to a halt on the sweep of gravel at the front of the house, Nick was out and running to the door.

Something made her say, 'Stay here' to Andy as she fumbled with her seat belt. 'I'm going to lock you in. I mean it, Andy. Stay right here and don't move.'

The hall sprang into being as Nick flicked the switches

and all the wall lights came on, illuminating the cavernous square space with all those doors and the elegant staircase twisting up to . . . No, Carol wasn't going to think about that, about Kathleen falling from up there.

'Dad?' Nick suddenly shouted, the word bouncing back at them from the far recesses of the hall. '*Dad?*'

The boy's handsome face was drained of colour in the sudden brightness, the adolescent softness transfigured into sharp angles and hollows under the wing of dark hair that flopped across his forehead. He pushed it back absently.

'Where are they?' he half-whispered.

And then he was running again, snapping on lights, throwing open doors, drafts hitting Carol from all sides as she trailed him – Carol wasn't built for speed – through the high-ceilinged rooms. It was still Kathleen's house. She was still everywhere here, in the restored fireplaces, the carefully chosen muted, authentic colours, the tasteful antiques and the chintzy armchairs and sofas.

She followed him along the panelled corridor to the kitchen.

Country house style, as Kathleen had called it.

Maggie wouldn't know country house style if she met it in her soup.

But at least the woman hadn't tried to put her own stamp on the place. It was all just as it had been in Kathleen's time, except for things like the David Bowie tea towel draped over the rail of the pale-blue Belling cooker and the orangey-pine rocking chair in which Maggie fed Isla. Clustered around the huge steriliser on the worktop were bottles of various sizes, the bottle warmer, the milk powder dispenser, and even the brush for cleaning them and the teat tongs, clutter Kathleen would have consigned to a drawer.

And there was Bunny, the mad-eyed grey rabbit Isla was always sucking on. He was lying on the floor by the fridge.

Carol bent and picked him up and thought of little Isla, just two months old. Despite being Maggie's, she was a sweet baby, like a little doll with that round face and big blue eyes.

Carol's back was prickling with shivers, although the room wasn't cold.

In fact, the kitchen was hot.

Very hot.

And then she saw the glowing red circle on the top of the Belling.

'The hob's on,' she said aloud, although Nick wasn't in the room. She could hear him moving about in the warren behind the kitchen. 'Nick! The hob's on!'

He appeared at a run, skidding to a halt next to her, staring, as she was, at that red circle. She put her hand over it, feeling the heat radiating out. And sitting on the worktop next to it was a pan filled with water and an open bag of oatmeal.

'Why were they making porridge?' said Nick. He turned and crossed the room to the table. 'And look. Three mugs, with half-drunk tea in them. And three bowls.' He picked one up and turned it over. 'Three empty bowls, for the porridge, I guess. Three spoons.'

'It looks like they were making breakfast,' Carol blurted, but managed to stop herself completing the thought out loud: *when something happened.*

'But we'd had breakfast. We'd cleared up the breakfast stuff. And why are there *three* mugs and *three* bowls? Isla isn't even on solids yet. And she doesn't drink *tea!*' He was staring at Carol now, as if she could help, as if she would have answers. 'Someone else was here. Who else was here?' And then his face collapsed, and she was reaching for him and he was shaking his head and backing off and oh, it was heartbreaking, watching him try to master himself, try to face this latest crisis in his short life.

'We need to call the police,' he choked. 'I *knew* something like this was going to happen. I've been trying to tell Dad – ever since Maggie moved in, I've been trying to tell him . . . get him to see what she's really like. But he wouldn't listen. And now she's *killed them*!'

'Oh, Nick, *no!*'

Finally, he let Carol pull him into a hug as he wailed: '*She has!* She's *killed* Dad and Isla!'

1

Lulu Clyde ignored the buzzing of her phone that heralded yet another text, got up from her chair and perched on the coffee table in front of Paul, her client. She needed to be close enough to perform the procedure but not so close as to invade his personal space. Her heart bumped as the familiar dread descended, but she spoke calmly and quietly. 'I want you to think about that day.' And as she saw his face change: 'No, no, don't worry. The *second* you feel uncomfortable, the *second* you want to stop, we'll stop. Okay?'

After a beat: 'I suppose.'

He was such an ordinary-looking man. Pushing forty, average height and build, mousy brown hair, pleasant, forgettable face. If you saw him in the street, walking along with his little dog, you would never guess that he carried a whole world of anger around inside him, day after day after day.

'Do you trust me?'

This time, the answer was immediate: 'Yes.'

'I'm not going to let anything bad happen to you. You're safe here.'

He was safe.

She had to keep reminding herself of that.

Here wasn't anywhere special: a small, rectangular, pale-green space with a really inspiring view of a brick wall. At the other end of the room were a desk and chair, and at this end, two comfy beige armchairs with a glass coffee table between them on which sat, in addition to Lulu herself, a jug of iced water and two glasses, a box of tissues from Tesco and a stunted maidenhair fern. On the wall behind the desk were her framed certificates, her Bachelor of Science from the University of Melbourne and her Master of Psychotherapy and Counselling from Western Sydney University.

Next to this room were a tiny kitchenette and a toilet.

And that was it.

Her office.

The place where miracles happened – although that made it sound like she had a God complex, and she wasn't deluded enough to think that the miracles were down to her. It was the clients, her brave, brave clients, who made them happen.

She was only the catalyst.

'I don't want Milo here,' Paul said suddenly, turning to look at the little dog who sat, so patiently, next to his chair.

Milo's stubby tail swished the carpet as he looked up at his owner with trusting brown eyes. He was a Jack Russell crossed with something hairy, an ugly little thing really, she supposed, but Lulu found him very cute. He had been in the dog shelter for months, apparently, with no takers, until her client had given him a home. Now they were inseparable, and Lulu suspected that Milo was a much more effective therapist than she was.

'Take him through to the kitchen,' she suggested. 'The bowl is in the cupboard under the sink if you want to give him some water.'

Several of her clients had emotional support dogs.

'Come on then, buddy. Ooh, what has Dad got here?' A grubby plastic object appeared from the bag at his feet. 'It's Piggy! It's *Piggy*, Milo!'

Milo trotted off happily with his 'dad', who told him he wouldn't be long and that Milo had to be a good boy and not chew anything but Piggy.

And then he was back, and there was no putting it off any longer.

Lulu took a deep breath. 'Let yourself think about that day. The sights and smells, the sounds, what you're doing, what's around you. Let the memories come. Narrate what you're experiencing, if you can. And as you're doing that, I'm going to slowly move my finger in front of your right eye. I want you to focus on my finger as you're remembering. Just go with the flow, and let's see where it takes us.'

It took them, as she had known it would, to a dark place.

A place Lulu really, really didn't want to go to. But she did. She went there with him, she grounded him in the present, and, as he relived the horror of that day, as Paul's face contorted unrecognisably and the anger threatened to rise up and overwhelm him, Lulu calmly told him to notice this or that image, to notice the anger; to let it in, to make space for it, to give it its due. And all the while, she slowly moved her finger in front of his eye and concentrated on making the movement smooth, on not letting her hand shake, and watched him watching it, staying in the present with her while he processed and filed away the terrible thing that had happened all those years ago.

EMDR, it was called – eye movement desensitisation and reprocessing. It involved moving your finger in front of the client's eye like a cartoon hypnotist, which seemed silly, but it worked. It was all about examining the traumatic memories from a place of safety in the present and filing them in the past where they belonged, in the vault of memory, so they weren't constantly accessible on a replay loop in the person's head. So they weren't constantly interfering with day-to-day life, reactivating negative emotions. It was about turning a constantly relived experience into something that had been terrible, yes, *so terrible*, but was over and done.

He was breathing fast.

Sweat was pouring from his hairline into his eyes.

You poor, poor man.

Lulu felt dizzy with the horror of it.

How could he possibly ever get over this?

She handed him the box of tissues, but she knew better than to try to pour him a glass of water. It was as if, now that she had stopped the finger movement, her hands felt they had permission to start shaking.

Stop thinking about it.

Her mentor at uni, Professor Karla Szubanski, had once told her, 'I have to teach a lot of my students how to empathise. But you're at the other extreme – you're going to have to learn to take a step back. Gain some objectivity.'

Easier said than done.

'Let's take a break,' Lulu said, managing to keep her voice level. 'I'll just – I'll just go and check on Milo.'

And she fled from the room. In the kitchen, Milo greeted her like a long-lost friend, and she sank to her knees and buried her face in his wiry coat.

'Oh, Milo.'

She granted herself a few seconds of comfort from the little animal as Milo licked the tears from her cheeks, before giving him a final pat, splashing water on her face and towelling it dry. She threw Piggy for Milo to chase, and then she returned to the room.

Paul was sitting back in the chair, looking dazed. 'That was – intense.'

She nodded.

'But when I think about it now, what happened . . .' His face suddenly cleared. 'It's not like *I'm actually back there*, you know? It's like I'm thinking about what happened in a film I once watched.' Tentatively, he smiled at her.

She felt a huge smile lifting her lips in response. 'That's great! It means you're starting to consign it to the past. The memories will still be there, but that's all they'll be – memories.' *Oh, this was so great!* And now tears were threatening again, but just at that moment there was another ping, giving her an excuse to turn away from him and go to her desk, pick up her phone and study the screen.

Damn. It was already past five o'clock.

She had six new texts from her husband.

They texted each other throughout the day, and when one of his messages pinged in after a harrowing session, often she felt like a drowning person grabbing a lifeline snaking through cyberspace. Even if it was just a silly description of his lunch or a colleague's bad hair day, each text was a tiny, just-for-her reminder that *Life is good, life is good, life is good.*

But the last one was asking why she wasn't replying to his messages.

Was she OK? Was she on her way?

She was supposed to be meeting him at the restaurant at 5:30 before going on to the National Theatre. They were seeing a play called *Why Pigeons do Backflips*, the ridiculousness appealing to both their weird senses of humour. It would take at least half an hour to get across town to the South Bank, even if she managed to snag a taxi straight away. But she couldn't stop now, right in the middle of a breakthrough.

She fired off a quick text:

*Won't make the restaurant. You go ahead and I'll meet you
at the theatre. Sorry!!! xxx*

Completing the session took another half hour. When it
was over, Lulu went to the loo for another brief cry, grimacing
at her puffy face in the mirror. She let down her long fall of
blonde hair and tugged a brush through it a few times, and
pinned her favourite enamel brooch to her dress, the one
Mum and Dad had given her for her twenty-first. The bright
pink and soft grey tones of the galah's plumage worked well
with the darker grey silk of the dress. She applied a little
make-up to her eyes and lips. Then she collected her jacket
and bag and ushered dog and client from the office.

As she was scrabbling in her bag for the key to lock the
office door – she had a talent both for losing keys and for
accumulating random ones in the bottom of her bag – Paul
said, 'It's like it's just hit me – *Why?* Why have I been so
angry? I mean, Dad's dead. And it wasn't even his fault.'

This was fantastic.

She took a moment to think carefully about what to say.
'PTSD isn't logical. You've held on to the anger because
you've been holding on to that angry child inside, all these
years. You've *been* that angry child.'

'Well, not any more.' And as he looked at her, he started
to smile, and it was like she could see inside his head, it was
like she was there with him as the past started to fall away
and his mind broke free of it, as he began to see the limitless
possibilities of the present, of the rest of his life stretching
ahead of him. 'I'm going to get back in touch with Samantha,'
he whispered, as if this were too incredible a prospect to bear
close scrutiny.

Oh my goodness!

This was why she did it. This was why she put herself
through it.

But neither of them should be getting carried away here. So she said, 'Okay, yes, you're making great, *great* progress, but baby steps? I'd hold off on contacting Samantha until we're a little further –'

'Aha!' The exclamation rang through the lobby, and there he was, striding towards them across the maroon carpet tiles, Saville Row come to Hammersmith. He lent the shabby space the glamour-by-proxy he seemed to take with him everywhere, like he was some kind of celebrity.

Her husband.

He'd come for her! He would know, of course, how drained the marathon session would leave her, how unequal to the task of finding her way across London she would be feeling.

She ran to him.

And now he was catching her in his arms and laughing, and she was back in her own wonderful world, the world he made afresh for her each day. It was as if he waved a magic wand and *whoosh*, all the rest was gone, all the dark places she travelled to with her clients. They'd just been a bad dream, and now she was awake again.

And she would have this, if she was lucky, for the rest of her life. The thought that *he was hers and she was his, forever and ever, amen*, still made her want to shout with joy.

He gave her an exaggerated smack of a kiss, and she clung to him, hardly able to believe that he was real, that she had found him, her soulmate, this man who looked like a film star and was rather vain about the fact and knew it, sending himself up at every opportunity.

'Enter stage left: the doting husband,' he intoned, 'who's just endured half an hour of casual racism, courtesy of an infeasibly stereotypical London cabbie, to rush to his wife's side with life-saving falafels.' Lulu's favourite food in the world and also, spookily, one of his. 'Your chauffeur awaits, ready, willing and able to blow your mind with his views on immigration.' He lowered his voice to a stage whisper: 'Best not to admit to being Australian.' And then, back in character, he swept an arm around the lobby. 'I've come to take you away from all this! I've come to whisk you off to la-la land where, for two shining hours, a load of luvvies will get deep and meaningful about the psychiatric issues of pigeons! Oh, the agony! Oh, the ecstasy!'

Milo was yipping excitedly.

'Idiot.' She laughed, pushing her husband away and rolling her eyes at Paul, who was staring at this apparition in rather wary bemusement. 'Paul, this is my husband, Nick. Nick, one of my clients, Paul.'

The two men nodded at each other.

Then Nick said, deadpan, 'So you're the man responsible for starving my wife.'

'Oh,' said poor Paul. 'I'm sorry, Lulu. I didn't realise you had plans.' He stooped to pick up Milo and looked at his watch. 'Oh, God – I've gone way over my time, haven't I? I'm sorry!'

Lulu smiled. 'It was completely down to me that we continued so long. There's nothing to apologise for.'

She'd forgotten to lock the office door. She left the three of them on the doorstep to do so, but when she came back out, she couldn't find the main door key.

'Why don't you keep them on the same ring, darling?' Nick murmured.

'That would be far too sensible. Ah, here it is!' She locked the door behind them. 'Well, same time next week, Paul? And Milo, of course?'

Paul set Milo down on the pavement and looked at Lulu for a long moment. Then he nodded. And then he was pulling her into a hug.

'Thank you,' he said into her hair. 'I don't know how to thank you. You've literally saved my life.'

Lulu didn't look at Nick, but she knew he'd be wearing a look of terrible patience. Nick's theory was that all the nuances of mental health issues were 'just a big con' invented by the woke brigade, while anyone with actual, genuine problems was 'a nutter'. It was one of the few subjects of contention between them, but she hadn't pushed it because she knew what was at the root of it. She knew he had a real horror of mental illness because of what had happened to his family, and he felt safer pretending there was a simple dichotomy of nutter versus normal.

She hugged Paul back. Physical contact with clients was generally frowned upon, but sometimes they hugged her, and Lulu was fine with that. When emotions were running high, sometimes a bit of human contact was what you needed.

She patted his back and said a few reassuring words, and gently detached herself.

'You're doing really well. You should be very proud of yourself.'

Paul gave her a rueful smile and dabbed at his face with a tissue. Then he turned, unexpectedly, to Nick. 'You should have seen me a month ago. My wife had just left me. I was a mess.'

You are a mess, said Nick's raised eyebrows. But he just murmured, 'Sorry to hear that.'

'I put my wife through hell – I don't blame her, she was better off out of it. She'd been trying to persuade me to get help with my anger for years, but it took her leaving me before I actually got up off my arse and did something about it. The day I came to Lulu was the best day of my life.' He looked at Lulu, his eyes moist with tears. 'I can't thank you enough, for what you've done for me.' He turned back to Nick. 'You're a lucky man. A lucky, lucky man.'

·   ·   ·

'*I'M A LUCKY, LUCKY MAN!*' Nick whispered in the silence of the darkened auditorium, walking his hand up under the hem of Lulu's dress, his fingertips on her bare skin sending desire shooting through her.

'*Not that lucky,*' Lulu hissed back, pushing the hand away, and the two of them giggled like a couple of teenagers.

The woman in the seat in front of Nick turned to glare at them. With her thick, short grey hair and penetrating gaze, she reminded Lulu of her Auntie May, who was never happier than when issuing reprimands to the neighbourhood kids.

'Sorry – I know, we're a nightmare,' Nick murmured with his trademark self-deprecating grimace. 'You might want to call security to throw us out.'

The woman's face relaxed in a reluctant smile as she turned back to the stage.

When the lights came up at the interval, Nick leaned forward between the seats and said, 'I feel I should offer to do penance. Let me buy you a drink. What's your tipple? No, let me guess – red? Merlot, if they have it?'

The woman laughed. 'That's really not necessary. Very kind, but not necessary.'

In the end, of course, she let Nick buy her a glass of Merlot, and a beer for her partner, and he came back with the drinks and a handful of bags of peanuts and crisps. 'Rustle away in retaliation,' he suggested.

The woman twinkled at him. 'Don't think we won't!' And she raised her plastic cup in an impish toast.

IT WAS A LOVELY, soft May night, and they decided to walk the five miles along the Thames from the South Bank to Chelsea Harbour. Outside the theatre, Lulu slipped on her Skechers and tucked her arm through Nick's. She never got tired of walking the streets of London. For a girl from Leonora, the buzz was incredible, the feeling of being right at the centre of things. Across the River Thames, through the line of old street lights along the Embankment, were Big Ben and the Palace of Westminster, all lit up and unreal-looking.

She let go Nick's arm and danced ahead, breathing in the sweet, rotten smell of the river flowing, as it had always flowed, through this dirty, noisy, self-important, wonderful city. Then she turned and danced backwards a few steps, watching him striding after her. She knew she wouldn't feel this way about London if she didn't have him to share it with. God, he was *so gorgeous!* Her Cath Kidston bag, bright yellow and covered in bees, looked ludicrous slung over the shoulder of his made-to-measure suit jacket, but he was such a gentleman that he would never dream of letting her carry her own bag while he carried nothing. He might joke about his vanity, but he never let it get in the way of being a decent guy.

'You're such a charmer,' she gurgled, taking his arm. 'That lady in the theatre practically asked for your phone number.'

He grinned, flicking back his Hugh Grant hair. 'She was only human.'

'I reckon her name is Irma. She's a retired doctor but she's always wanted to be an actress. She lives in St John's Wood with her boring husband Jeremy, but the man she was with tonight was her lover – her lover Eduardo.'

'One of them,' said Nick. 'Her regular Friday night date. Eduardo challenges Irma's sense of propriety. He'll wait until the auditorium has emptied and then before she knows it they'll be having sex on the stage.'

She shouted with laughter. Nick was *the best* at this. Ever since she'd been a lonely little girl on Braemar Station, stuck out there in the bush with two bratty little brothers, ten miles from Leonora and all her friends, she had made up stories about the people she encountered: the farm workers on the station, the vet, the guy who came selling feed, the people in the cars that trundled past the pickup on the school run in annoyingly obscuring orange dust clouds.

It had been a solitary pleasure – until Nick.

As it had been a solitary pleasure for him. He said he used to do the same thing as a teenager as a way, she supposed, of trying to control a world that had spiralled into chaos. And she used to think *she* was lonely! She couldn't bear to think of him, the boy he had been, left all alone. She wanted to reach back through time and grab him into her arms.

'What would I do without you?' She sighed, leaning her head against his shoulder as they walked, slipping her hand up inside the lean, solid muscularity of his upper arm.

He squeezed her hand against his side. 'Bad day at work?'

He always knew.

'Not bad, exactly, but . . . difficult, I suppose.'

'Are they ever anything else?'

Lulu sighed again. 'Nothing worth doing is easy. Isn't that an inspirational quote I've read somewhere? But today definitely ended on a high. Paul's making really, *really* good progress.' She shouldn't be telling him that, though.

Silence for a few steps. Then: 'Lu, I'm not sure I like the idea of your being alone with someone with "anger management" problems, as you'd probably describe them. What did he do to his wife? He referred to putting her through hell – is that a euphemism for "I'm a psycho who beats up women"?'

She longed to tell him no, Paul had never been physically violent to Samantha, but she couldn't betray client confidentiality to reassure Nick on this point. 'I can't talk about my clients. But you don't need to worry about Paul.'

'The guy's a creep. The way he looked at you . . . And he *hugged* you, for God's sake. You're always so concerned about playing by the rules, but surely that's not allowed? Pawing the therapist, like some kind of sex offender?' He stopped walking and turned her to face him. '*Is* he a sex offender?'

'Paul isn't dangerous in any way,' she said levelly. 'Not everyone with a mental health problem is potentially violent. If that were the case, half the population would have to be locked up.' Here was her chance to nudge him towards all the things he didn't want to talk about, but she knew not to push it, that he'd back right off if she did. So she contented herself with, 'Mental health problems are very, very common.'

'Oh, I know it's fashionable to have one. But this Paul guy – he really seems obsessed with you. The day he met you was the best day of his life? Combine that with the fact he's a psycho –'

'He's not a "psycho"!'

Nick moved his hands on her shoulders, rubbing warmth into them, making her realise for the first time that the night air was a little chilly. 'You're so bloody *trusting*, Lulu, and I love that about you, but it means you're . . . you're vulnerable to being played by these people. You're just the type of woman men obsess over. I know you don't see it, for some crazy reason you don't think you're attractive, but you are *beautiful*. You're beautiful and you're kind, and you always think the best of everyone. Let's face it – you're a nutter magnet.'

'Uh, thanks – I think! But you know I hate that word.'

'Okay, *psychopath* magnet. That better? But seriously, I really didn't like the way Paul acted with you. I think you should stop seeing him.'

'Oh, Nick! I can't do that! Paul's *not dangerous*.'

'So you keep saying, but how can I know that, if you won't tell me anything about him?'

'I can't break client confidentiality.'

He dropped his hands from her arms, hitched the bee bag

more securely onto his shoulder, and turned away to the steps up to Westminster Bridge. She hurried after him. She wanted so much to try to get him to talk to her about his step-mother and father and sister and what had happened, but, for all her training as a therapist, she was at a loss to know how to do that. How to help her own, beloved husband who was so perfect on the outside and so damaged on the inside, she didn't even know where to start.

They had only been married two months. She had only known him for six. That was what she kept telling herself. When she got to know him better, she'd be better placed to give him the help he obviously desperately needed, to break down the wall he'd built around himself and defended with facetiousness and humour and charm.

And with silence.

Nick was a master of the silent treatment, particularly when he was thwarted.

'I'm not in any danger from Paul, or from any of my clients,' she tried, trotting to match his long stride as they approached the centre of the bridge, with its jaunty triple lantern lights. She was very conscious of the river flowing unseen beneath them, the wide, brown river that flowed past their penthouse apartment at Chelsea Harbour and that she loved so much but that also, at times, gave her a vague feeling of unease.

There were more than fifty 'jumpers' a year, Nick had told her the first time they viewed the apartment. People who jumped into this river. People who had watched it, perhaps, day after day, and felt its pull. And one day that pull had been too strong.

She stopped walking.

After a few steps, he turned and came back to her, as she had known he would. He would never leave her here. He never tired of reminding her of the number of women who were raped in London every year (over five thousand) and the number of murders (one hundred and twelve). He made her carry an illegal can of pepper spray in her bag, which he'd got from God knew where.

He'd made her promise to keep to the main thoroughfares when she was alone, and never take shortcuts up quiet, dubious alleyways. And she had to keep her phone switched on at all times in case she needed to call 999.

As he walked back to her, his expression contained, wary, her heart suddenly went out to him and she grabbed him into her arms and hugged him tight, *so tight*, the bee bag bumping awkwardly against them. She felt his chest heave with suppressed emotion.

Talk to me, she wanted to say. *Talk to me about them.*

Nick's mum, Kathleen, had died in an accident when he was fourteen – she'd fallen from the galleried landing of their big Victorian house in the Scottish Borders while Nick, oblivious, was upstairs in his room. He had found her body. She thought of Paul, so traumatised by finding his father's body that he'd been unable to let go of the experience, to let go of the rage, all these years. But Paul had had the loving support of his mother and extended family.

Nick had lost what remained of his family less than two years later, and in the worst possible way. She couldn't stop thinking about him as he'd been then, sixteen-year-old Nick, coming home from a fun day out with his best friend and his best friend's mum to find his family gone. Without a trace. And the police had been convinced that they'd just upped and left, leaving Nick behind.

What had that done to him?

At first, Nick had acted like he was amused by Lulu's attempts to 'psychoanalyse' him, as he put it. Now, he just shut her down.

When they eventually moved apart, he lifted a hand to

her face and smiled at her and said, 'I'm sorry, Lu. I didn't mean to add to your stress.'

'You haven't. You could never do that. When I'm with you, all the stress goes away.'

'I just want you to be safe.'

She nodded, she smiled, she stroked the thick, soft hair at his temples. 'I know. Oh, Nick, I know. But I *am* safe.' She pulled him back into a fierce hug. 'You're not going to lose me.' *Like you lost them* remained unspoken in the cool, river-smelling air that eddied around them. 'I *am* safe.'

2

As Duncan turned into the drive and smiled at her and said, 'Welcome home,' Maggie managed to smile back, but God, it took all she had. Ten minutes ago, about a mile out of Langholm, she'd been forced to ask him to stop the car so she could get out and piss at the side of the road. She'd blamed the baby squashing her bladder, but it had been pure nerves. There she'd squatted, bare arse glowing like a beacon in the evening sunshine, as a couple of cars had passed by. One had slowed right down. She was hoping it might just have been a pervert, but knowing her luck it would turn out to be one of Duncan's neighbours.

Oh, ugh – no, children, don't look.

That's not the common little thing Duncan Clyde's got himself married to, is it?

It is!

Oh dear God.

And now she'd better subtly check that the folds of her maternity dress hadn't got trapped in her pants, like had happened on the cruise. She smoothed the cheap floral polyester under her legs. Naw, she was fine. Well, not *fine*. She looked terrible. It was like this dress and Duncan's crisp white shirt and navy chinos shouldn't exist in the same universe, let alone the same couple.

The honeymoon had really brought home how far out of her league Duncan was. Maggie had expected the cruise to be all about stuffing your face and lounging in the sun and being deafened by the cabaret, but it hadn't been that kind of ship. It had been a 'boutique' cruise with less than a hundred passengers, ninety per cent snobby bastards. The food was magic, aye, but there was no cabaret, just lectures on the botany and archaeology of the places they stopped off at. And none of the other women were wearing polyester maternity dresses from a dodgy market or leggings from Topshop, and Maggie had had to keep washing out her new East sundress and hanging it up to drip-dry in the lav so she could wear it again. Duncan said he didn't care what she wore, but how could that be true?

Any minute now, he was going to do a double take and realise this wasn't his classy wife Kathleen sitting next him, this was some wee minger from Paisley that had got herself up the duff to worm her way in and needed kicking into touch pronto.

Maggie wished she could stop thinking about Kathleen, but she'd only died eighteen months ago and they'd been together forever, so how could he be over her? And what would Kathleen be thinking if she could see Duncan now, married to wee Maggie McPhee and all excited to be bringing her here, to Sunnyside, to the home Kathleen had lovingly created with her blood, sweat and tears?

Maggie felt bad for the woman, but that didn't mean she wasn't secretly going *Yes!* inside as the Range Rover purred round the side of the massive, *massive* house and there was the lawn stretching down to the shrubbery and the bonnie fields and woods, like something out of *Midsomer Murders* if you didn't look too closely at the big bleak hilltop at the back of the view. Maggie didn't like that hill, with the rocks and heather at the top. It always made her think of Billy McLetchie that used to live in the flat above Ma's, and the bloody scabs sticking out his greasy hair.

But the house was amazing. The summer evening sun was hitting the stonework, making it glow pink like a Disney palace.

She rested her hand on her belly.

This wee one was going to have it all, growing up here in the lap of luxury. He or she would have a ma and da and big brother that loved them, and bought them more toys than they could ever play with, and let them choose whatever sweets they liked in the shops. They weren't going to be stunted because they were malnourished. They were never going to have to pick manky cold chips and chicken wings up off the pavement that folk had dropped the night before and eat them because their ma was lying in the flat in her own piss, out her face on drugs.

They were never going to have to stay off school because their ma had forgotten her own rule of *not the face or the hands*. They were going to be so safe and loved and happy they wouldn't even know it. They wouldn't even know how it was to be anything else, in the honest-to-God pink palace that the Clyde family called home.

'The welcome committee!' said Duncan, stopping the car at the front door, where his sixteen-year-old son Nick was standing with Duncan's snobby sister Yvonne and her husband Michael. Yvonne was tall and willowy and wearing one of her trademark power-dressing black trouser suits. She looked like an accountant or a lawyer or a corporate bitch, not a farmer's wife who made cheese. Right enough, it was upmarket cheese pregnant folk couldn't eat because pasteurisation was for plebes, but it was still just cheese. Michael, on the other hand, was a real Farmer Giles, with his red nose and flat cap and one of those cream shirts with a pattern on it like the squared paper you used to get in school. He ran the big farm across the fields that had been in Duncan and Yvonne's family for a hundred and seventy years. Maggie was hazy on the family history, but it seemed the Clyde family had once owned most of the land round here, but a lot of it had either been sold off or parcelled up amongst different Clydes in the 1960s, and Duncan had ended up buying Sunnyside off his cousin when his uncle died.

Yvonne and Michael had big false smiles on their faces like they were going, *It's shit that you've got that common wee piece pregnant, you silly bastard, but look, we're trying to make the best of it here, all right?*

'God's sake,' went Maggie. 'I feel like I should be giving them the royal wave and asking if they've come far.'

Duncan laughed but, as if he had an idea what she was thinking, he rested his hand on top of hers where it cupped her belly. 'It's going to be fine. When they get to know you properly, they're going to love you as much as I do.'

'Do you love me?' The words were out before she could stop them.

Now that the honeymoon was literally over, now they were back to reality, was he going to change his mind about wanting to be with her?

His handsome face softened into a big smile. 'Of course I love you, you daft bitch.'

Duncan had been an officer in the Army when he was a young man, before and just after he and Kathleen were married, so Maggie guessed he must have used swear words all the time when he was giving the men a bollocking, which, judging from what she'd seen on TV, would have been twenty-four/seven. But now he never swore, except when the two of them were alone together, when, as he said, he could let rip with impunity. Swearing, belching, farting, you name it. Duncan said he'd never felt so at ease with anyone as he did with her, and he'd certainly never have carried on like that with Kathleen. If he and Kathleen had been in bed together and he'd felt a fruity one building, he'd always take himself off to the en suite to let it out rather than polluting the airspace of the marital bed.

He had no such qualms with Maggie, chuckling away and lifting the duvet and inviting her to get a noseful of that one.

He had no inhibitions with her, she guessed, because, unlike Kathleen, Maggie McPhee was no lady. But she couldn't say he didn't treat her like one. Now, he came round the car to open her door and take her hand to help her out, even though Nick had come running across the gravel giving it, '*Dad!*' Duncan was leaving him hanging, just saying, 'Well, it's good to be back – how are things? Yvonne and Michael don't seem too frazzled after two weeks of your company,' and not going in for a hug until Maggie was safely out of the car and waddling towards the house.

She put on a fake smile and did a daft dance with Michael – did they hug, did they not? – finally going for a loose folding of arms around shoulders as he asked about the journey and the traffic. Why was it that men were obsessed with traffic? Yvonne didn't make any sort of move towards her, which was fine by Maggie. All she said was a tight, 'Well, we'll be off. Let you get settled in.' *Let you get your feet under the table, you frightful little oik.*

Maggie smiled sweetly. 'Thanks, Yvonne.' *Aye, piss off, bitch.*

An image came into Maggie's head of her fist connecting with that sour mouth, teeth flying, the long willowy length of Yvonne smacking back on the fancy hall tiles, the back of her skull cracking open, blood spilling over the tiles and seeping down between them.

Just like what happened to Kathleen.

The psychiatrist they'd made her see in the young offender institution had said Maggie should try to immediately think about something else when thoughts of violence came into her head, and she'd played along, nodding and saying things like, 'Aye, right enough, that makes sense.' But what was the harm in a nice wee fantasy now and then? What had that bastard known about real life anyway, stuck up there in his ivory tower? He'd been a laughing stock in the YOI. Borderline, they'd called him, because that was the diagnosis he gave everyone, Maggie included: borderline personality disorder.

Load of crap.

All that was wrong with Maggie, with most of the others, was they'd had a shit childhood, and how was it possible to come out the other end of that skipping through the daisies like everything in the fucking garden was rosy?

She'd tried, with this bitch Yvonne. She'd even asked her to the flat for coffee, not long after she and Duncan had got together, because she wanted to get on with his family and make an effort and not judge a book by its cover. She'd given the place a deep clean the day before and even used upholstery products on the couch, which had suffered a bit, right enough, from Maggie's habit of lying there perching a curry on her tits while she watched the telly.

One of the benefits of having a coffee shop and living right above it was real coffee and homebakes on tap. But Yvonne had turned her nose up at the variety of coffees on offer, and the scones (choice of cheese or fruit) and cakes (choice of carrot, lemon or chocolate), and asked for a cup of fucking tea.

And then she started on the telly.

'Oh my goodness, that's a whopper.'

Maggie knew that wasn't a compliment, but she acted like it was. 'Aye, it's a nice big screen, eh?'

'It really dominates the room.'

Maggie nodded. 'Almost as good as being in a cinema. Want to see the picture?'

'Oh, no, thanks. I don't really watch TV.'

That was what they all said, all the middle-class bints who were regulars at the coffee shop. They were always bragging about how they never watched television, in the same tone of voice they might use to say they never mainlined heroin. But if one of them slipped up and mentioned the latest crime drama or soap storyline, all the others had somehow seen it.

Out of badness – and she was impressed with herself for managing this – Maggie turned the stilted conversation from the weather to the formation of the universe. 'What do you reckon to the oscillating model?'

Yvonne stared at her. 'The what?'

'The oscillating model of the universe? A whole load of big bangs alternating with big crunch thingmies? I'd rather believe that was what happened than just one big bang. If there was just the one, what was there before it, eh?' And she shoved a big piece of scone in her gob and muttered through it: 'Blows your mind.'

Yvonne's mouth had actually dropped open at that point.

'Some of the evidence is against it, though, according to this programme on BBC Two last week. I try to make the time to keep myself informed about the big questions, you know? If you don't watch yourself, it's easy to get bogged down in the mundane wee things, washing socks and going to the supermarket and doing the books for the business, and forget there's a whole other higher plane out there where folk are pondering the big stuff, how life evolved, how the universe came to be – pure dead amazing, eh? I always think it's a shame that so many people go through life never knowing that that higher plane *even exists*.' She'd bit into her scone again and chewed for a few seconds, enjoying the look of pure hatred on Yvonne's sour face. 'Aye, I try to take advantage, when I can, of the brilliant resources out there now for the lay person to educate themself.' She'd slapped more butter onto her scone. 'BBC Two at eight o'clock on a Tuesday, if you're interested. But maybe you've not even *got* a telly?' And Maggie had favoured Yvonne with a look of pure pity.

Now, she hardly even glanced at the bitch.

'Wait, wait, wait!' Duncan shouted from behind, and here he was, sweeping her up in his arms and pretending to stagger under the weight of her – even thirty-six weeks pregnant, Maggie was only seven and a half stones – and carrying her over the threshold, and Maggie was yelping and laughing as he pretended to drop her, while poor Nick tramped along behind, humphing their cases like a porter.

Nick was a good lad, and she felt bad for him, losing his ma and now having to cope with his da's new woman, and out of respect for that she'd hardly ever visited Sunnyside. She and Duncan had mostly spent time together in Langholm, in the coffee shop or the flat. According to Duncan, Nick was 'coping remarkably well' with Kathleen's death and had no problem with Duncan's new relationship, but Maggie wasn't buying that. There was bound to be resentment in the boy, no matter how much nicely-brought-up middle-class politeness he layered on top of it.

Even now, when he must be dying inside, as he came into the hall after them and set down the cases with a thump, he gave her a wee smile and muttered, 'Welcome to Sunnyside, Maggie. How are you feeling after the journey?'

'Oh, thanks, Nick! It's really good to be here. I am a *little* tired.' She'd noticed that, when she spoke to Nick, she subconsciously took the edges off her Paisley accent and tried to speak 'proper'. Her telephone voice, as Duncan called it. It was as if she was trying to prove to the boy that she was a worthy successor to Kathleen.

Who was she kidding?

Not, she was sure, Nick Clyde.

'How about a nap, while I rustle up something for dinner?' Duncan suggested, heading for the cases. 'I'll take these up, but we can unpack later.'

'I'll do it.' Nick hefted the cases. 'Not an entirely altruistic move. The sooner you get in that kitchen, the sooner my stomach will realise that no, it's okay, my throat hasn't been cut.'

'What a lovely analogy.' Duncan grinned, giving the boy another half hug as Nick went past him to the stairs.

This was where Kathleen had died. She'd fallen, the forensics folk had decided, from the landing onto the hard Victorian tiles and been killed instantly. Maggie couldn't help looking down at those tiles and wondering where, exactly ...

Poor Nick. Poor lad, having to walk here every day and remember what had happened, what he'd seen.

Maggie put the image out her mind and began the trek up the stairs. She'd only been upstairs in Sunnyside three or four times, most lately on a Saturday a couple of weeks before the wedding, when she and Duncan had redecorated the bedroom that was to be the nursery and arranged the new furniture in it.

She opened the nursery door and stepped inside.

'Your room,' she whispered, stroking her belly.

Leaf-green walls and a Winnie the Pooh frieze. A white cot and chest of drawers and changing table. An antique trunk for all the toys. Shelves already filling up with a collection of soft animals. A thick, firm-piled alphabet rug.

The familiar feelings of excitement and panic filled her.

She was going to be someone's ma.

She'd never thought she would be. How could wee Maggie McPhee give a kid what they needed? How could she keep them safe?

Someone was there. Behind her. She swung round, her heart, for no reason, hammering. The baby moved, as if to go, *Steady, Ma!*

It was just Nick, standing in the doorway.

Poor wee bastard.

She wanted to tell him that she would never try to take his ma's place, even if she could. But all she said was, 'Hi, Nick.'

'Dad's room is next door. But maybe you know that.'

'Yes, I remember. Thanks.'

She walked towards him, to the doorway, but he didn't move to let her past.

Was there something he wanted to say to her? She smiled at him, and when he said nothing, tried, 'Thank you for making me so welcome. I know it can't be easy, having someone you hardly know living in your house.'

'That's okay. I'm used to it. We often have guests staying.'

And there it was. Oh aye, he resented her, right enough.

He moved back into the corridor, and went ahead of her to Duncan's room, opening the door and walking in. 'Aunt Yvonne has given it an airing – badly needed given the ability of Dad's feet to stink up a room.'

The room was big and square, with windows on two sides, all open to let in a breeze that rippled the curtains. It was a right bonnie room, the walls painted dark pink, the woodwork white. There was a massive antique wardrobe made out of swirly, glowing wood, and tasteful paintings on the walls of cows in fields. The bed was a king-size oak one with a padded headboard in pale green, made up with crisp white sheets and pillows and duvet cover. All she wanted to do was kick off her shoes and crash on it.

'Thanks, Nick.' She lowered herself to sit on the edge of the bed with an 'Oof!'

He just stood there looking at her.

Aye, what? she wanted to rap out. But: 'I'll try to keep away from the whole evil stepmother thing,' she said, smiling up at him. He was tall, as tall as Duncan. 'Although I can't promise to always let you win at Scrabble.' The three of them had played a couple of times, and Nick had won by miles. Maggie had joked about letting him win, and Nick had seemed to appreciate the attempt at humour.

And now, again, it raised a smile. 'Oh, hasn't Dad told you? I always win at everything. I'm insufferable that way.'

Maggie laughed. 'So I've noticed.'

Nick's smile turned into a grin as he left the room.

She always thought it must be like having to deal with a different species from his charming, perfect son, Duncan having to wrangle all those young offenders, all those losers, on the programme he ran out of The Phoenix Centre in Langholm for a charity that tried to rehabilitate yobs. It was how he and Maggie had first met. She'd been a nightmare of a twenty-year-old, assigned to the programme by her social worker in a last-ditch attempt to keep her out of adult prison. She'd been angry at the world, as Duncan put it. He used to call her Little Miss Prickles. On her twenty-first birthday he'd given her a card with a hedgehog in a party hat on it, but she hadn't been able to work herself up to take offence, as she would normally.

Because it was Duncan.

She'd been in love with him by then. Oh aye, she'd fallen hard! But she'd known he was out of her league and nothing was ever going to happen between them. Duncan was fourteen years older than Maggie. A former Army officer. Posh.

And she knew he didn't think of her that way. All he saw was a troubled young woman who needed help. And anyway, starting something with someone on the programme would probably have got him the sack.

After she'd 'graduated' from the programme six years ago, she and Duncan had kept in touch. He'd helped get her onto the course at catering college, and then he'd sponsored her for the grant that had allowed her to open Maggie's, her wee coffee shop. He and Kathleen used to pop in maybe once a month. Latte for Duncan, double-shot cappuccino for Kathleen, lemon drizzle cake for both. Kathleen had been mad for Maggie's lemon drizzle.

When Kathleen had died, Maggie had cried for an hour straight – for Duncan, if she was being honest, rather than for Kathleen herself – but then the evil thought had popped into her head that now Duncan was fair game. Fair game and grieving and in need of support from an old friend. He'd started coming into the coffee shop for his lunch every Tuesday. Usually soup and a toastie or a baked potato, but Maggie had started adding pies to the lunch menu on a Tuesday because she knew Duncan loved them. Chicken and leek. Steak and kidney. Good old Scotch pies. He'd joked that he'd put on half a stone in a month. They joked around a lot, Maggie and Duncan, and she liked to think it was a bright spot in his week, that Tuesday lunch. Then he'd seen the advert she'd put in the window for an assistant, and suggested she might want to give this young lad who'd just left the programme a try. His name was Liam and he'd been sucked into the gang culture in Glasgow in his early teens and done a long stretch in a young offender institution for GBH and armed robbery, but now he was turning his life around. If she could take a chance on him, with her example in front of him and 'our support', Duncan was hopeful the lad could make it.

Our support.

Maggie didn't give a stuff about this Liam. The least sympathetic folk in the world when it came to wee yobs were reformed wee yobs. She didn't want some mad GBH bastard in her coffee shop, putting the frighteners on her regulars.

But *our support.*

Liam Clarke had started at the coffee shop the next day. And aye, at first he'd been the nightmare she'd expected, giving her lip and smoking in the kitchen, dropping fag ash in the tuna mayo. Smashing glasses accidentally on purpose. Getting all his dodgy pals in to sit around with cans of lager up their jumpers, boasting about their court appearances and clearing the place. But Maggie had read him the riot act, and Duncan had read him the riot act, and he'd pulled his socks up pronto. Two weeks later, he was asking her if maybe the punters might like an avocado-based baked potato filling, maybe with sour cream and spring onion and a wee touch of chilli for a kick.

Liam turned out to be a natural.

Duncan started coming in every day for his lunch to check on his progress.

And then, one red-letter day, Duncan asked Maggie out to a fancy hotel for dinner to thank her for all her help with Liam. They had a lovely meal, and she soon forgot that she was showing him up with her common ways. They laughed and laughed. They drank a fair bit, of course, which helped. And then, walking her back to her flat, Duncan started crying and muttering about Kathleen.

She hugged him.

He kissed her.

And then he started crying again.

'How can I be feeling the way I do about you, when Kathleen ... when Kathleen ...' And it all came pouring out. That he'd been attracted to Maggie from the start, from when she'd been in the programme. 'Little Miss Prickles.' He admitted that he'd enjoyed her company so much that he used to dread the time she'd leave the programme. 'We just clicked, didn't we? We had so much fun. I felt I'd known you all my life.'

Maggie couldn't believe it. It was like she'd just stepped out of her real life and into her wildest dream.

But she knew she should go slow. She told him it was too soon. He was still grieving for Kathleen. Aye, she had feelings for him too, and aye, she agreed that they'd 'clicked' all those years ago – in fact, she'd had a massive crush on him – but they should just stay friends, for now at least.

The sexual tension this embargo had produced had been incredible.

A month, he'd held out. A long, frustrating, electric month of 'accidental' touching, as she handed him his coffee or his change. She'd reeled him in good and proper.

And now look!

She knew it was going to be fine. She knew Duncan Clyde loved her, maybe even more than he'd loved Kathleen.

She kicked off her shoes and pulled up the duvet and sighed as she sank onto the comfy mattress, lying on her side as she had to now. There was a window right opposite with a view across the lawn and the fields to the hill that she had to stop thinking of as Billy McLetchie. It was pure dead gorgeous. Everything here was gorgeous. Even the window was a posh old wooden one with four panes in it, framing this view of the bonnie Scottish Borders countryside.

Maggie shut her eyes, sinking into sleep, breathing in the cool, clean, fresh country air.

For the first time in her life, she had a real home and a real family.

For the first time in her life, she felt safe.

3

The blood was like threads, threads that thickened into string, into rope, coiling through the bath water, coiling over the doughy, pale grey skin of the person who lay there, on his side, his back turned towards her so she couldn't see his face.

Lulu was clutching the door handle.

She couldn't let go the door handle.

It was a strange room, gloomy and dingy with peeling paint and a grubby floor, but the bath in the centre was the bath from Braemar Station, the big cream enamel bath with the chip in the side where her brothers had hit it once with a cricket ball.

She needed to get to him, but she was caught in a thick, heavy inertia, as if the air around her wasn't gas but solid, and there was nothing she could do, she couldn't get to him and she couldn't stop what was happening.

He flopped over, and she saw his face.

It was Dad.

And then light was searing through her eyelids and she

was awake, all of a sudden, awake and weeping, staring at the bright wall of glass opposite the bed.

The blinds were rolling up and music was blaring from the integrated sound system.

'Close to You' by the Carpenters.

Thank God, thank God, thank God, it was a dream!

She closed her eyes.

That had been hellish. Even worse than usual.

Every night, as soon as she closed her eyes, her brain seemed to take this as a cue to go back over her clients' traumas, but not with Lulu as an objective observer. Oh, no. Lulu *was* her clients, as she imagined the events they'd experienced happening to herself. And when she eventually managed to drop off, this often bled into her dreams.

She felt like she'd only just fallen asleep, but it must be 7:30 already. Instead of an alarm, Nick set a different track to come on for her each morning. But she didn't feel ready to face the day. As Nick had slept like a baby through the night, she had lain awake for hours, battling against the urge to take a zolpidem. On the advice of the private doctor Nick had insisted she see, she was trying to wean herself off her prescription sleeping pills. She was currently allowed one tablet every three nights, and this hadn't been one of those blissful occasions. She'd grabbed her phone at intervals to chart the progress of her wakefulness – ten to one, quarter past two, half past three, four o'clock.

That meant she'd had a maximum of three and a half hours' sleep.

Not enough. She knew that wasn't enough to get her through the day in anything like decent shape. Her head ached already. But at least tonight was a pill night – not that she generally felt any better when she woke after taking one, her head muzzy and stupid, her mouth dry and sticky, her bowels rebelling. There was no easy answer, it seemed, to what the doctor had referred to as the 'chronic anxiety-related insomnia' caused by the stressful nature of her work. Nick had pounced on that, of course, as yet another reason why she should give it up and do something else.

But she couldn't help but smile as she listened to the song.

Nick was a big fan of cheesy retro romantic stuff.

She forced herself upright and padded across the soft white carpet to the wall of glass which gave an uninterrupted view across the wide brown expanse of the Thames to the new high-rises that loomed above the old brick buildings of Battersea. Standing here was like you were floating right over the river. The master bedroom floor formed the roof of the big balcony underneath, so between this window and the riverbank there was only the width of the walkway.

Showered and dressed, she stumbled downstairs and into the maze, as Nick called it, the series of right-angle turns in the white-walled and mirrored corridor that took her past all the other bedrooms and the study and out into the big open-plan living space, which Lulu always secretly thought was a bit like walking into an upmarket department store – all clean white lines and marble and glass and tasteful soft furnishings in shades of beige and grey. Light was streaming in through the slanted glass roof above the double-height area in the middle of the room, from which you looked up to the gallery that led to the master bedroom. She had worried, when she'd seen that on the house tour, that it would be triggering for Nick, but when she'd tentatively broached the subject, he'd assured her that the apartment was so different from Sunnyside in every way that it wouldn't pull any 'triggers' on him. 'You don't have to worry that you'll come home one day to find me chewing the back of the sofa like a neurotic spaniel you've left home alone.'

But I do worry! she'd wanted to yell at him. *Stop using humour to deflect!*

All this light was making her head pound.

She crossed the expanse of white floor to the glass wall looking over the little marina that was Chelsea Harbour, and then she turned and paced the length of the room – all forty-six feet of it – to the opposite glass wall overlooking the Thames. An apartment this size was obscene in London, she'd discovered after they'd bought the place, when she'd been giving Jenny and Beth, her two best friends from Leonora, a virtual tour on Zoom. They had sat there with their mouths open. 'Is Nick some sort of oligarch?' Jenny had said in wonder, peering through her geek-chic, heavy-framed glasses. 'How much was it?'

Just over six million pounds was the answer. Lulu had still been getting used to converting to Australian dollars, so it was only then that it had struck her just how wealthy Nick must be. 'I suppose that *is* a lot of money,' she had said sheepishly as the two of them had done their usual 'Oh, *Lulu!*' She had a – totally undeserved – reputation as the ditzy dreamer of the group, who went around with her head in the clouds.

'No, but really, how can Nick afford it?' Glamour-puss Beth had broken her own no-frowning rule ('Frowns give you *wrinkles*, people!') to glare at Lulu. 'Is he a mafia boss?' They knew he was a City trader at the London Stock Exchange, but this was Beth's none-too-subtle way of saying that Lulu should be careful, make sure she knew what she was getting into before she married some bloke she'd only known four months.

Lulu had frowned sternly at Beth across nine thousand miles of Zoom. 'He's eight years older than us, remember – he's had seventeen years since he left Oxford to make "obscene amounts of money", as he puts it.' What she hadn't mentioned to her friends, because it would have felt like a breach of his privacy, was that she was sure that Nick's undiagnosed PTSD meant he'd been obsessed with making himself 'safe' by accumulating wealth – until he'd met Lulu.

Now, it was her actual, physical safety he was obsessed with.

But she hadn't told Jenny and Beth that either.

'I guess he must be a bit of a Rockefeller,' Lulu had admitted. 'It's not like he boasts about it – or not much – but I reckon he must be one of the most successful traders in the city. He's super-bright.' To emphasise this point, she'd panned across the floor-to-ceiling cabinet set into one wall, in which his collection of Roman artefacts was displayed, and then across the wall on which hung his genuine, real-life Alma-Tadema, a sumptuous Victorian oil painting depicting a beautiful trio of Roman girls about to be undressed by their slaves, the glassy water of a garden pool in the background. 'The Swim' it was called. It should have looked out of place in this ultra-modern setting, but somehow it worked, injecting a bit of soul into the rather impersonal space.

What she hadn't shown Jenny and Beth was the wall opposite, on which Nick had placed the three big studio portraits of Lulu, one in which she faced right, one straight ahead, and one left. The photographer had flattered her with clever lighting so she didn't look like herself, she looked like the beautiful woman Nick was always saying she was.

Now, she opened the glass doors to the big balcony that overlooked the Thames. She had gone on and on to Nick about wanting to live on a boat when she was a little girl growing up in the parched, dusty outback. She used to long to sit on a boat, dabbling her feet in the water. And when he'd brought her here, and they'd stood out on this balcony together and she'd turned and looked back through the long room to the marina on the other side, she'd realised that being in this apartment was the next best thing. And he'd read her mind, and murmured, 'Well, you couldn't seriously expect me to pump out the bilge every morning, or whatever one has to do on those insanitary things.'

'It's perfect!' And she had broken down and cried.

She needed coffee.

The kitchen area was tucked away in an offshoot of the main space, behind the island with its row of bar stools. It was all reflective surfaces – three oven doors and an array of shiny black cupboards. She laughed out loud when she saw what was stuck, incongruously, to the one in which they kept the breakfast cereals.

A yellow sticky note with a drawing of a comical wombat on it and the question: *Why did the wombat cross the road?*

She opened the cupboard. Attached to her muesli was another sticky note, this one with the answer: *Because it was stapled to the chicken!* and another drawing of the goofy wombat being dragged across a road by a giant chook.

That was terrible! He had exactly her silly sense of humour!

The pain between her eyes eased a little.

Nick was up and at 'em two hours before she woke – he needed to be at his desk early so he could get up to speed with developments in the markets – but he always left something for her to find, whether a silly joke or quote or a beautifully arranged fruit salad or, one morning after she'd had a particularly bad case of the runs, a single red rose. But this was Nick and Lulu, so it wasn't on her pillow or the chaise longue, it was on the toilet seat!

Today, there was another sticky note on the framed montage of photographs by the lift that documented their relationship, from a fuzzy snap of Lulu in a lounger on the terrace of the villa in Ithaca, to a selfie taken on their first night in the apartment, both of them raising a glass of champagne, to their wedding in Leonora (Dad: 'Well, if you're sure, love.' Mum: 'He's an absolute dreamboat!').

Nick had stuck the note on a photo of Lulu paddling in a pond on Hampstead Heath. *My gorgeous girl! Love you forever!*

The soppy idiot.

On the other side of the lift was a wall of memories of his dad, Duncan. Her favourite was one of the two of them playing football: Nick a tiny, tousle-headed child of three or four, Duncan a tall, dark, handsome man with long legs who looked spookily like Nick. There was another which was almost professional in quality, a candid shot of Duncan's face in profile, in repose, a slight smile on his lips, his eyes focused on something off camera. A really good-looking man. Completely different in mood was a snap of him being a silly dad, wearing a back-to-front baseball cap and crossing his eyes, one arm slung around teenage Nick. Nick must have been about sixteen in that one, so the photo had probably been taken not long before it happened.

Before they all disappeared.

His father, his stepmother, his baby sister.

Nick had told her tersely when she'd asked about his family, one hot night in his villa in Ithaca soon after they'd met, that his stepmother had murdered his father and his baby half-sister and disappeared. And of course Lulu had immediately Googled *Clyde family murder, Scottish Borders* and discovered that this was only Nick's interpretation of what had happened.

There'd been a documentary made a few years ago, 'The unexplained disappearance of the Clyde family', and Lulu had found it on YouTube and secretly watched a bit of it, fascinated to see a photograph of Maggie, Nick's stepmother, in her wedding dress – a tiny woman with a strong face, smiling so happily into the camera – before stopping because it felt like a betrayal. She didn't want to go rummaging around in his trauma without his permission. But basically, it seemed that the police had decided there was 'no evidence of a crime'. It looked like Duncan and Maggie had taken little Isla and just up and left one day, leaving Nick behind. There was something about a murder at Duncan's workplace a few weeks before involving dubious characters which could, it was suggested, have caused them to panic and run. One unexplained thing was that there were three mugs and three bowls left on the table, not the two you'd expect, but the police had explained that by postulating that Maggie might have started unloading the dishwasher (her fingerprints had been all over it) and collecting dirty crockery from around the house, but Duncan had told her to just leave it, they didn't have time for housework. Lulu had shaken her head over such gender stereotyping. She supposed DNA technology must have been in its infancy in 1997, and it hadn't been possible to get DNA profiles from the tiny traces of saliva on the mugs. Duncan and Maggie's fingerprints were on two of the mugs, but the third one had yielded nothing, which seemed odd.

When she tried to talk to Nick about it, all he'd say was that the police were useless and everyone knew Maggie had killed them. No way would his dad have abandoned him like that.

'She was convicted of GBH when she was seventeen after *she attacked a girl and left her brain-damaged*,' he had half-shouted at Lulu, his mouth contorting. 'She spent three years in a *fucking young offender institution*! She was still dangerous. She was still violent – had been on a number of occasions since she moved in with us. She was a suspect in a murder. She was a *fucking psycho*! What other explanation is there that makes any sense, other than that *she killed them*? I don't know why there was a third mug and a third bowl. Maybe she had an accomplice.'

'It must be so awful, not knowing –'

But, as he always did when she tried to get him away from the subject of psycho Maggie and into the more difficult area of his feelings about his dad and sister, he had clammed up. She saw this all the time with her PTSD clients: anger was so much easier than pain.

Gently, she unpeeled the sticky note from the glass over the photo of herself and, as she descended in the lift, read the words again. When Nick had first left her one of his notes, the morning after they'd moved into the apartment, she had told him that evening that she'd loved carrying it about with her all day, like a talisman. 'A talisman,' he had repeated slowly. 'I like that.' And then, almost shyly, diffidently: 'Will you always take one with you? It would make me feel . . . I don't know.' But he didn't need to say it. She knew what he was thinking, as they so often knew one another's minds. It would be as if the physical evidence of his love could act as protection when he wasn't with her. But this was soppy, illogical nonsense, so of course he couldn't say it out loud.

'Of course I will,' she had said.

The lobby the lift opened onto had security cameras everywhere and a porter's desk with pigeonholes behind it for mail. There was a 24-hour porterage service, and Lulu always felt sorry for the poor guys who had to sit here all day.

She couldn't blame them for deserting their post rather frequently. Nick had complained about it a couple of times to the company that supplied the porters and CCTV cameras and the security for the building generally, and they'd assured him they would 'address the issue raised'. But Harry, who was on most days, was just a young bloke, and Lulu felt it wasn't fair to expect him to sit there on his skinny behind doing nothing all day. He seemed to spend a lot of time walking round the block and lingering on the Thames walkway under their balcony, and checking out the boats in the harbour, as if it were entirely possible that the multimillionaires who hung out on them could be a security threat.

Harry wasn't at the desk now, which was a little annoying as she needed to speak to him about something. Her fuzzy brain wouldn't immediately tell her what – the caffeine hadn't kicked in yet. And then she remembered. She needed to tell Harry about the delivery she was expecting. Last week, he'd signed on her behalf for delivery of a rug, her attempt to add some colour to the apartment, not realising he was signing a form to say he'd checked the goods for damage, which he hadn't. The rug must have been caught in machinery or something as it was being rolled up – it had a big, black, greasy line down it, and she'd had a terrible time getting them to accept a return and send a replacement.

She went round behind the desk and looked about for a pen and paper. There was a small notebook on the shelf under the desktop. She took it out and opened it, intending to tear off a sheet of paper.

Inside was some sort of log of dates and times, with comments opposite. She leafed through, looking for a blank sheet, but then her eye was caught by one of the comments. It was dated 12 May. A week ago.

Happy, chatted.

Weird.

And the next one, for 13 May, was *Seemed preoccupied and tired.* Followed by *Small cut on right hand, about 1 cm long* for 14 May.

She looked down at her right hand, at the now fading cut on the base of her thumb, where she'd scratched it opening a tin of sardines.

Harry had been watching her?

Making notes about her, timed and dated?

Why?

She knew what Jenny and Beth would say, rolling their eyes: *Because he's a creep!*

Harry?

Lovely Harry, with the nervous blink? *Really?*

And the thought hit her: was it possible that Nick obsessed about her safety not because he was unreasonably paranoid, but because Lulu was a ditzy idiot who lost her credit card about once a month and got herself locked in shops and hadn't a clue that the lovely young porter she bantered with was a sleazy creep who was –

The front door swished open.

Lulu ducked down behind the desk, the notebook clutched to her chest.

She held her breath as footsteps clomped across the polished floor. Coming closer . . .

Coming, suddenly, round the desk!

And then Harry's face was looming over her, eyes blinking rapidly. 'Mrs Clyde! Are you okay?'

She scrambled away from him, the notebook still clutched in one hand, and then she was up and running for the door, and he was running after her shouting, 'Hey, Mrs Clyde! No, wait!' but Lulu was out of the door and off, her trainers pounding the cobbled wharf that ran round the harbour, and there were people here, a couple on one of the boats, a woman walking ahead of her with a heavy bag on her arm, a man talking on his phone who looked up at her in surprise as she ran past.

When she'd reached the other side of the harbour, she stopped and turned. Harry was standing at the door of the building, watching her. When he saw her looking, he shook his head at her in a defeated gesture.

Lulu pulled out her phone and called Nick.

4

Nick picked a chunk of green icing off his cupcake. 'Practically radioactive! Is this a challenge to see how many e-numbers you can get into us, Mags? And what the hell's *this*?' He tapped the floral plate she'd put the cupcake on. 'You been raiding a skip, Mags?'

Maggie hadn't brought much with her to Sunnyside, having donated most of her stuff to charities, but she'd thought this set of vintage tea plates a customer had given her last Christmas would be classy enough to slide under the radar at Sunnyside. Seemed she'd been wrong.

'Stop calling me Mags, you wee monster,' she said, like she still found it funny, like it wasn't seriously pissing her off. She'd told Nick, when they were looking through the wedding cards, that she hated being called Mags, but some of her friends couldn't seem to help themselves. 'Oh, okay, *Mags*,' he'd grinned, and it had become a joke between them, that he called her Mags. But he'd started using the name in every second sentence, and it had stopped being funny.

'Not that Meebs is bothered.' Nick pointed his fork at Andy Jardine, who was sitting opposite him at the kitchen table and had already lifted his cupcake to his mouth and taken a big bite. 'He'll hoover up anything you put in his path. You know why he's called Meebs? Short for amoeba. Because amoebas are pretty much the lowest form of animal life there is? Don't even have a ganglion, Mags, let alone a brain. But also because they phagocytose anything within range that's vaguely edible.'

Andy just took all this, keeping on chewing like his life depended on it. Nick looked at him, the way a scientist might look at a not-very-interesting specimen.

'Hey, Meebs.' Nick flicked the piece of green icing at him. It bounced off Andy's face and landed on the table.

Andy picked it up and added it to the food already in his mouth.

'QED!' Nick laughed. 'Bloody QED!'

Andy just smiled his lopsided smile. Poor Andy had a scar running through the side of his mouth, deforming his lips and pulling down the left side of his lumpy face, so when he smiled, only the right side of his mouth turned up. Maggie couldn't help thinking he looked like one of those clowns in a horror film.

He was a weird best friend for Nick to have, this big lummock of a boy with about as much spark as a brick. The conversation between the two of them, from what Maggie could make out, wasn't the usual banter between teenage boys. Whatever Nick batted at Andy, Andy just let whistle past without even attempting to hit it back.

'You'd better watch that Andy doesn't phagocytose you, you cheeky wee bugger,' she said, determinedly cheery.

'Well, granted, that's always a worry, Mags.'

She couldn't say exactly when her interactions with Nick had gone to pish, but it had been going on for days, this sniping at her, but always in a jokey way, so if she'd pulled him up about it she'd look like she was having a sense of humour failure.

Carol Jardine, thank God, arrived ten minutes later to take Andy home. You could easily tell she was Andy's ma, over-weight and with the same lumpy face, but she was all smiles and chat. It was like Carol's spark had somehow not made it through on the genes she'd passed on to Andy. Or maybe it was down to Andy's facial deformity. That must be hard for a teenager.

Carol was all over Nick, asking about school, saying he must be looking forward to the start of the rugby season and how she'd heard great things about his chances of making the national squad this year, despite being at least a year younger than most of the other boys in the first fifteen.

'He's such a star, isn't he?' she gushed.

Maggie made like she hadn't heard, clattering about at the sink.

Nick was sooking up, all smiles and compliments, and Carol was giggling, the daft cow. On the way out, she tapped her son on the arm. 'What do you say?' like he was a fucking five-year-old.

'Thanks very much, Mrs Clyde,' muttered Andy.

Half an hour later and it was Duncan sitting at the table drinking tea and eating a green-iced cupcake. Finally, Maggie could relax, sticking her upper lip over the rim of her mug to suck up tea from long range. Best way to cool it down, and it made the surface of the tea ripple like a stormy sea, which always gave Maggie childish satisfaction. She'd taught Duncan the method, and he was doing it too. A slurp duet.

Duncan demolished his cupcake almost as fast as Andy had done and belched, arms stretched out like an opera singer. If Kathleen could see him now! 'Delicious. I needed that. Sometimes a sugar rush is the only way to go.'

'Bad day?'

'Oh, well, you know . . . Dean.'

Dean was a 'troublemaker', in Duncan-speak. Translation – wee bastard. Face like a rat and habits to match. His first written warning had been for pissing in another kid's bag.

'He broke into the sports equipment cupboard and liberated the basketballs and footballs while he was meant to be playing five-a-side with Jemma's group. I was in the meeting room. One of the kids suddenly pointed at the window and there was Dean, plus Darren and Stu, kicking the balls across the road into the oncoming traffic. Could have caused a smash.'

'So that's him out, eh?'

The rules of the programme were strict – three strikes and you're out. And Dean had already had two written warnings about his behaviour.

'We're giving him one last chance.'

She knew how that meeting would have gone. Jemma and Ross, the other mentors, would have wanted Dean gone because he led the other kids astray. But Duncan was the Programme Leader, so it would ultimately have been his decision. 'You old softy.'

He half-smiled and changed the subject. 'So, Andy came over?'

'Aye.'

'You don't like Andy, do you?'

'I've no feelings about him either way. But he seems a weird choice of best pal for Nick.'

'Oh, well. They were thrown together as toddlers, Carol and Kathleen being thick as thieves, and I suppose . . . Well, Nick doesn't always find it easy to make friends.'

Interesting. 'Do you think Nick might have some . . . socialisation issues?' Maggie knew all the buzz words from her time in the system.

Duncan took another slurp of tea. 'Not in the usual sense.

He's socially adept with adults. But with his peers . . . I don't know. I suspect he won't find his "people", as they say, until uni. He's one of those irritating kids who excel academically without even trying – and he's not above rubbing the other kids' noses in the fact. In his prelims this year, he got a hundred per cent for maths, and over ninety per cent in all his other subjects – ninety-seven per cent for chemistry, ninety-three for history . . .'

Typical of Duncan to have memorised the numbers. She supposed she shouldn't be surprised that he was such an OTT da, given that he'd chosen a career helping young folk and that he'd been a single parent for the last eighteen months, but she sometimes wondered if Kathleen's death had made him fixate on Nick too much.

She nodded, digging her fingernail into a knot in the surface of the table and thinking of the way Nick had looked at Andy, his best pal – his only pal, from the sound of it. With no emotion. Watchful, assessing. Waiting for a reaction.

It was the same way he looked at her.

There was something not right about the boy.

And for the first time, she admitted it to herself:

She didn't like Nick.

'Well, I don't think it's healthy,' she said.

'I know – must be about a week's worth of the recommended sugar intake.'

'Naw, I mean Nick having no friends. Apart from Andy.' Who hardly even counted. 'Don't you think there might be a bit more to it than the other kids being jealous? I know you think he's coping okay with Kathleen's death, but is he, really? Or is he pushing people away?'

'*I am the cat who walks by himself,*' said Nick's voice, and Maggie jumped in her chair. She hadn't heard him come into the room. 'Thanks for your concern, Mags, but I'm fine.' He dumped a pile of kids' books on the table and turned to

Duncan. 'Found these at the bottom of a cupboard. Thought the rug rat could have them.'

Duncan pulled a book towards him. '*Where the Wild Things Are*. We used to call you King of the Wild Things – remember?'

'Yeah, yeah, I was – am – a brat.' Nick grinned. 'Embarrass me in front of Mags, why don't you.' He was looking over Duncan's shoulder while he turned the pages. 'I used to love this one. Especially the part where Max puts on the wolf outfit.'

To give them some space, Maggie heaved herself upright, muttering something about the laundry, and headed off down the passage that led off the kitchen to all the other wee back rooms.

And stopped.

On the flagstones of the passage was a scattering of yellow plastic.

Her set of measuring spoons.

Smashed to bits on the floor.

The measuring spoons Mrs Greenlees had given her when she left school with her one O Grade in Home Economics. The measuring spoons that meant more to Maggie than any of her other possessions.

With a wordless sound, she put a hand on her belly and squatted down and then she somehow managed to get down on her knees so she could reach them, so she could reach the pieces and touch them. And then Duncan's arms were round her and he was asking what was wrong, was it the baby, and she was shouting, struggling free of him, rounding on Nick, who was standing there looking at her, of course he was, the fucking wee bastard.

'He's done this! He's smashed my spoons!'

Nick raised his eyebrows. 'Uh – what?'

'My spoons!' She threw the handful of yellow plastic

pieces at him, and he dodged out the way, his face going: *Nothing to do with me.*

'Maggie,' went Duncan in her ear, putting his arms back round her. 'It's okay. You're okay.'

'I haven't done anything, Dad.' Nick had picked up a piece of yellow plastic and was examining it. 'I guess this is her measuring spoons? They've been stood on?'

'*He* did it!' Maggie pushed Duncan away and grabbed at Nick, grabbed for the yellow plastic in his hand. 'Leave that alone, you wee *fucker*! *Leave it!*'

'Uh, okay.' With exaggerated care, Nick set the shard of plastic back down on the flagstones. 'Dad, I don't think this is good for the baby.' He was staring, now, at her belly, frowning like he was all worried. And then, as Duncan made reassuring noises, rubbed her arm, tried to ease her to her feet, Nick met her eyes and a shiver of shock went through her.

Those blue eyes of his shone with pure evil, like he was doing terrible things to her in his head.

She knew that look, because she was giving him the same one back.

She took a deep breath, and sighed, and said, 'Oh God, I'm sorry, Nick. Blame the pregnancy hormones.' And she made herself smile at him. 'I'm *so sorry*. Of course it must have been an accident. Those big feet of yours! It's okay, it's fine. I don't know what I'm making all this fuss for.' And she made a wee *I'm that ashamed of myself* face at Duncan.

Duncan grimaced sympathetically. 'I know how much those spoons meant to you.'

She nodded, real tears coming now.

Duncan pulled her into a hug.

'I didn't break the spoons,' went Nick. *Ha!* He was raging that she'd turned this round and suggested that he'd broken them and not wanted to own up, but that she forgave him.

'It's okay, it doesn't matter.' She buried her face in

Duncan's jumper so he couldn't see her triumphant grin. Nick was going to find he was messing with the wrong woman here. Aye, maybe Maggie McPhee was a stunted wee plebe from Paisley who only had one O Grade, but she was a graduate of the school of hard knocks and she'd come up against mad fuckers a whole lot more scary than Nick Clyde.

ON SUNDAY MORNING, Maggie slept late and found Yvonne in the kitchen, washing dishes at the sink like it was her own house. She turned to Maggie, drying her hands on a tea towel and lifting her eyes to the clock.

So it's 11:30. Want to make something of it?

'I've been having a lie-in,' went Maggie, trudging to the kettle.

'Evidently. I hear Nick's been giving you grief?'

Maggie looked at Yvonne. The woman was smart-casual in stiff, unflattering jeans, an orange jumper and one of those posh silk scarves with horseshoes on it. Interesting choice of words, though – 'Nick's been giving you grief', not 'You've been getting your knickers in a twist about poor Nick.'

Maggie leant back against the worktop, stretching her back.

Yvonne shrugged. 'Kids are vile.' She looked at Maggie's belly. 'Sorry, but let's face it, they're not worth bothering with until they're at least twenty-one. You're older than that, aren't you?'

'I'm twenty-eight!' puffed Maggie. 'Still get asked if I've got a young person's railcard, mind,' she conceded. 'Even with this.' She patted her belly.

'I had the opposite problem. Five foot nine at the age of thirteen. I once got mistaken for the teacher.'

'Aye, I can see that!' The words were out before Maggie could stop them. She could just imagine Yvonne at thirteen, a forty-year-old in a wee lassie's body. She was two years younger than Duncan, but you'd think she was ten years older.

Yvonne raised her eyebrows.

'Aye, Nick.' Maggie poured boiling water into a mug and dumped a teabag in after it. 'He's being a nightmare.'

'Duncan spoils him rotten. Even before Kathleen's death, dear little Nick could do no wrong as far as he was concerned. Kathleen was always complaining that Duncan didn't discipline him and left it all to her. Wanting to be the cool dad. But of course it meant poor Kathleen had to be the strict one. Make sure you don't make the same mistake with this one. Make sure Duncan steps up to the plate.'

What did Yvonne know about bringing up a child? Duncan said she'd never wanted her own kids and wasn't much of an auntie to Nick.

'Where's Duncan?'

'He and Michael are in the garage, I think. There's something wrong with Nick's bike and the two of them will be out there staring at it for an hour before they finally give up and admit they need to take it to the bike shop.'

Maggie took the shortcut across the lawn and down a path overhung with wee trees and roses. So she was coming at the garage from the side, rather than along the track off the drive that led to the front of it. She was about to step onto the gravel when she heard Duncan's voice say, 'I just hope being pregnant, and vulnerable emotionally, isn't starting to reactivate old behaviours.'

She stepped off the path and onto the grass at the side of the garage, moving silently right up to the edge of the door.

'Are you worried about how she's going to cope with the baby?' That was Michael's gruff voice.

Duncan sighed. 'A little. I mean, how's she going to deal with a needy newborn, if she can't handle a relatively well-behaved teenager? Nick has his moments, but as teenagers go, he's a positive paragon. She says he resents her, but I can see no evidence of that – can you?'

Silence. She imagined Michael shaking his head.

'She says he's been saying things to hurt her, but that can't be true. Nick's not nasty like that. Maybe he's been a bit tactless when he's been joking around, but I can't see him saying anything to hurt her *deliberately*.'

A bit tactless.

Joking around.

On Friday morning, when Duncan had been out at work, Maggie had been sitting on the couch in the lounge – no, the *sofa* in the *drawing room* – looking through the wedding album, and suddenly Nick's voice had gone: 'Lovely.'

He was there, right behind her, looking over her shoulder.

The photo was one of Maggie on her own, in her wedding dress, big belly sticking out, thin mousy hair put up by the hairdresser into a 'do' but already straggling out of it. Maggie liked the photo, though. She looked dead happy, grinning away.

'Sun spotlighting my schnozzle,' she pointed out. 'Not my best feature.' Maggie had, she assumed, inherited her large Roman nose from her father, whoever the bastard had been.

Nick went, 'A face only a mother could love, hmm?'

Terrible silence.

And then he was all, 'Oh, God, sorry! I didn't mean . . .' He dropped onto the couch next to her and put a hand over hers, leaning too close.

She pulled her hand away.

'Oh God, Mags, I'm an insensitive idiot! I'm *so sorry!*'

He knew about Ma? Duncan had told him about the abuse?

Nick gave her a sickly, sympathetic smile. 'I shouldn't have said that.'

Shut up, shut up, shut up! she wanted to shout at him. She wanted to grab that thick floppy hair and pull his head down and give him a Glasgow kiss, as they called it when you used your own thick skull to smash someone's face in. She wanted to hurt the wee bastard, and hurt him bad.

He must have seen it in her face, because he had suddenly leant back and said, 'You're not going to go for me with an ice bucket, are you?' Those blue eyes had been bright, eager, as if he was almost hoping she'd go for him because then Duncan would kick her into touch.

She'd heaved herself up and walked away.

She'd walked out of that room and across the hall and into the library. Of all the 'strategies' she'd been taught to control her anger, it was the only one that worked: *Just walk away.*

She hadn't told Duncan exactly what Nick had said. But maybe she should. Then he'd see. She was that riled up now she wanted to march into that garage and let rip at the two of them. Duncan hadn't a fucking clue. He hadn't a fucking clue about his own son.

'She's becoming paranoid,' he was saying now. 'She accused Nick of smashing up her plastic measuring spoons. You should have seen her going off on one at him. Like a little wildcat.'

'Well, Dunc . . .'

'What? I hope you're not going to say *I told you so?*'

'Far be it from me. No, I like Maggie. I've a lot of respect for the girl, making something of her life, after the childhood she had. That mother of hers.'

'Oh, don't get me started. Social Services have a lot to answer for there. Beggars belief that they missed all the signs of neglect, not to mention physical abuse, year after year.' She heard him suck in his breath. Then: 'I know everyone thinks I'm mad. I know it's not the done thing, having a relationship with someone I used to mentor on the programme. But that was over six years ago. She's twenty-eight now, Michael – an adult. And yes, she's damaged, as Jemma kept telling me – you and Yvonne weren't the only ones to warn me off Maggie. But the simple fact is . . . I love her. And I'm prepared to do whatever it takes to help her. She's going to be a good mother to this child.'

Maggie backed away and then she was waddling back along the path, her heart hammering. That bitch Jemma! What business of hers was it if Duncan and Maggie wanted to get together? What business was it of Michael and Yvonne's?

But what she couldn't get out her head, as she stumbled across the lawn and back to the house, was Duncan's voice as he'd told Michael he loved her, that he was prepared to do whatever it took to help her, that she was going to be a good mother. It had been almost like he was trying to convince not *Michael* but *himself.*

She was sobbing as she lurched through the hall and up the stairs, hauling herself up using the bannisters. At the top, she stopped to get her breath, and then there he was. There he was in front of her.

Nick.

'Get away from me!'

'Mags – what's wrong?'

'Nothing!'

He made a long, sympathetic face at her. 'Oh God – have I upset you again? If I have, I really didn't mean to. Sometimes I open my mouth and these horrendous things come out. It's the last thing you need, isn't it, eight months pregnant and some oaf of a teenager is pushing your buttons? Bringing back all those traumatic memories?'

She moved to go past him, but he blocked her way, reaching out to take her arm.

She moved back against the bannisters.

'People with borderline personality disorder . . . that's what you've got, isn't it? I know that means you have big problems with relationships. I know it's an emotional rollercoaster and you find it really hard to control your mood swings, and being pregnant, hormones swirling, must be making it so much worse . . . and I'm making it worse by going on about it, aren't I?' He grimaced, all *What am I like?* 'Look – from what I understand, the most important thing, with someone with BPD, is to make them feel "heard". So, you know, Mags, any time you want to talk about anything . . . I mean, I know I'm probably the last person you'd want to talk to, just now, anyway, but – what's the phrase? I'm here for you?' Another self-deprecating grimace, which morphed charmingly into an uncertain smile.

And for a moment, just a moment, she wondered if Duncan was right. If she was paranoid. If she'd got Nick all wrong. She had a bad tendency to think people were picking a fight when they were just trying to be nice. That was something Duncan had pointed out to her, all those years ago when she'd been in the programme.

Little Miss Prickles.

But then it happened.

Nick shoved a hand at her belly, so hard she felt the baby squash back against her spine, wriggling like it was trying to get away, and Maggie was trapped against the bannisters as Nick smiled into her face and said, 'I'm really looking forward to being a big brother.' Slowly, he increased the pressure, and pain shot through her.

She pushed him away and aimed a kick at his balls which, impeded by her big belly, lost most of its force by the time it connected, almost overbalancing her, but he winced, and she yelled at him: '*Get the fuck away from me!*' and he put his hands out towards her, like he was fending off a wild animal, and said, 'Easy, easy! Sorry, I just wanted to see if I could feel the baby kick. Maggie, come away from the bannisters. *Come away from the bannisters!*'

But she couldn't move away from the bannisters because he was there, blocking her way, and as he reached for her she had a sudden image of him reaching out to Kathleen like this.

But no. *No.*

He couldn't have killed his own mother.

Could he?

'*Get away from me!*' She shouted it at the top of her voice, and thank God, *thank God*, here was Duncan running up the stairs, going, 'What the hell?' and Nick was speaking to him and finally, finally, she got away; stumbled to the bedroom and slammed the door behind her and leant on it.

'Maggie!'

The door was pushed open, sending her staggering forward, and then Duncan was in the room and holding her, and Nick was behind him, eyebrows raised, observing the specimen, and '*Evil wee bastard!*' was coming out her mouth, and Duncan, ill-advisedly, was going, 'Now, Maggie,' and she was rounding on him, on Duncan, on the only man she had ever or would ever love, spitting at him and trying to punch his face.

WHEN SHE WOKE, the light had faded. She was in their bed, lying on her side facing the window and the green velvet armchair where Duncan sat looking at her. When he saw she was awake, he got up and came and sat on the bed and put his hand to her hair.

'How are you feeling?'

'Okay.' Her mouth was so dry it was hard to speak.

'Water?'

She nodded.

He disappeared into the en suite, and she heard the gush of the tap – he always ran it for her because he knew she liked water that was nice and cold. And then he was back with not just the glass of water but a cool cloth for her forehead.

She struggled upright, holding the cloth in place. 'Thanks. You're so good to me. I'm sorry. I'm sorry for going mental. But Nick . . . he was . . . he shoved my belly, he tried to hurt the baby, and then he . . . I think he was going to push me over the bannisters!'

'Nick just wanted to feel the baby kick. And of course he wasn't going to push you over the bannisters, you silly bugger.' The smile he gave her was very gentle. 'He was worried you might fall. He tried to grab you because he was worried . . . You know that's where Kathleen . . . that's how Kathleen died. She fell over the bannisters.'

Maggie nodded. But she wasn't to be deflected. 'It's no big surprise that he resents me. He gets at me all the time. But this –'

'*Gets at* you?' Duncan was smiling, like there was no way this could be true.

'He said I had a face only a mother could love. He knows about Ma, I'm guessing? What she did to me?'

Duncan's face fell. 'Well, yes, I told him about that, but – are you sure, Maggie? Are you sure he said that?'

'I'm dead sure.'

He sighed. 'I'm so sorry. That was – really crass of him. He was probably just joking around with you, or trying to. I'm afraid he can be a bit gauche. Teenagers . . . well, we both know how obnoxious they can be.'

'This isn't just normal teenage badness. Nick hates me.'

Duncan shook his head.

'He wants to hurt me.'

'Oh, Christ, Maggie!' He grabbed her hand. 'No. Of course

he doesn't! You're making something out of nothing here! Nick's a good lad! Ask anyone. Ask Carol and Steve –'

'Aye, Carol's a fully paid-up member of the Nick fan club, right enough. But she hasn't seen what I've seen. He's – he's –' And then she was gulping for air, and Duncan was calming her, rubbing her back.

'Breathe. Just breathe. Slow and deep. Imagine . . . imagine you're standing by a cool mountain stream. Maybe that stream we paddled in, in the Eildon Hills – remember? You were being a right grumpy bastard because you were too hot and I was walking too fast, and you flung yourself down by the stream and told me to go on – "you sadistic fucker", I think were your exact words – and you'd just die there? And I made you paddle in the stream, even though you were convinced the fish would nip your toes. Think of that. The water's so clear you can see every detail of every stone. And there's the tinkling sound it makes as it flows off down through the valley . . .'

She shut her eyes and went back there.

She was holding Duncan's hand and watching the water swirling round her bare feet and thinking to herself that this was what it felt like to be happy.

Duncan was the only person who had ever been able to calm Maggie down. It was like, when he touched her, he was connecting her physically to a different world, a world she hadn't even known existed until Duncan had come into her life, a world where there was happiness and warmth and most of all – and this was something she could hardly even believe – love.

Love, but not just love in general.

Love for Maggie McPhee.

She opened her eyes. 'Sorry.'

'No. No need.' He held her close. 'You're safe, you know.

No one's going to hurt you and no one's going to hurt our baby. I won't let them.'

She choked on a sob.

He went on soothingly, 'Don't you think this stuff with Nick . . . don't you think you could be projecting your fears onto him, your fears about bringing a child into a world that's hurt you so much?'

All she could do was shake her head.

She thought of Nick, and his face as he said how much he was looking forward to being a big brother. She had come up against mental bastards like him in the system – the real headcases, the ones that looked at you with those ice-cold eyes, and you knew there was nothing there, nothing at all, nothing human you could appeal to.

She opened her eyes, stared right into Duncan's face, willed him to listen as she said, 'Nick hates me and he wants to hurt me.'

He sighed. 'He doesn't. He really doesn't. This is just the trauma of what happened to you when you were a kid, coming back now you're about to be a mum. And the pregnancy hormones, making you hypervigilant and ultra-protective of your unborn child. It's nature's way of ensuring the safety of a pregnant woman, I suppose. Making sure they avoid any dangerous situation by making them a bit . . .'

'Paranoid?' she suggested, her lips twisting round the word.

And suddenly she wanted to hit him again.

Her hands made fists under the covers.

But he smiled at her, her wonderful Duncan, and how could she even have *begun* to want to hurt him?

She made her fingers relax, and smiled back at him, and said, 'Maybe.'

He got into bed beside her and spooned her, pulling her

close into the warmth of his body. And for a while, five, ten minutes, it was fine. It was good.

But then, lying there looking out at the trees, she started thinking.

What would happen when the wee one was out in the world, outside the protection of her womb?

What might Nick do then?

Duncan must have felt her tense up, because he held her even closer and started to whisper in her ear about the mountain stream, and she closed her eyes and visualised Nick there: the stream was swollen by floods, all churning and foaming, and he was standing there watching it. Maggie came up behind him with a rock and smashed it onto the back of his head and he fell forward into the water and went under.

Bye-bye, Nick.

Finally, she closed her eyes.

And that was when the first wave of pain hit her.

5

'Good morning, Mrs Clyde.' The porter at the desk, an older guy called Adeel, nodded to Lulu and then went straight back to reading his paper. No doubt the porters had all been told to give her as wide a berth as possible. They were bound to know the reason Harry had been sacked last week and probably blamed her.

'Hi, Adeel,' she said briefly, and went on past and out of the building.

She fell asleep on the Tube, missed her stop and had to get another train back to Hammersmith. As she ascended from the mineral, hot-engine smell of the Underground into the early morning London air, a mix of fumes and dusty pavements and cooking and, somehow, grass, every step shuddered pain into her head. Her phone buzzed with a text message from Nick:

Just checking you're OK

Sighing, she messaged back:

Fine. Can't always text you on the hour every hour.

And she left it at that. She wasn't going to justify herself. It wasn't reasonable to expect her to text him every hour as he'd requested. She was finding his smothering behaviour, after what had happened with Harry, increasingly hard to deal with. He didn't let her go out alone after dark, saying he wouldn't have a moment's peace for worrying about her. He'd even started following her about the apartment. If she went to sit on the balcony for a few moments to herself, he'd join her. If she went back in to watch TV, he'd be there, snuggling up to her.

It was such a relief to be out of there. Even when he wasn't physically present, there were all the damn notes. She'd taken them with her, as usual, but as she passed a bin, she rooted in her handbag for them. As she turned to drop them in the bin, she was conscious of a man some way down the pavement wheeling round and walking in the opposite direction. He was a fair distance away, but from here he looked a bit like Harry. Same lanky frame, same very narrow bum.

Oh, for crying out loud!

She was becoming as paranoid as Nick.

In her office, she just sat for a moment, eyes closed, centring herself before the first client of the day. Putting all thoughts of stalkers and overprotective husbands out of her mind.

Her phone buzzing woke her up.

'Urrrgghhh!' she vented, picking it up.

But it wasn't a text from Nick.

Hi Lulu, sorry, I'm really sorry. I know I'm not due to see you until Friday but I need your help. Please. Please, Lulu, I really need to see you NOW but I can't face it, leaving

*here and crossing town. I can't face any of it. Can you
come here? I'm sorry. I know I'm being a terrible, terrible
nuisance but I need to talk to you pretty urgently. Thanks.
Paul*

Oh my God!

What did he mean, he needed her help?

What had happened?

She quickly replied to say she was on her way, sent texts
to the clients she was due to see that morning saying they
would have to reschedule, and left the office.

PAUL'S STREET was a brick Victorian terrace typical of thou-
sands all over London. Used to the wide-open spaces of
Australia, where even the cities were spacious, Lulu couldn't
get her head round the way people lived here, cheek by jowl,
one on top of the other. As she identified Paul's impossibly
narrow little house, the unedifying thought popped into her
mind: *Thank goodness Nick is rich.*

There was a tiny front garden – at least, presumably it
had once been a garden, but it was now just two small
squares of paving on either side of a concrete path to the
front door.

Which was standing half open.

'Paul?' She rang the bell, and when there was no
response, pushed the door wide. 'Paul, it's Lulu.'

She stepped into the narrow hall and, through the open
kitchen door, saw his legs and his feet.

Dangling.

Dark jeans. Polished brown leather shoes, swaying gently
in the slight breeze from the open front door.

Then she was in the kitchen, grabbing his legs, grabbing
the overturned chair and jumping up on it so she could hold

him up, so she could hold him round the hips and lift him up to take the pressure off –

She looked at his face only once.

There was blue nylon twine round his neck, tied above his head to an old hook in the ceiling. A pair of eyes goggled at her, not Paul's eyes, not those intelligent, troubled eyes she'd got to know, but ghastly fish-like orbs. His mouth was open, tongue slightly protruding as if in mockery of her vain attempts to save him.

He was dead.

Of course he was dead.

But she held onto him, she spoke calmly and reassuringly as she would have in one of their sessions. She pulled him to her with her left arm while with her right hand she fumbled in her bag for her phone.

And then she saw him.

Milo.

The little dog was cowering under the table, trembling all over, his head dipped submissively, ears folded back. He was gazing up at her.

'Oh, Milo,' breathed Lulu as she stabbed 999.

He didn't stop shaking, but at the sound of his name his stubby tail moved, tentatively, back and forth.

6

MAGGIE - AUGUST 1997

'And here they are!' Duncan was grinning all over his face as he and Nick came into the room.

Maggie was slumped back on her pillows chewing wine gums – recommended after a C-section to 'restore bowel function' as quickly as possible – and wondering if she needed to call a nurse for a painkiller top-up. She felt like she'd been hit by a truck. And the nurses here were sadists, making her stand up and move around to get things moving down there, so the first morning in Isla's life had been filled with her ma's farts and her da's chuckles. Maggie tried not to laugh because it hurt too much.

It was dead weird, being here in this room with the baby the two of them had made. She'd never known anything like it. Waves of pure joy kept washing through her, leaving her crying like a baby herself, but at the same time she felt like nothing would ever bother her again.

She couldn't stop staring at Isla, sleeping in the cot thingmy next the bed. She was two weeks premature and was a wee bit poukit, as Mrs Greenlees would say – a wee bit on the puny side – but she didn't need oxygen or anything like that. She was fine.

She was amazing.

She was a beautiful, tiny wee human being and she was Maggie's daughter, 'an actual person who's come out of me,' she remembered blethering to Duncan after the C-section as he handed her a slimy wee thing with arms and legs that moved. She had expected a new baby to just lie there and couldn't get over the fact she *moved* so much – funny, jerky movements of her arms and legs.

Maggie would never, ever get tired of watching her, drinking in every wee wriggle, every sound. She had cute bandy legs that Duncan said would straighten in time and her skin wasn't peachy like Maggie had expected, it was dry and flaky, but Duncan said that was also normal. Her tiny face was perfect, with those big blue eyes, soft gummy wee mouth opening and closing like a wee fish.

Isla had latched on immediately, as if to say, 'It's okay, Ma, it's going to be fine,' and Maggie had sat in the recovery room with her baby – *her actual baby* – feeding like a pro, and Duncan sitting with his arm round them both.

It really helped that Duncan had done this before.

He knew how to be a da, and what Maggie needed to do to be a ma.

Everything that had happened to her up to now didn't matter because it had led to this.

To Isla.

So when Nick appeared, big fake cheesy smile on his face, Maggie found she was telling her former self off, her pre-Isla self, for taking against the boy like she had, for thinking he was deliberately saying and doing things to hurt her, to threaten her. Duncan was right, eh? Nick was just a teenager being a teenager. He was bound to have some issues with his new stepmother. It would be surprising if they *didn't* butt heads. .

They'd work through it.

The Clydes were going to be fine.

She smiled at Nick and said, 'Meet your new sister,' and while Duncan went off to the shop to get more wine gums, Nick looked down at Isla in her cot.

As the door closed behind Duncan, Nick laughed. 'And I thought *you* were the ugliest thing I'd ever seen in my life, Mags. Christ. It's *disgusting*. It looks like a piece of raw meat that's gone off.'

Before she was even aware of thinking about moving, Maggie was out that bed and on him in mother tiger mode, pushing him away from the cot and yelling:

'*Get away from her!*'

As the door crashed open and Duncan came flying back into the room, Nick fell to the floor like a footballer angling for a penalty. Isla yowled. Maggie just stood there in her nightie and bare feet, glaring at Duncan, fists bunched, ready to defend Isla from the both of them.

But it wasn't Nick that Duncan rushed to.

It was Isla.

He scooped her up gently and cradled her against his chest. 'She's premature,' he snapped at Nick. 'You have to be *very* careful around her and *not* mess about!'

Ha!

'I didn't do anything!' Nick got to his feet. 'I didn't even touch her!'

'You were messing about.'

'I wasn't! Maggie pushed me for no reason!'

'He was tormenting her,' went Maggie. 'He made her cry.' Which was true, in a way.

Duncan gave Nick a long, long look. 'Not on,' he said quietly, rocking Isla. 'That's just not on.'

. . .

THE FIRST WEEK after Maggie and Isla came home was 'challenging', as the midwife put it. Isla latching on so well after she was born had lulled Maggie into a false sense of security. Now it was a struggle to get her to take enough milk. Maggie had started expressing it and, while Maggie dozed, Duncan would sit with Isla in the armchair by the bedroom window, trying to outwit her with the bottle using all kinds of tricks, like holding her facing out rather than into his body, swaying her, or tickling her upper lip with Bunny, the daft grey rabbit he'd bought her from that posh baby shop in Langholm.

Isla was Duncan's wee princess, his 'little darling' as he called her, and no wonder. She was a wee cracker. You could tell she was bright as a button, the way she looked at them with her big blue eyes, Maggie and Duncan, as if she already knew that these were the two people who loved her the most and always would be.

Duncan spent hours talking to her, making faces at her, just gazing at her like a daftie. He was rapidly filling the nursery up with things he 'thought Isla might like', and he'd decided that the mobile they'd bought her wasn't 'stimulating' enough for such a genius baby and was making one for her himself, a Noah's Ark, a complicated affair of pairs of wooden animals surrounding the bright red Ark, where Noah and his wife stood cradling a baby. Had there even been a baby on the Ark?

When Duncan knocked back Nick's suggestion of a kickabout because he had to work on the mobile, Nick was all, 'Neither of you even believes in God, let alone the story of the Ark.'

Maggie made sure never to leave Isla alone with him.

Duncan had taken time off work but had been called in a couple of times for 'crisis meetings' about Dean. The rat-faced wee bastard was trying to blackmail Duncan into giving him £1000, saying that if he didn't cough up, Dean would tell the police that Duncan had hit him. Maggie had persuaded Duncan to go to the police himself. 'That has to be nipped in the bud pronto,' she'd insisted. 'What if he *does* make allegations? You've got to get in there first. And let the other mentors know what's happening. Chuck the wee bastard off the programme.'

Of course, it wasn't that simple. There were meetings to be sat through and boxes to be ticked. The final meeting with all the 'stakeholders' involved in wrangling Dean had been fixed for this afternoon, a Friday, and Duncan had promised this would be an end to it – he'd be at home all next week.

When he'd left for the meeting, Maggie sat in the lounge – the *drawing room* – in her favourite wee purple chair with Isla, looking out over the lawn to the fields and the scabby hill, praying Nick wouldn't be back from school before Duncan – Nick got the school bus the four miles to and from Langholm – when the door came open and there was Yvonne, a big shopper over one arm.

Did the woman not know how to use a doorbell?

'Brought you some meals,' she said briskly. 'I don't imagine you'll be up to cooking at the moment, catering college diploma or no. And Duncan's repertoire is what you might call limited. I've got mince and tatties, spaghetti Bolognese and two home-made quiches.'

Maggie hated quiche.

Did Yvonne think she couldn't even cope with making the dinner, now she had a baby? Had Michael and Yvonne decided they had to rally round because Maggie was liable to fall apart and have a nervous fucking breakdown if she didn't get help?

'Thanks,' she managed.

Yvonne looked down at Isla, who was snuggled in a soft

yellow blanket in Maggie's arms looking pure adorable. 'Nice little thing, isn't she?' she said, almost reluctantly. Then she backed off, maybe worried that Maggie might suggest she hold her. 'Right, I'll put these in the fridge.'

'Okay. Thanks, Yvonne, that's good of you to take the trouble.'

Yvonne nodded in agreement and left the room.

A few minutes later the door crashed open again and this time it *was* Nick, barging in and whacking his schoolbag down on the couch.

'Hi, Mags!' he half-shouted.

Isla stirred.

'God, it's still so *tiny*. Failure to thrive, they call it, don't they?'

'*Keep your voice down!*' Maggie hissed. 'You're going to wake her.'

'*Sorrreee!*' he mouthed in an exaggerated whisper.

'She's fine,' Maggie murmured. 'The midwife says most slightly premature babies soon catch up.'

Nick nodded. 'I'm sure that's the case, normally. But, Mags – I'm sorry to bring this up, but there are a whole load of studies showing that abused children make terrible mothers. A small percentage repeat the abuse. A much larger percentage are merely neglectful. Their babies fail to thrive, have health problems that go unnoticed, don't get proper nourishment, fall into deep-fat fryers, et cetera, et cetera. Wouldn't it be terrible if something happened to it because you couldn't look after it properly?' He grimaced down at Isla.

'*You little bastard!*' The words shot across the room, and Yvonne came striding in. 'You poisonous little *bastard.*'

Nick, Maggie was glad to see, had gone pale. 'I was just trying to help,' he muttered, looking off.

Yvonne didn't bother responding to this. She just stood there until Nick had collected his bag and slunk from the room. Then she puffed out a breath. 'Maggie. I'm so sorry. I had no idea it was that bad.'

'He's only like that when he's alone with me.' Maggie put a catch in her voice, gazing up at Yvonne and blinking. 'Duncan doesn't think there's a problem. He thinks Nick's just a bit tactless, not in any way . . . *threatening*.' She blinked again and was pleased to find she could still cry on cue, a trick she'd mastered in the young offender institution when she needed to play the victim.

Not that she was playing the victim now. She *was* the fucking victim.

Yvonne's gaunt face was grim. 'Well, that's going to have to change.'

DUNCAN, as usual, was a right wetty with Nick, sitting him down at the kitchen table with Maggie and Yvonne to put to him the 'suggestion' that he 'see someone'. Duncan had been leaning towards a counsellor who worked with the kids on the programme, but the woman was shite. Maggie knew this from personal experience and had shut this idea down pronto. So Yvonne had got the name of a psychiatrist with a private practice from Carol and Steve Jardine, who had tried to take Andy to him once. Andy had refused to go – which was a surprise to Maggie. She wouldn't have thought he had the gumption.

'You don't have to go if you don't want to, obviously,' Duncan assured Nick. 'But I think talking things through with a professional might help.' He looked at Nick across the kitchen table with a little smile, as if he was sure his darling boy wasn't going to let him down.

Nick looked from Duncan to Maggie to Yvonne. 'I was only trying to *help* Maggie. She's not looking after Isla properly.'

'That's rubbish,' said Yvonne calmly.

'Maggie's a great mum,' Duncan said at once.

Maggie lifted her eyebrows at Nick and said gently, 'It's perfectly understandable that you resent me, and maybe Isla too. This isn't about blame.'

The fuck it wasn't.

As she'd hoped, this provoked the real Nick to rear his ugly head. His lips curled away from his teeth like a mad dog someone had poked with a stick.

But it was Maggie who should be raging here. Duncan had ignored what she was saying about Nick until Yvonne had put her oar in. 'Maggie feels threatened, and she's every cause to,' Yvonne had rapped out at her brother. 'Nick's bullying her. How you've let it get this far, I don't know. Apparently you haven't believed Maggie.'

Yes!

Maggie couldn't have written Yvonne's script better herself.

'It's not that I didn't *believe* her,' Duncan had said, a face on him like a smacked arse. 'I just didn't see any evidence that Nick resented her in any way.'

Yvonne had snorted. 'Of course you didn't. He only picks on her when you're not there.'

'Oh, Christ!' Duncan had touched Maggie's arm, but Maggie had pulled away from him. 'I'm sorry. I should have . . . Okay, I accept that he's maybe got issues. He maybe hasn't been coping with Kathleen's death as well as I thought. And now he's maybe feeling excluded, struggling with the new family he finds himself in . . . But he would never do anything to hurt you or Isla.'

'How can you know that?' Yvonne had asked.

'Because *he's my son!*'

And now, he was giving Nick an out. 'I think we need to do this, yes? But, obviously, it's entirely up to you.'

Nick must know that Andy had refused to go to the psychiatrist and got away with it.

So it was a big surprise when he nodded, and gave Duncan a wee smile. 'If you think it's for the best, Dad. But really, you've got this all wrong.'

'Good man, good man!' Duncan beamed. 'We're going to sort this out. Don't worry. It's going to be fine.'

THE PSYCHIATRIST, Jamie Stirling-Stewart, MBBS, MSc, FRCPsych, was a youngish, poncy man in red trousers with floppy hair like Nick's and an office in the New Town in Edinburgh. He had refused to discuss Nick with Duncan and Maggie until after the third session, when he'd scheduled a 'chat' for after the consultation.

'Nick has agreed that I can talk to the two of you about how we've been getting on,' he said, sitting down in one of the armchairs at a coffee table and waving at Duncan and Maggie to do likewise. 'Would you like some water?'

Maggie hoped this was a good sign, that he felt they'd need reviving after he dropped the bombshell that Nick had psychopathic traits, was a danger to Maggie and Isla and needed sectioned. Both of them accepted the offer.

But 'Nick seems a bit anxious,' he began, crossing his long red legs. 'And his mother's death obviously hit him hard. He's having a few issues adjusting to the new status quo.'

'He hates me and Isla,' said Maggie.

The psychiatrist smiled. 'No. In fact, he seems fond of you. He actually broke down when I suggested he'd made you feel unsafe.' He looked past Duncan and Maggie like he was in search of inspiration to help him explain the complexities of the human psyche to these two numpties. 'In the teenage brain, the prefrontal cortex – which is responsible for things like rational decision-making and impulse control – is very much a work in progress. So the amygdala, which is where emotions stem from, is used instead by teenagers to process information, and there's no "brake" on it from the prefrontal cortex as there is in adults.' He smiled again. 'Teenagers often have very poor judgement and impulse control, don't think things through, and are more vulnerable to stress. Their emotions can very often get the better of them, and they can say some really terrible things that, as the teenager themselves will say, they "don't mean". In other words, they know on some level they're being irrational and maybe hurtful for no good reason, but they can't control what's coming out of their mouths.'

Duncan breathed out. 'So, you don't think he could be in any way . . . dangerous?'

Maggie hadn't thought the guy's smile could get any more patronising, but he managed it. 'Only to the extent that any teenager can be said to be "dangerous" through this inherent lack of control. But in Nick's case, I would say the prefrontal cortex is further on the road to maturity than in many sixteen-year-olds. He has insight into the effect his behaviour has had on you, Maggie. Which is ninety per cent of the way to addressing it. He was in tears when he was recounting some of the things he's said.'

'What, so everything in the garden's rosy? That's what you're saying?' Maggie turned to Duncan. 'This is a fucking joke. How much are we paying this so-called fucking expert?'

That at least wiped the smile off the guy's face.

'*Maggie*,' muttered Duncan.

'As I say,' the psychiatrist said stiffly, 'Nick accepts there's an issue. At the root of his anxiety seems to be a – completely unfounded, I'm sure – worry about *your* mental stability, Mrs Clyde. Which may explain his desire to keep you at arm's length. But with a bit of *understanding and patience*, I think he'll be fine.' He eyeballed Maggie.

Jesus! Blame the victim, why don't you?

'Oh aye, *he'll* be fine. It's me and my wee lassie I'm worried about, pal.'

His mouth pursed up like a wee arsehole. He didn't like that, being called *pal* like he was any random off the street. Which he might as well be for all the use he was, the fucker.

He got up and went to his desk. 'Here's something that might, I hope, reassure you. I find it's often helpful to get my patients to draw – it's a sort of shortcut to the subconscious mind.' He handed them some sheets of A3 paper.

They were bad drawings of a happy family – big tall da, tiny ma, boy and baby. The drawings showed them sitting round a table eating or going for a walk or playing on a beach. Maggie leafed through them, handing each one to Duncan after she'd glanced at it.

Then the f-bomb was out her mouth again.

This one showed the da character hugging the boy, who in turn hugged the ma, who was holding the baby. They all had manic grins apart from the baby, who had no face, and he'd drawn the tiny ma with wide, I'm-shitting-myself-here eyes. 'Do you not think this one is maybe *just a wee bit disturbing?*' She showed Duncan and then the psychiatrist. 'Isla has no face. And look at me.'

'Uh, Nick's artistic skills aren't the best,' said Duncan.

'Sometimes,' Mr Psychiatrist said quietly, 'we can read into this sort of thing what we expect – what we're *afraid* we might find. It's the sentiment that's important. There's a lot of affection here, wouldn't you say, for his family?'

But Maggie didn't want to look at the drawing again.

Two days later, having put up with Nick's sickly smiles and exaggeratedly concerned questions long enough, Maggie decided to go on the offensive and search his room, a long,

low space up in the eaves of the house with a prime view of
Billy McLetchie Hill from four wee windows. It wasn't the
typical teenage boy's room – it was dead tidy. And there was
nothing personal in it apart from three framed photographs
of Nick and Duncan on top of his chest of drawers – one of
Nick as a wee boy playing football with his da, one of the two
of them on top of a hill, and one of them standing in the
garden, Duncan making a daft face, arms round each other.

She found the psychiatry textbook at the bottom of the
wardrobe.

A library book called *The Human Mind: What we Know*.
She took it to one of the windows and thumbed through it.

She supposed it was meant for professionals in the field
or maybe medical students. He must have used this to work
out what to say and how to act to fool the psychiatrist into
thinking there was no harm in him.

She slammed it shut and took it outside. Duncan was in
the garden somewhere with Isla. As Maggie marched across
the lawn, a bird cooed from a tree and a bee buzzed right past
her nose. On the rough grazing on the side of the hill, cotton-
wool sheep troddled about. Right enough, it was like she'd
rocked up in the Garden of Eden.

Shame about the snake.

A deep rumble cut through the sounds of nature and
brought her back to reality as a massive lorry passed on the
road at the foot of the garden. Then another. There was a
forestry operation about a mile away, and at five o'clock every
afternoon two lorries stacked with timber thundered past. A
piercing cry rose up, allowing Maggie to pinpoint where
Duncan and Isla were.

Duncan was pushing the pram round the rose garden. As
he turned to her with a smile, Maggie shoved the book
at him.

'This was in Nick's room. He's obviously been using it to bamboozle that fuckwit of a shrink.'

Nick appeared without making a sound, as he often did.

'You've been in my room?' he asked mildly, a hand on the roof of the pram. 'Rummaging around? That's a bit of an invasion of privacy, Mags.'

'I was cleaning it.'

Nick reached out for the book and opened it. 'I was reading up on the effects of –' He lowered his voice. 'Childhood abuse. I was trying to understand you.' He turned his bright blue eyes, all concerned, on Maggie. 'What happened to you was so terrible. I wanted to try to understand why you fly into rages the whole time. And your issues around trust.'

'My *what*?' Maggie half-screamed. Jesus – he was turning this round on her?

'Apparently, childhood abuse can stop the prefrontal cortex developing properly, which can lead to problems with rational thinking –'

'You *little fucker!*'

'– And impulse control,' he finished in a small voice, stepping back. He looked at Duncan. 'Can make people lash out for no reason.'

She just lashed out for no reason. That was what the prosecutor had said at Maggie's trial for GBH when she was seventeen. Had Nick somehow got hold of the trial report in the local Paisley paper? He was crafty enough to have found it. To have sent off for it to a press cuttings agency.

Her lawyer had tried to argue that Maggie hadn't been in her right mind at the time of the assault in the nightclub, which was true enough. Something that bitch had said or the way she'd said it had conjured up Ma, and before she knew it Maggie had picked up the ice bucket and walloped the lassie on the side of the head. It was like it was Ma standing there laughing at her, and Maggie wasn't a helpless bairn any more, she was a grown woman with an ice bucket in her hand.

Gillian Menzies, her 'victim' had been called. Maggie still sometimes wondered about her, how she was doing. She'd been in a coma for two days, and when she came out of it she wasn't right. Wobbled when she walked. Had cross eyes. Problems concentrating.

Maggie had been in a fugue state, her lawyer had argued. Having a flashback to her traumatised childhood. The sheriff hadn't bought it, and Maggie had been sentenced to three years in a YOI. Which was fair enough.

She took a deep breath. She nodded at Duncan, to tell him *I'm fine, I'm not losing the head here.* And then she turned and walked away from them both.

But on the other side of the line of wee trees, she stopped.

Nick was going, 'Mr Stirling-Stewart said I have to be more accepting of Maggie and her problems and stop panicking all the time that she's about to kick off. But . . . Dad, I'm still worried. I'm still worried about what she might do.'

'We've been through this,' went Duncan.

'I know, but . . .'

'Maggie's offending behaviour stemmed from what she suffered as a child and was effectively addressed long ago. Yes, she's been a little short-tempered lately, but that's because she's in protective new mum mode. You have to cut her some slack and remember her bark is worse than her bite. In fact, she doesn't even *have* a bite.'

'But what if she got *really* angry with me or you? Or with Isla?'

'For God's sake, Nick. You're being ridiculous now. Maggie would never hurt any of us.'

'But how can you be so sure? I know you do all that amazing work with troubled people. I know you've already helped Maggie a lot, but maybe she needs, I don't know, more specialist help?'

'Maggie's fine,' said Duncan. 'She doesn't need "help".'

Maggie didn't wait to hear any more. She marched along the path and across the lawn and onto the gravel, her C-section scar nipping like a bastard. There was a wee stone urn by the door with bonnie flowers in it. She kicked the fucker.

It went over, and all the earth and flowers fell out.

'Maggie, are you okay?' said Duncan's voice behind her.

Fuck.

She turned. Duncan was there with the pram, and Nick right next to him. They'd followed her.

'Fine. Tripped.'

'Let me do that.' Nick got down on his knees and scooped everything back in the urn. As he patted the earth in place around the plants, he whispered, 'Nice one. QED, Mags. QED.' He got to his feet with a smile. 'There we are. No harm done.'

7

LULU - JUNE 2019

L ulu stood in the middle of her office looking at the view of the brick wall. Probably some sort of metaphor for what she was feeling. But how could she be standing here thinking of herself and metaphors when Paul . . . when Paul . . . But if she allowed herself to think about Paul, about what he must have gone through as he positioned the chair, as he tied the length of blue nylon twine around his neck, as he said goodbye to Milo, she would lose it again.

She'd had no idea he could be suicidal.

What sort of therapist did that make her?

Typical Lulu.

Typical ditzy Lulu. Always losing things.

Karla, her old tutor at Sydney Uni, had reassured her in several tearful Zoom conversations that she shouldn't blame herself. 'Our clients, by definition, are troubled souls. People undergoing therapy are more likely to go through with suicide, but studies have shown that there isn't a causal relationship. They're in therapy *because* they're troubled, and they complete suicide for the same reason, not because of the therapy.'

And Lulu knew, with her head, that this was true. But her heart . . .

Nick had been trying to persuade her to take a break from work. Last night, he'd held her in bed when the tears had come, yet again. He'd gently chided her for taking a zolpidem off-schedule, and she'd half-yelled at him that she knew she wouldn't sleep without it. He had hugged her tight and murmured reassurances. 'The human mind is a mysterious thing. You keep saying yourself that even the most brilliant neurologists are only beginning to understand it. Don't be so hard on yourself. There's no way you could have seen this coming.'

But she *should* have seen it coming.

She stared at the wall.

Maybe she should take a break from work. She'd already stopped taking on any new clients.

She picked up her tablet and slipped it into her bag. She'd downloaded papers on risk factors for suicidal ideation but hadn't been able to face looking at them. She needed to do that. She had half an hour before her next appointment. She owed it to her existing and possible future clients to work out where she'd gone wrong with Paul.

She went across the road to Ravenscourt Park, found a quiet bench in the shade of three big trees in the middle of the grass, and started to read. The papers told her what she already knew – that one of the main risk factors for suicide was having a family member who'd killed themselves. There was a genetic component to it, apparently, but there was also the problem that it loomed large if someone close to you – your father, for instance – had completed suicide.

Oh God.

She *knew* that, so why hadn't she seen it coming with

Paul? He hadn't displayed any of the warning signs. He hadn't, as far as she knew, attempted suicide before, in all the thirty-odd years since finding his dad's body in that bath. He wasn't depressed or particularly anxious. He didn't have a problem with alcohol. He hadn't expressed feelings of hope-lessness – quite the opposite, in that last session.

The screen blurred.

She couldn't stop thinking about Milo, cowering under the table. She had wanted to take him, when the police and the paramedics had arrived, but they wouldn't let her. After she'd made her statement, she'd browbeaten one of the police officers, a DC called Tariq Akhtar, into revealing where Milo had been taken. He wasn't, as she'd hoped, with friends or family. He was in a dog shelter. In one of those concrete cells, probably, watching everyone who went past, his little tail starting to wag in the hope that it might be his dad come to get him.

'Can we take him?' she'd asked Nick impulsively.

'Pets aren't allowed here,' he'd said quickly, but with a grimace, trying to make out he wished it were otherwise. 'You know that. Which makes sense, with no garden. Someone will take him. If he's as adorable as you say he is, he'll be snapped up pretty quickly, I'll bet.'

But Milo wasn't an attractive dog. The chances were that people walking past his cell would just keep on walking.

Oh God!

She looked away from the screen across the park.

A man was coming up the grassy slope towards her.

Harry.

Wasn't it?

Yes, it was porter Harry!

He must have been staking out her office and had followed her in here!

Heart bumping, she looked around.

There was no one nearby.

She grabbed up her bag and started to run across the grass, skirting a line of shrubs on the other side of which, she knew, was the pond. There would be people there. She had opened her mouth to shout something when a hand clamped across it and she was being knocked sideways into the bushes.

She landed hard on the packed, dusty earth, with Harry on top of her. His hand was still over her mouth. She kicked out behind her and had the satisfaction of feeling him wince.

They were in a cave-like space roofed by thick vegetation – invisible, probably, to anyone out there walking past.

She tried to scream, but he pressed his hand harder against her mouth and rasped into her ear: 'I'm not going to hurt you. I'm sorry, Mrs Clyde. I just need to talk to you. I'm going to take my hand away. Please don't scream. I'm in enough trouble as it is.'

As he released her, Lulu scrambled away from him on all fours, leaving her bag where it lay. She crashed out of the bushes, a twig scratching her face, and stumbled, almost falling, giving him a chance to catch up to her and say, his acne-dotted face full of earnest contrition, 'I'm so sorry. But I need to tell you what happened. Your husband, Mrs Clyde – he's a nutjob.'

WHEN NICK GOT in that evening, Lulu was sitting on the balcony, watching the river and nursing a white wine she didn't want. The Thames was always this muddy brown colour, not, as she'd first assumed, because of pollution but because of the silt that was continually churned up from the riverbed. It actually wasn't badly polluted any more, and, if you watched for long enough, you could see fish jumping, ducks bobbing by, herons and cormorants and occasionally a seal or a dolphin.

'Oof,' Nick groaned, subsiding on the long couch beside her and sticking his legs out under the coffee table. 'I'll have that, if you don't want it.'

She waited until he'd drained the glass to say, 'I spoke to Harry today. Harry the former porter. The one you got sacked.'

He went still.

'And before you start on about psychos and how it's not safe for me out there – no, he wasn't stalking me. Or not in the usual sense. But then, you know that, don't you?'

He looked at her, his blue eyes narrowing in the way they did when he felt himself under attack, as if to stop her seeing inside his head, to close himself off from her.

'Harry told me that you paid him to keep tabs on me. To tell you if he saw anyone talking to me. And you also paid him to give you the passcode to the CCTV software so you could check the footage whenever you wanted. *You're* the one who's *stalking* me, Nick!' She got up and went to the rail of the balcony, pressing her hands down on it, breathing the muddy, weedy river air.

'But – you don't *believe* him, Lu, do you?' The charm was back. He gave a little laugh, and came and stood beside her. 'The guy's a –'

'Nutter? Funny, that's what he said about you. And yes, I believe him. Why would he make it up? It's not going to get him reinstated. Presumably, what he did for you is also a sackable offence. Arguably, it's even worse.' Near the far bank of the river, a boat was chugging along. 'After he told me about the CCTV, I remembered something. One night, must be a month or so ago, I'd gone to bed to read, but the story was all about a chef and it made me hungry, so I came back down to raid the fridge, and you were sitting at the island watching something on your laptop. Footage of the area at the front of the building. You said the security firm had sent you a random sample of images so you could check them for quality. Remember? If I ask them, will they confirm that?' At last, she turned and looked at him.

For a long moment, their gazes locked.

'Lulu,' was all he said.

'You paid Harry to spy on me.' And suddenly her legs were shaking. She pushed herself away from the rail and strode inside. She didn't know where she was going.

Out.

She needed to get out of this apartment.

'Lulu, I'm sorry!' Nick was behind her. 'I was only trying to protect you! I've brought you here, to a strange city, a strange country where you know *no one*. You're not streetwise. Not London streetwise. I know you lived in Sydney, but it's not the same. And you're not well. You're not sleeping, you're exhausted all the time, you forget things. I only looked at the CCTV footage to check you were okay, to check there were no dodgy types hanging around, following you, whatever. And yes, I asked Harry to keep an eye on you, to look out for you, but I didn't tell him to keep *notes*, for God's sake! I'm so sorry, Lu – I didn't realise I was facilitating a stalker. Because that's what he is. He followed you, presumably, when you left the building.'

Halfway to the lift, she turned. 'No. It was in Ravenscourt Park that we spoke. I guess he must have followed me from my office.'

'So he found out where you worked. Christ, Lu, he must have followed you from here all the way to your office.' Nick subsided onto the massive L-shaped sofa in the sitting area. He put his head in his hands. 'I'm sorry. God. What was I thinking?'

Lulu sighed, and walked back to him, and put a hand on

his shoulder. The muscles of his shoulder, his neck, were knotted like ropes.

'I really don't think he's a stalker. He just wanted to come clean. I'm okay.' Gently, she pressed the knots with her fingers. 'But you need to talk to me, Nick. *Please.* You need to work through why you worry about me so obsessively, for no good reason. I know it's to do with what happened to your family.' And she left a space.

Normally, he'd fill this space with humour. Say something like, 'Are you charging me by the hour for this?'

Now, though, he just mumbled, 'I can't lose you too.'

Here was where Lulu had to be tough. She sat down next to him and took his hand. 'The only way you're going to lose me is if you carry on like this. I can't live this way, Nick. You're smothering me, laying down rules, not letting me have any time to myself.'

'Oh God, Lu, I'm sorry! I won't any more!'

'I know you don't mean to do it. But I think the only way you're going to be able to stop is if you address *why* you're like this. *Talk* to me, Nick. About your family. *Please.*'

He let go her hand and stood, and walked to the TV that was set into the wall, and turned to face her, as if standing on a stage giving a lecture. She often found that her clients physically moved away from her when they first started to open up. It was as if they needed space around them to feel safe.

'They had gone,' he said, staring at her. 'They'd just *disappeared,* all three of them, into thin air. When I got back home that day . . . I'd been in Edinburgh doing museums and galleries and stuff with my friend Andy and his mum. I was looking forward to telling Dad all about it. Then the house . . . the house was in darkness, and *they'd gone.* The police decided there were no suspicious circumstances and they'd left of their own accord, and it wasn't a police matter. I was sixteen and theoretically an adult, so it wasn't a case of child abandonment. But *no way* would Dad have done that to me!'

He turned towards the river, then towards the marina, and then he suddenly walked off into the corridor and came back with one of the framed photos, the one of him and his dad with their arms round each other.

'Look at us!' He thrust it into her hands. 'Dad and I – we were really close. I loved him *so much*, and he loved me. I know he did. He would never, *ever* have just gone off like that, leaving me all alone. Leaving me not knowing what had happened.' He choked on a deep breath.

'You can see how much you love each other,' Lulu said quietly, touching the glass over the photo with gentle fingertips.

'It was like the *Mary Celeste*, Lulu! Nothing was disturbed, which is why the police presumably ruled out violence. But it didn't add up. They hadn't taken their passports or withdrawn any money from their bank accounts. I know the breakfast things were cleared up before I left that morning, so why were there *three* mugs and *three* bowls and *three* spoons on the table, when it was just the two of them in the house, apart from Isla? One of the rings on the hob was on. There was a pan of water and oatmeal next to it, as if Dad had been about to make some porridge when . . . whatever happened happened.'

'You think your stepmother did something to your dad and your sister,' she prompted.

'There's no other explanation that makes sense.'

'But does *that* explanation make sense?' Lulu made her voice gentle. 'She was a small woman, wasn't she? Could she really have done it?'

'She could have had an accomplice – hence the extra mug and bowl and spoon. Or maybe she was trying to set *me* up for it, make it look like I was there when it happened. She'd been a young offender, for God's sake – convicted of GBH. She was violent. I was *scared* of her, this tiny woman . . . When we were alone together, she used to stare at me, like she was . . . I don't know. Like she wanted me gone. And she did things like trample a set of plastic spoons she had and try to blame me. She used to call me a wee bastard, a wee fucker . . . Okay, I was an annoying brat, and I definitely went out of my way to push her buttons, but I can see now that she really overreacted to that. She was scary, Lulu.'

Oh God. 'What did your dad make of her behaviour?'

'Dad was a bit like you.' A small smile. 'Always saw the best in people.'

He turned away from her and paced to the glass wall, his back to Lulu. 'I should have tried harder to make Dad see what she was really like.'

'But you don't *know* that Maggie was responsible. You don't know what happened to them. Probably you'll never know – and maybe you're going to have to accept that.'

'There was blood.' Nick turned back to face her. 'On the drawing room carpet and in the hall. When the police had it tested, they found it had Maggie's DNA. They concluded it was irrelevant to what had happened, that Maggie maybe cut her finger or something. But I think that must be where . . . where she did whatever she did to Dad. He must have put up some sort of a fight, but – he wouldn't have wanted to hurt her, you see. Everything in him would have been screaming that he couldn't hurt a woman.'

There was a long silence. Then Lulu said, 'It must have been so hard, losing them and then being packed off to boarding school, living amongst strangers . . .'

His face twisted. 'Dear Auntie Yvonne and Uncle Michael were kind enough to arrange that for me. Yvonne got herself made what they call a judicial factor loco absentis, which let her take control of Dad's affairs until he was declared officially dead. She organised the letting of the house to give me an income. And they allowed me to stay with them for a week at Christmas and a week in the summer, but not at Easter or half term or any other time. They pretty much washed their hands of me.'

'Your whole world imploded,' she summarised, going to him and pulling him into a hug as the tears came, for both of them.

'I've blown it, haven't I?' he sobbed. 'I've pushed you away!'

She wasn't going to lie to him. She took a deep breath. 'You haven't *blown it*, Nick, but I do think the way this relationship is developing is unhealthy. Getting Harry to spy on me . . .' To soften the impact of her words, she rubbed his back. 'That crossed a line.'

'Oh God! *Please* give me another chance! I'll never do anything like that again!'

She kept rubbing his back. 'That's easy to say. But the first step in making a change is to accept that you have a problem. There's nothing terrible about having a mental illness.' She had to tread gently here. 'It doesn't mean that you're like Maggie.'

He made a wordless sound and broke away from her, staring into her eyes as if scared of what he might see there.

'There's nothing to be ashamed of in admitting that you need help.' She took both his hands in hers.

It was strictly against the code of ethics she'd signed up to, to treat a member of one's own family. She could lose her licence for this. But so what? She wasn't sure she even wanted to be a therapist any more. And anyway, Nick was more important.

'I love you, Nick. I'll always love you. You're not going to lose my love by letting me help you through this. Quite the opposite. Please, will you let me help you *heal*?'

After a long moment, he nodded.

She squeezed his hands. 'I know you're very frightened, but you don't need to be. Therapy for PTSD now doesn't involve making you talk endlessly about the trauma – that method has been totally discredited. It's been shown to make things worse for people, if anything. Oh, Nick, were you worried I would make you do that?'

Another nod.

'I only use evidence-based therapies.' Safe therapies, she had been about to say . . . but then she flashed on Paul, crying after the EMDR session. Karla had assured her that EMDR *was* safe, but Lulu had stopped using it. She'd switched her remaining clients on EMDR to other, equivalent ways of revisiting their trauma. Just in case there was something *she* was doing, some quirk in her application of EMDR that had caused Paul to end his life.

She wasn't about to take that chance with Nick.

She felt she needed to *really* be there with him as he revisited the trauma, not just sitting moving her finger in front of his eyes as he went back there alone.

It took a huge effort to continue to speak calmly, but this was what she had been trained to do – to make the client feel safe with her. 'The therapy I'm thinking of using – yes, you have to revisit the trauma, but only briefly, and I'll be with you, *physically* with you, in every way I can be, grounding you in the here and now and putting the past back where it belongs. The idea is to stop you being trapped in the trauma – which I think you are. I think that's why you're behaving the way you are with me.'

He heaved in a huge sigh.

'At least give it a try. Show me you care enough about this relationship to try.'

'Of course I do. Yes. I'll do anything you want. *Anything*, Lu. Literally *anything*.'

Her heart was bumping, her mouth dry, and her words came out in a sort of croak: 'Would you go back there?' She swallowed, cleared her throat, made herself hold his gaze steadily. 'Back to Sunnyside? To properly revisit what happened, I think we need to take a trip back there. If it's a holiday let now, presumably you can cancel a booking or two so we can stay there?'

'You mean, actually in the house? In Sunnyside?'

'I was thinking of taking a break from work anyway, after . . . after Paul.' She put a hand to his face. 'I really think we need to do this, if we're going to have a future together. We need to go back to the place where your family vanished, because, really, I don't think you've ever left.'

8

MAGGIE - SEPTEMBER 1997

'Okay, Nick, it's seven-ten,' went Maggie. 'Leaving in five minutes.'

She was dropping Nick at his school in Langholm for a rehearsal of a Shakespeare play, and then she was going on to the coffee shop to have a proper catch-up with Pam and Liam. Her pal Pam from catering college was 'between jobs' and had jumped at the chance to fill in for Maggie while she was off on maternity.

Nick turned to her from the sink. 'Okay, I'll just finish up these last few things. Could you dry that and put it away?' He nodded at the knife on the draining board.

The knife had belonged to Duncan and Yvonne's ma and was something of a family heirloom. Duncan always insisted it be dried immediately to stop it rusting. Maggie picked it up, dried it and put it away in the rack.

'Thanks,' said Nick.

If she hadn't known better, she'd have thought a miracle had happened – that Nick had turned over a new leaf. But she *did* know better. His nicey-nicey act had got to be fake. In the week since her latest meltdown, she'd been waiting for his next move, but nada. He'd smiled and smiled and brought her cups of tea. She hadn't drunk them, mind. You never knew what the wee bastard might have put in them.

It was doing her head in. Just like when she was wee, waiting for Ma to turn on her. The waiting had almost been the worst bit.

She expected him to maybe start on her when they were alone in the car, but he just sat there in silence. Maggie looked at the scenery and tried to relax. The humpy hillsides, Billy McLetchie and pals, became more threatening towards night-time, like Billy himself when he'd had a few. But the cute cottages and the trees just starting to get their autumn colour, and the fields with the bales in them throwing long shadows across the stubble, the harvests gathered in – all that was magic.

As she stopped outside the school to let Nick out, she even found it in her to say she hoped he had a good rehearsal.

'Thanks, Mags, I will. Enjoy your catch-up.'

Maggie drove through the old square and over the bridge across the River Esk. This was where the bonniest houses were, big old stone ones like Sunnyside. She turned right along the High Street, passing the wee lane she knew so well because up there was the house where her bedsit used to be. Most of the yobs attending The Phoenix Centre were bused in from the local area, but some were from further afield, like Maggie and Liam, and were put up in that house, which was owned by the same charity.

Maggie had thought she'd died and gone to heaven, living in this barry wee town nestled in the hills. The locals weren't mad about the whole arrangement, but Duncan maintained it was carrying on a long tradition of accommodating hoodlums. Langholm was just eight miles from the Scotland/England border, and back in the day this whole area had been

Scotland's equivalent of the Wild West. Outlaws, reivers and all-purpose mad bastards had called it home. Those days were long gone, of course, much to the disappointment of most of the yobs on the programme.

She got to the coffee shop at twenty to eight, just as the sun was setting. It was in a prime location near the town hall, in a narrow stone building squashed between a bank and an estate agent. Maggie had painted the door and window a fashionable pale grey and done her best with red and white gingham to make it look bonnie.

The place closed at four, but they did the stocktake and paperwork every second Thursday evening, and it was all lit up. Pam and Liam were at the table in the window with sheets of paper spread between them. Liam seemed to have even more gel in his spiky blond hair than usual, like a character out *The Broons*.

'Hi there!' Maggie breezed in, and the two of them looked up with big grins that made her feel ten feet tall.

'Maggie!' whooped Pam, coming over to hug her.

'Have you left Duncan minding the baby?' went Liam.

Maggie clapped her hands to her face. 'Oh my God! The baby!' And as Liam's eyes widened: 'Of course he's minding her, you wee bampot.'

She had to admit it – she'd got to like Liam. The boy had a good heart, and he made her laugh, although not always intentionally. As Pam bustled about getting Maggie a coffee and a slice of carrot cake, and top-ups for herself and Liam, out of badness Maggie got out her wee album of Isla photos and made Liam look through it.

'Aye, and that's her in the *blue* sleepsuit. Dead gorgeous with her blue eyes, eh? Why should girl babies not wear blue, is what I say.'

'Uh,' went Liam.

Pam grabbed the album off him and pored over it. Maggie

was going on about how they were tempting Isla to feed when the phone behind the counter trilled. Maggie went and answered it.

'Hello, Maggie's?'

'Is that Maggie Clyde?' said a crabby voice. 'Duncan Clyde's missus?'

'That's me.'

'Door's standing open at the Borstal place.'

'You mean The Phoenix Centre?'

'Aye, whatever. God knows what those wee bastards are up to now.'

'Oh. Right. Thanks very much for letting us know, Mr . . .'

But the guy had rung off. Probably one of the pissed-off neighbours who'd had to put up with all kinds of crap from the young offenders over the years. Maggie better get her arse over there pronto. It was only five minutes' walk, and she carried keys to The Phoenix Centre in her bag.

Liam offered to go with her, but she shook her head. 'Probably just that airhead Jemma left the door open.'

She was half expecting to meet some of the kids on her way there. You sometimes saw them in wee groups, hanging around the streets trying to bring the tone down, mouthing off to passers-by and trying to get drug deals going, but nine times out of ten some busybody like Maggie would send them off with a flea in their ear. It was a culture shock for the wee bastards, used as they were to decent folk showing them the respect they thought they deserved and looking the other way. But Langholm wasn't that kind of a place.

The Phoenix Centre was in an old building that used to be a school, set back from the road behind a low wall and the car park, and a bit of grass where the kids played football. In the gloom, Maggie could see that the heavy old front door, a big Victorian effort in two halves, was indeed standing open. She walked inside, giving it, 'Hello? Anyone in here?'

Silence.

The smell of the place took her back – sweaty shoes and polish and disinfectant. The walls were painted in the institutional favourite of dark green below waist height, light green above. Her shoes clopped on the vinyl floor as she walked down the long corridor, opening doors to check inside rooms as she went, clicking lights on and off again. The meeting room, the kitchen, the classrooms, the sports hall – all empty.

She'd never been in here on her own in the evening.

It felt weird.

She had a bad feeling, like someone was in here with her.

She stopped and listened, turning a slow three-sixty, looking back down the empty corridor, squinting in the glare of the fluorescent lights. She couldn't hear anything. No footsteps, no sounds of breathing . . .

'Pull yourself together, Maggie,' she said out loud, and carried on down the corridor.

The door at the end, the door to Duncan's office, was, unlike all the others, standing open.

'Hello?' she tried again.

She walked into the room.

It was a cramped wee office with a window looking over trees at the back of the building. In it there was just a filing cabinet, a table, a desk and three chairs.

And Dean Reid, lying on the floor, a knife sticking out his chest.

His wee rodent mouth open in a snarl.

The blood was still shining wet.

This had just happened.

Maggie recognised that knife. She recognised the worn wooden handle. It was the kitchen knife that had belonged to Duncan's ma, bought before the War and, Duncan never tired of reminding everyone, still a better slicer than any of the new ones. They made things to last in those days.

Nick had got her to handle it. So her fingerprints would be on it.

And that must have been him on the phone, his voice disguised.

Nick had done this.

The fucking psycho had killed Dean Reid and set her up for it.

And off down the corridor, she could hear voices. Footsteps.

'Police! If there's anyone in here, show yourself!'

And then he'd called the cops.

It was like an out-of-body experience. Maggie got a baby wipe from her pocket and wiped the handle of the knife. Then she was up on the filing cabinet and out that window.

Keeping low, she ran from the building to the trees and clambered over a wall, onto a path that ran behind the back gardens of a row of houses. Lucky they all had high fences. She could hear sounds of people, a kid laughing, the smell of a barbeque.

She took a second to calm down. Then she put up the hood of her jacket and made her way back to the coffee shop, where Pam and Liam were now in the kitchen checking the stock.

Pam stared at her. 'Maggie, what's up?'

Catching her breath, she told them what had happened. What Nick must have done.

'Oh my God,' said Pam.

'The wee prick,' said Liam, with his usual talent for understatement.

'Someone could have seen me,' Maggie got out. Her heart was hammering, adrenaline still pumping. Was it really possible? Nick had actually *killed someone* to get rid of her? So she'd be arrested and charged and convicted and sent to prison? Bye-bye, Mags? He'd gone that far?

'Aye, well, if they did, it's our word against theirs,' went Liam. 'We'll give you an alibi.'

'You don't have to,' said Maggie at once. 'You don't have to lie for me.' And as the thought hit her: 'For all you know, I *could* have killed the lad.'

Liam just snorted.

'Why on earth would you do that?' Pam shook her head. 'Of course I'll give you an alibi. They might not believe Liam, but I'm a law-abiding citizen without as much as a conviction for speeding. We'll say you were here the whole time.'

'You have to go on home, Maggie,' said Liam, 'like nothing happened. Pick Nick up at the school, acting like everything's hunky-dory, and drive home.'

Maggie nodded.

Blindly, she stumbled to the toilet and threw up.

As MAGGIE ARRIVED at the car park at the school, twenty minutes early, she had to make her clawed hands release the steering wheel. She clocked Carol Jardine sitting in her car, presumably waiting for Andy, and slouched down in her seat. She couldn't be doing with chirpy Carol right now. She wiped her sweaty palms on her jeans and went through again in her head what she'd say to Nick.

She kept thinking of that boy lying in his own blood, the knife sticking out of him.

Would Pam and Liam really lie for her, once the police got at them? Would Liam risk it, now that he was turning his life around and determined to stay on the straight and narrow? And what about Pam? Pam came from a nice middle-class family. How was she going to cope under questioning?

Now gaggles of kids were streaming out of the school.

Nick wasn't in one of the groups. He walked alone across the tarmac to the car.

If he was surprised to see her, he didn't let on. He ducked into the passenger seat and flashed her one of his charming smiles. 'Have a nice catch-up?'

'Really good, thanks. How was rehearsal?'

She couldn't stop staring at his right hand as it pushed the catch of the seat belt. She imagined that same hand, less than an hour ago, pushing the kitchen knife into Dean Reid's chest.

Really?

Could this boy *really* have done that?

But what other explanation was there for the Sunnyside kitchen knife, the one Nick had made her touch, being used as a murder weapon on Dean Reid? Could Dean and some of the other kids have gone to Sunnyside, maybe to see Duncan, and Dean stole the knife? And then they went to The Phoenix Centre, and there was a fight between them?

Nick dropped the left side of his mouth and went, in a dull monotone: '*How now spirit whither wander you.*' He chuckled. 'Whoever cast Meebs as Puck has a great sense of humour.'

Maggie eased out of the car park.

'But yours is the lead role, aye?' she made herself ask.

'Yeah, King of the Fairies. Gives all those Neanderthals something to pin on me. I'm not gay, by the way, in case you're wondering.'

It was the last thing on her mind. But now the thought of Nick with a partner flashed into her head. *Jesus.*

They waited in the queue of cars at the exit and then Maggie turned right. Soon they'd left the outskirts of Langholm behind and were into the trees.

What the hell was she going to say to Duncan?

She had to tell him she'd been there in The Phoenix

Centre, tell him the truth about what had happened. She had no choice. But as Nick blethered on about the funny things that had happened during the rehearsal, her heart plummeted. Would Duncan believe her version of events, her accusation that Nick had set her up, over Nick's? He must have left the rehearsal, somehow arranged to meet Dean at The Phoenix Centre, killed him, rushed back . . .

But the folk at the school must have noticed he was missing!

Maybe someone had even seen him going into the Centre.

But would Duncan believe her about finding Dean, that she'd done him no harm? Or would he go straight to the police with what she told him, blowing her alibi out the water? He'd been having doubts, right enough, about her mental health.

Usually, the bonnie drive through Eskdale lifted her spirits and calmed her down at the same time. Now, the fields sweeping down to the river looked all weird in the moonlight, like she'd never seen them before, and the dark hillsides against the lighter sky were spooky humps.

She looked over at Nick.

He smiled at her.

The scenario he'd set up, she supposed, was Maggie investigates a possible break-in at The Phoenix Centre, finds Dean in there and loses her rag. Volatile Maggie – God knows why she was carrying a knife from the kitchen at Sunnyside – stabs the poor lad.

When she turned up the avenue to the house, she immediately saw the police car, the fluorescent markings bright in her headlights. She wanted to throw the car into reverse, but she took a deep breath and went, 'Is that a police car?' like it wasn't obvious. Like they didn't both know why it was here.

Nick went, 'Well, I wonder why the police are here? Been up to your old tricks, Mags?'

So the gloves were off. 'Naw,' she replied calmly, stopping the car next to the police car by the back door. 'And I've got an alibi to prove it.'

Nick raised his eyebrows.

As they got out of the car, Yvonne came running from the back door, Isla swaddled in her arms. 'They're taking him!' She shoved Isla at Maggie and ran back to the door, where Duncan appeared, his hair rumpled. His hands were hand-cuffed in front of him, and a big cop had a hold of his arm.

'What the *hell*?' Nick suddenly screamed. 'No! *Dad!?*' He went for the massive policeman, grabbing him, trying to pull him off Duncan.

The other policeman grabbed Nick. 'Okay, son, okay. We're just taking your dad to the station to answer some questions.'

'What questions?'

'This is all wrong,' went Maggie.

'It's okay.' Duncan's gaze bounced from Nick to Maggie. 'I haven't done anything. Dean's been murdered, and they think I had something to do with it because yesterday we had a massive row in the High Street. He went for me and I had to defend myself. I didn't tell you . . .' He took a shuddering breath. 'Didn't want you to worry about it. It's the blackmail thing. They think I –'

'Okay, sir, let's go.' The big cop eased Duncan into the back of the car and shut the door on him.

'But this is *ridiculous!*' Nick yelled, struggling in the arms of the other cop. '*Dad* would never hurt anyone! What about *her*?' He pointed at Maggie. 'She's a *headcase*. She's been in prison for assault. Where's *she* been tonight?'

Maggie rapped back: 'In the coffee shop, as you know fine well. Yvonne, could you . . .' She handed a grizzling Isla over to Yvonne, who carried her back inside. Maggie held the big cop's gaze, willing him to see sense. 'You need to look at this one,' she went in a low voice, not wanting to add to Duncan's trauma, as she indicated Nick. '*He's* the one who's psychotic! You need to process him, get forensics onto him. There'll be traces on him. *He* did it. *He* killed that boy. I want to make a statement.'

'So do I!' yelled Nick.

TWENTY-FOUR HOURS LATER, Maggie and Yvonne sat at the kitchen table, Isla cosy in her carry cot by Maggie's chair with Bunny tucked in beside her. There was no way Maggie was letting Isla out her sight. After they'd got back from the police station last night, Maggie had gone her dinger at Nick. 'You'd better not come near me or Isla, or I *will* use a knife on you, you *psychotic little fucker!*'

'*Piss off!*' Nick had screamed at her. '*Piss off, Mags!*' And he'd run off inside. She hadn't seen him since. If he was going to stay in his room the whole time, that was fine by her.

'Thanks for staying,' she said now to Yvonne. 'I wouldn't feel safe on my own with him.'

Yvonne waved her thanks away.

After Nick and Maggie's allegations against each other, they had both undergone fingerprinting and forensic examinations and the clothes they were wearing had been taken away. Nick had been wearing his school uniform. Maggie had told the police he could have changed, after the murder, into a fresh set of school clothes and disposed of the ones he'd been wearing, and they should check the bins between The Phoenix Centre and the school.

'I don't think they took it seriously,' went Maggie now. 'The possibility that Nick could have done it.'

'They were so intent on charging Duncan,' Yvonne agreed.

Maggie had told Yvonne everything. She didn't know why.

She didn't even like the woman, but she trusted her. Maybe it was the fact that Yvonne reminded her in some ways of Duncan. She had the same straightforwardness about her.

'We've *got* to break Nick's alibi,' went Maggie.

'But how?'

He had a cast-iron alibi. The police had established that he hadn't left the school play rehearsal, and there were folk who could vouch for that. He'd either been on stage or in the wings with the other actors and teachers, apart from a twenty-minute break when he'd gone outside for a fag – alone, but one of the other kids had joined him after ten minutes, which wasn't even close to being enough time for him to have got to The Phoenix Centre, murdered Dean, and got back to the school.

Maggie sighed. 'How can it be possible to tell whether he sneaked off for a bit?'

'But it would have taken him what, half an hour at least to run across town, kill the boy, run back . . . call you to lure you to the Centre. He had the main part in the play. Oberon. Surely he'd have been missed? No. I think he must have got someone else to do it and set up an alibi for himself, so he'd be in the clear.'

'But who?'

'Could he have something on one of the kids in the programme? Could he have blackmailed them into doing it?' Yvonne grimaced. 'At least *your* alibi is holding up.'

Aye, right enough, that was the only ray of hope in this whole mess. Pam and Liam said their police interviews had been very short. The cops obviously weren't seriously looking at Maggie.

Because they were convinced they had their man.

Duncan's altercation with Dean had been in the most public place possible, outside the newsagent on the High Street with about twenty folk watching. There had been a scuffle. Dean had howled about how Duncan was attacking him 'again' and had appealed to passers-by for help.

Open and shut case.

Duncan had been charged with murder and remanded in custody awaiting trial.

9

Lulu had been dozing in the passenger seat, on and off, all the way from London. Nick had insisted on driving all the way to give her a chance to catch up on some sleep. She was now down to one zolpidem every four days and was finding it pretty hard going. And when she did manage to fall asleep, often the dream would come. The dream where she was hugging Milo, and then tying the blue twine round her neck, pulling a chair under the big old hook in the ceiling . . . Sometimes she tied twine round Milo's neck too.

Don't think about it.

Don't think about Milo.

They were travelling, now, through a secret valley, an idyll of green fields and woods hidden amongst the desolate hills of the Scottish Borders.

'You wouldn't think, to look at it now, that it was such a hotbed of anarchy, would you?' Nick smiled. 'Cattle reivers and outlaws and running battles between the Scots and the English.'

It helped him, she supposed, to talk about what had

happened here five hundred years ago rather than twenty. But Lulu could just imagine them, those leather-jerkined desperados, peering out at the road from the cover of the trees.

'It was known as The Debatable Lands in the 16th Century.' Nick slowed the car as they rounded a bend in the road and a particularly beautiful scene was laid out before them: blowing verges of cow parsley, grey drystone walls, peaceful fields of grazing cattle and sheep. In the near distance was a stone cottage set in a colourful garden, the wooded slope behind it rising to a bleak hilltop. 'A kind of no-man's land. So lawless and dangerous that neither Scotland nor England wanted responsibility for it. There was even a decree, issued by the English but agreed on by the Scots, wiping their hands of the place. Pretty much the only time Scotland and England have agreed on anything. We had to learn it by heart at school. *"All Englishmen and Scottishmen, after this proclamation made, are and shall be free to rob, burn, spoil, slay, murder and destroy all and every such persons, their bodies, buildings, goods and cattle as do remain or shall inhabit upon any part of the said Debatable Land without any redress to be made for the same."'*

Lulu felt a shiver on the bare skin of her arms. 'Wow.'

Nick suddenly grimaced, and she knew he was reflecting, as she was, on what he believed Maggie had done here, five hundred years later, with similar impunity.

They turned off the road that ran alongside the River Esk and into the lane that led to Sunnyside. Nick was wearing sunglasses, so she couldn't see his eyes as he focused on the road, but she could see how tightly he was gripping the wheel.

She needed to think of something to puncture the tension.

At his temple, she could see the single strand of grey hair

they called Tiberius. It had all started one day, just before
they were married, when he'd sent her a text message:

*!!EMERGENCY!! I just found my FIRST GREY HAIR!!! In
desperate need of therapy!!*

On the way home, Lulu had scoured the shops until she'd
found the perfect card, with a grey fox on the front and the
message *To my favourite silver fox.* They had spent a giggly five
minutes trying to locate the hair on the back of Nick's head.
He'd been checking with two mirrors that he didn't have a
bald patch developing and had found, instead, the hair.

'Aw, it's lovely,' Lulu had crooned when she'd located it.
'I'll take a photo. Hold still.'

Nick had pushed away the screen of Lulu's phone with
the image of the hair on it and pretended to collapse on the
couch, traumatised. She had sat opposite him in therapist
mode.

'Okay, Nick, I do realise that it's a big shock for you, but
this is – how shall I put it – not really a valid reason for a trip
to A&E?'

'I need an operation to remove it!'

Her gaze fell on the cabinet of artefacts. 'Would it help if
we named it? How about Julius, after Julius Caesar?'

Nick had groaned. 'Okay, I see where you're going with
this. The next one will be Augustus, I suppose. Then
Tiberius.'

'Ooh, *yes!*' Lulu had gurgled.

'Hmm. I'm not sure how *loveable* the Roman emperors
were.' He had grinned at her. 'Caligula's idea of entertain-
ment was to have his minions construct elaborate structures
in the arena onto which the condemned men would climb,
thinking they'd be safe up there from the lions and bears –

but the structures were designed to be unstable and collapse under their weight. Oh, how he laughed.'

'Okay, we can skip Caligula.'

Now, Lulu reached up and caressed the hair at his temple: Tiberius and all the other nameless dark ones. 'Ooh, I think I've just found . . . whoever comes after Nero.'

'Galba,' said Nick, deadpan. 'God, really? We'll probably be onto the Byzantine lot by the end of these two weeks.' His mouth quirked in a smile. And then: 'Here we are.'

He indicated right and eased the Audi up a steepish driveway between trees, a tunnel of green, the trees like two lines of silent giants performing some strange Scottish dance, leaning over to touch the tips of their branches together, forming an archway for Lulu and Nick to pass under.

'Sunnyside.' He said the name as if it were in inverted commas.

And oh God, it was an old-fashioned brute of a place – huge, high stone walls and a forest of chimneys. Very grand, she supposed, as Nick pulled up at the front door and they got out, stretching and breathing in the fresh air. No other houses in sight from here, just woods and fields and hillside.

The Debatable Lands.

She didn't like to think about what it must have been like to live here in the 16th Century, in a place so anarchic that both Scotland and England had given up trying to impose the rule of law and had just let everyone get on with robbing and murdering each other. But what if you were an ordinary family just trying to get by? Knowing that you were completely at the mercy of bands of desperate men roaming the countryside? That robbery and murder were even officially sanctioned?

She linked her arm through Nick's. 'It's a beautiful house.'

He took off his sunglasses and raised his eyebrows.

'It's only for two weeks,' she added, and they both laughed.

She wanted to ask him how he was feeling. She wanted to know what was going on behind those narrowed blue eyes as he looked up at the house, but he would have to confront his memories head-on soon enough. For now, it was enough that he was here.

'Home, sweet home,' he said brightly, hauling their cases from the boot.

At the door, he just stood for a moment, then squared his shoulders. 'Okay, let's do this. Yvonne said she'd leave the door open, so . . .' He walked forward.

Inside, it took a while for Lulu's eyes to adjust after the bright sunlight. The place was huge. She followed Nick from room to room, exclaiming with false enthusiasm over the admittedly very pleasant rooms, big and square and furnished with real antiques. But there was an odd feeling to the place. Maybe it was because she knew what had happened here, but there was an expectant quality to it, as if the house were waiting, not for its next holiday let guests, but for the family to return and find it just as they'd left it.

Duncan and Maggie and Isla.

And Nick.

It was as if the chintzy chairs and sofa grouped about the fireplace in the 'drawing room' were positioned ready for them all, ready to resume a conversation broken off twenty-two years ago. They were the same chairs, she was sure. The same vintage creamy carpet with a pattern of vines twining over it. The same brass matchbox holder with an embossed sunflower just waiting for a Clyde to pick it up again and light the fire.

'Dear Auntie seems to have kept the place up, at least,' said Nick as they climbed the stairs, Nick with both cases, as ever the perfect gent. 'An agency organises the bookings and the cleaners and what have you, but Yvonne oversees the whole thing. I give her a cut of the profits. Yvonne doesn't really do altruism.'

At the top of the stairs, he stopped and turned.

This must be where his mother fell.

She touched his arm. 'Where are we sleeping?'

'I asked them to make up one of the guest rooms.'

Of course he did. He wouldn't want to use his parents' room or his own childhood one. Which was fine by her. As she followed him along a wide, rather gloomy corridor, she kept looking over her shoulder to check there was no one – nothing – behind them. She wanted to grab Nick's arm and pull him away, back down the stairs, back into the car. She didn't want to be here. This was where Nick's whole family had just *disappeared*.

'This is lovely,' she said brightly as they entered a large, sunny bedroom overlooking the back of the house.

There was a four-poster bed. Gleaming antique furniture. A surprisingly modern en suite complete with walk-in shower. She had a pee, and then she and Nick went back downstairs to the big old-fashioned kitchen, where someone had stocked the fridge with milk, cheese, butter, tomatoes and juice. And there was a loaf of crusty bread on the worktop.

'This would be your aunt?'

'Mm.'

'It's going to be . . . interesting . . . to meet her and your uncle.'

'That's one way of putting it.'

Lulu didn't have long to wait. They had eaten a sketchy lunch and were wandering about the garden, by tacit agreement getting out of the house itself as soon as possible, when a tall woman Lulu guessed was in her sixties appeared round the side of the greenhouse and lifted a hand stiffly. She was elegantly dressed in a navy trouser suit, with a slash of colour at her neck in the form of a cerise silk scarf, jauntily tied.

'Yvonne,' said Nick grimly as they approached one another.

Yvonne nodded at him. There was no attempt at a hug or even much of a smile, just a questioning look at Lulu. The stocky man who appeared behind her, in contrast, was beaming nervously.

'Lu, this is my Aunt Yvonne and Uncle Michael,' said Nick tonelessly. 'My wife, Lulu.'

'Pleased to meet you!' burbled Michael, offering his hand. 'Well, well, this is a turn-up for the books, eh?'

Lulu took his hand briefly, her own automatic smile fading fast.

She wanted to scream at them. She wanted to throw it in their faces, what they'd done to sixteen-year-old Nick. He'd lost the whole of his immediate family. Any decent aunt and uncle would have taken him in, but no, they'd abandoned him too, virtually. Okay, so they had made sure he was secure financially, and found a good school for him, and 'allowed' him to visit them for a week at Christmas and in the summer. That had been the word, heartbreakingly, that Nick had used.

Allowed.

They'd allowed him two weeks of family a year.

The rest of the holidays he'd spent at his boarding school with strangers.

You horrible, horrible people! Lulu wanted to snarl at them, but contented herself with a slight lift of her upper lip which she hoped conveyed the sentiment.

'Much traffic on the way up?' said Michael.

'We've brought you some more food,' said Yvonne, indicating the bag she was carrying.

'Thanks,' said Nick coldly, 'but we'll be doing a shop

tomorrow. And we'll probably eat out tonight. We don't need anything more.'

Not from you was the unspoken message.

'Well, we've bought it now,' said Yvonne, as if this were Nick's fault. 'I'll leave it in the kitchen, and you can do what you like with it.' And she moved past them, off along the path towards the house.

No.

No, Lulu couldn't let this go.

As Michael started on about the farm and the changes Nick was going to see – something about one of the sheds being replaced and the problems they'd had getting planning permission – Lulu hurried after Yvonne.

She caught up with her in the huge, high hall and just blurted it out:

'Why didn't you take Nick to live with you?'

For a long moment, Yvonne said nothing, her face blank as she looked at Lulu, almost as if she were looking through her. 'I don't do children,' was all she said, eventually.

Rapid footsteps sounded on the tiles behind her, and Nick said, 'Lulu! I turned round and you'd gone! Why did you just take off like that?'

He spoke too loudly, his tone harsh, and as she turned to him with a reassuring smile – she was humouring, for now, his need to keep track of her every movement – she was conscious of Yvonne flinching. And she wanted to round on her again, to tell her *she'd done this*. She'd contributed, at least, to making Nick the way he was, making him panic and talk too loudly and offend her sense of what was reasonable behaviour.

'Sorry, darling,' Lulu said softly, taking Nick's arm.

This is on you, she wanted to yell at the woman with the pursed little mouth in the neat navy trouser suit. *You should have taken him in, you should have helped him through it, you should have* loved him.

You should, you should, you should.

SHE REALLY DIDN'T WANT to do this.

But she had to, for Nick's sake. For both their sakes.

They waited until dusk had fallen, to more closely replicate the dark November evening when Nick had returned to Sunnyside with Carol and Andy Jardine. In June in Scotland, Lulu discovered, the days were long, and it was after ten o'clock when she and Nick stepped out of the house and onto the big area of gravel in front of it.

'Mr Nutter takes a holiday,' Nick murmured. 'One of those silent French films. Lots of close-ups of my face girning as ghosts and ghoulies chase me about a haunted house.'

Lulu shivered. 'Stop it.' She wasn't going to let him sabotage this with his usual facetiousness.

'And poor old Mrs Nutter is wondering what the hell she's let herself in for. Lots of close-ups of you rolling your eyes.'

Lulu took his hand. 'I'm going to hold on to your hand the whole time, okay? So you know I'm with you, wherever you might go in your head. You're with me and you're safe.' But there was also, she admitted to herself, a reassurance for Lulu in holding Nick's hand.

'Oh God, Lu. I'm not sure about this.'

'I know. We can stop any time.' She squeezed his hand. 'Think of it like being in a waking dream.' Her specialist subject, she reflected dryly. 'It's thought that dreams are a way for the brain to process what's gone on during the previous day but also sometimes stuff that's happened in our lives a while ago but still troubles us. Dreams are a way of going back through events to make sense of them and take whatever we need from them, as we consign what we've been through to memory.'

'But how will it help, reliving it all yet again?' He turned and looked up at the house silhouetted against the evening sky.

'We're going to ground you in the present so we can force your brain to process what happened as *past events*, to integrate your repressed memories into your "normal" memory bank, so you can acknowledge the trauma and move on. We need to really examine each thing you remember. Do you think you can do that?'

A curt nod. 'Let's just get it over with.'

They got as far as the hall.

'Keep breathing in and out and noticing those breaths,' said Lulu, 'while you think about what happened.'

He exhaled slowly. 'The whole house was in darkness. It smelt . . . This sounds weird, but it *smelt* empty. I switched on the lights . . .' He moved to the switch, and Lulu went with him, keeping hold of his hand. 'And I shouted. I shouted for Dad.'

'Okay. Take a deep breath and let how you were feeling then come back.'

She felt him tense. And suddenly he gripped her hand so tight it hurt.

'Dad!' he screamed. '*Dad!*'

'Okay, Nick, you're okay.' She put her arms around him. 'I'm here! You're okay! I'm here, I'm here, my darling!'

THE HOUSE WAS DARK. Lulu knew she had to find the kitchen – it was really, really important she find the kitchen where Mum and Dad and her brothers were – but this wasn't the old farmhouse at Braemar Station, this was a strange warehouse of a place full of huge antique furniture that loomed over her as she ran from one room to the next, calling their names.

The kitchen.

Where was the kitchen?

Where were Mum and Dad and Dennis and John?

And then she was awake, and Nick was stroking her hair and telling her it was all right, she was all right, it was just another bad dream.

10

Maggie didn't know what to do.

At least they were safe in here. She'd bought a bolt and fixed it to the bedroom door so Nick couldn't get in while she was asleep. And she had brought up to the room a supply of food and nappies and bin bags. The one good thing about the situation was that Isla had discovered her appetite, latching on like a wee limpet, as if she was picking up on what was happening and was getting comfort from Maggie in the only way she knew how.

Maggie waited until she heard Nick's footsteps brattling down the stairs, and then she got up from the chair, wincing at the pull on her C-section scar and the sore skin on her thigh. She took Isla into the bathroom across the corridor, which overlooked the drive, carefully locking the door behind them. When Nick appeared in his school blazer, bag slung over his shoulder as he jogged off down the drive, she unlocked the bathroom door and carefully went downstairs, Isla held safe against her body.

'Oh, Duncan, Duncan,' she groaned, collapsing into her

rocking chair in the kitchen and undoing the buttons on her top with her unbandaged left hand so Isla could feed again.

Duncan was in prison in Dumfries. He'd been denied bail because of the seriousness of the charge. And Nick was raging about this too, of course. He obviously blamed Maggie for wriggling out of it and putting Duncan in the frame.

Michael and Yvonne were visiting Duncan today, and Maggie was going tomorrow. It would be brilliant to see him, but she was dreading it, too. Dreading speaking to him about Nick.

Should she go back to the cops and admit that her alibi was false, that she'd been there at The Phoenix Centre, that she'd found Dean? That she was set up by Nick? Then they would have to look more closely at Nick's alibi. But what if it really was watertight? What if Nick had got someone else to do the dirty work, as Yvonne suspected? And if Maggie got arrested and banged up, that would leave Isla at Nick's mercy. Duncan was a total diddy when it came to Nick. In his eyes, Nick was a fine young man with just a few 'typical teenage issues'. Duncan wouldn't be able to protect Isla from him.

She looked down into her daughter's big blue eyes and smiled, stroking the soft skin of her cheek.

Such a wee scrap, to be the centre of her whole universe.

Was there some way of proving that Duncan couldn't have done it, at least? She and Yvonne and Michael had gone round in circles on that one. Duncan had been driving about with Isla on the evening Dean was killed, trying to get her off to sleep. But of course, he couldn't prove it.

Yvonne had stayed with Maggie and Isla for two days after Duncan's arrest, but she couldn't stay forever. She'd gone back to the farm, and the next morning Nick had suddenly been all smiles. 'Thank God the witch has gone. Why don't you go through to the TV room and relax properly, and I'll bring you a cuppa, and we can talk about what we're going to do to get Dad out of there?'

'But shouldn't you be getting off to school?'

'This is more important.'

She'd been knackered. Isla had been waking through the night and then not settling back to sleep for what seemed like hours. Hoping she and Isla could doze off, she'd sat them and Bunny down in a big armchair in the TV room. Maggie had easily persuaded Duncan to swap the wee telly that had been in here for her one. He watched as much telly as she did – 'But don't tell anyone. The hobbies on my CV are kayaking, hillwalking and Roman history, not shoving Maltesers in my face and watching *EastEnders*.'

Nick had come in with a tray on which he'd set a mug of tea and a plate of chocolate biscuits. Maggie had decided not to eat or drink anything he gave her. She'd wait until he'd gone and then get rid of them. He'd offered the tray to Maggie, and as she'd been about to pick up the mug, the tray had suddenly tilted, and she'd grabbed the handle to stop the mug toppling.

Pain had shot up her arm from her hand.

She had shouted and dropped the mug, and the hot tea had splashed onto her leg, onto Bunny, narrowly missing Isla and burning Maggie through the thin cotton of her trousers.

'Oh, I'm sorry.' Nick had raised his voice over Isla's screams. 'I didn't realise the mug was so hot.'

He must have superheated it in the oven or the microwave.

She'd driven herself and Isla to A&E, where they'd patched her up – the burns nipped like a bastard but were superficial – and bought the bolt for the door. When they'd got back, she'd fetched a screwdriver and drill from Duncan's shed and fixed the bolt in place, and locked them into the bedroom.

That evening, Nick had tapped on the door. 'Maggie? Maggie, are you okay in there? Do I need to call the GP? Maybe get you a referral to some sort of mental health service?'

Two hours later, he'd been back.

She'd been woken by his footsteps coming along the corridor. Stopping at the door.

The handle had slowly turned.

She could hear his breathing.

And then a soft laugh.

She felt like she was being a right nugget, letting him do this to her, letting him get the better of her, but what could she do? She was a wee five-foot-nothing woman and he was an athletic, six-foot teenage boy who was prepared to do God knew what to get rid of her.

She could go to Yvonne and Michael's, eh? Stay with them?

But the farm was just ten minutes' walk away, down the track that wound its way through the fields and woods. They wouldn't be safe from him there either. At least here, in her own home, she called the shots. If she wanted a bolt on her bedroom door, she got one. That might not be possible at the farm. She could imagine Yvonne pursing her lips and going, 'Well, I really don't think that's necessary.'

At least she had most of the day without Nick.

When Isla had drunk her fill and gone off to sleep, making the wee snuffling noises that always made Maggie smile, she gently eased her into the car seat and drove to Langholm, to the coffee shop, to Pam and Liam. They were both shocked by her injuries.

'The wee prick!' Liam growled. And, as Pam bustled off to get Maggie a glass of water – hot drinks had lost their appeal – he muttered, 'He needs dealt with.'

'I know.' Maggie jiggled Isla, who was screwing up her

face, working up to a tantrum at her nap being disturbed. 'But what can I do?'

'I know people.'

'Oh Jesus, no, Liam. No.'

'Why not? Wipe the wee prick out.'

'*No.*' Maggie rocked Isla, who was making the experimental noises that meant she was about to kick off. 'What I need to do is think how I can get Duncan in the clear. Then deal with the whole Nick problem.' She dropped her voice and said, under cover of Isla's crying, 'Look. I'm flattered you'd do that for me . . . but no. *That's not happening.* Right? It would break Duncan's heart if he lost Nick.'

'Okay.' Liam gave her a stern look, like Maggie was the one being unreasonable here. 'It's your funeral.'

Back at Sunnyside, she put Isla down in her cot in the bedroom and did a deep clean of the kitchen. She had always found that housework cleared her mind and was hoping she might have some brainwave about how to get Duncan off the hook.

Aye, it had been dark, but was there a chance someone had clocked him in the car, driving Isla around? She could ask him about the route he took.

The baby monitor on the worktop suddenly came to life, distorted wails bouncing off the kitchen's hard surfaces.

'Okay, okay, missie, I'm coming.' Maggie went quickly to the sink to wash her hands.

'Don't cry, little sister,' crooned Nick's voice.

She was out that kitchen and up those stairs in a heartbeat.

Nick was up here!

She barrelled into the bedroom.

Isla was writhing in the cot, her face purple, mouth wide, eyes scrunched shut. There was a big red bruise on the side of her head.

Maggie snatched her up and turned a three-sixty.

The room was empty.

Holding Isla to her, she flung open the door to the en suite, but that was empty too.

'Nick!' she called out. 'Nick, I know you're here!' She was sobbing now, rocking Isla, whispering, 'It's okay, it's okay. You're okay.'

She bolted the bedroom door and set Isla down on the bed, gently stroking her poor wee face as she looked at the bruise. It was big, a couple of inches across.

Jesus!

He'd done this? He'd hurt a gorgeous wee innocent bairn? What had he done? Hit her with something? Oh Jesus, she couldn't even think about it! She'd been telling Isla, ever since she first knew she was pregnant, that she would keep her safe, that no one would ever hurt her, and now this had happened and Maggie had been downstairs happy as Larry doing her Mrs Mop act while up here in this room, Nick . . . Nick . . .

She was sobbing again, her hands shaking like an alkie's. She needed to get a cold compress on that bruise, but she didn't want to leave the room in case Nick was out there.

'Oh, my wee one,' she crooned. 'It's okay. Your ma's here now.'

She had to get ice.

She eased open the door and crossed the landing to the stairs, whispering to Isla all the while. On the stairs, every few steps she stopped and listened, but the house was still. In the kitchen, she got an ice pack from the freezer and wrapped it in a tea towel, and held it against the bruise for ten seconds at a time.

When she was just a wee lassie, Maggie had discovered this was the best way to take the nip out a bruise.

Another sob rose in her throat.

She was never letting Isla out her sight again.

It took over an hour for Isla to stop yowling, a sound that went right through Maggie to the place inside her that wanted to call Liam and tell him to do it.

Get some Glasgow ned to wipe Nick out.

Instead, she called Nick's school. He had PE that morning, she remembered – she'd had to wash his kit. She made up a story about wanting to check that he was okay because he'd had a sore foot and she'd suggested giving him a note to excuse him, but he hadn't wanted to miss the lesson. Could she speak to his PE teacher?

When the man came on the phone, she was expecting him to be all confused, to say that Nick hadn't been in the class that morning, but he breezily reassured Maggie that Nick had had no problems and had, in fact, easily outdistanced the rest of the boys as usual.

How had he done it?

She was sitting on the bed, the door bolted, when she heard noises on the landing, in the corridor. Quick footsteps. Nick's cheery voice: 'I'm back, Mags!'

The doorknob jiggled.

'Mags? Are you okay in there?'

Maggie put her hand to her mouth to stop the huge sob that was rising up.

'How's Isla been?'

'You *fucking wee monster!*' Maggie choked. 'I've got evidence now. I've taken a photo of the bruise –'

'The *bruise*? Oh, Mags, what's happened? Let me in! What have you done to her?' A little chuckle. 'Do I need to call social services?'

11

L ulu sighed, and stood, and stretched. She was too restless to sleep. While Nick worked, she'd come out to the little summerhouse with the intention of snoozing in the big wicker chair, but sleep wouldn't come. She was too worried about Nick. This was their third day at Sunnyside, and the 'therapy' had ground to a halt because Nick had asked for a break from it which had somehow dragged on for two days.

She'd had another nightmare last night about the house, and this time it had been more recognisably Sunnyside. She'd been running through the rooms looking for Nick but had known, sickeningly, that he wasn't there, that somehow he had never been there.

She walked back across the lawn towards the house. Nick would still, presumably, be working in the study. He had arranged with his boss that he could have two weeks off at short notice provided he clocked in at the vital times, at the beginning and end of the trading day, early in the morning and from three to four-thirty in the afternoon, so he was going to be closeted away in the study at those times on weekdays.

Lulu had wanted to take the car for a drive but hadn't been able to find the keys. Presumably, Nick had them, and she hadn't wanted to interrupt his work.

As she walked into the hall, she wondered if it had been a mistake to try to take him through the events of that night chronologically, starting in here – confronting him not only with his family's absence but with the memories of finding his mother's body.

It had been too much.

How could she have made such a stupid mistake?

THAT NIGHT, Lulu expected Nick to make some excuse to postpone the therapy session yet again, but come ten o'clock it was Nick himself who said, 'Are we going to do this or what?'

Lulu took his hand and led him into the kitchen.

'I searched the back rooms,' he said, pulling her with him as he marched down the flagstone corridor and started opening doors to storerooms, a larder, a laundry room. 'There was some chicken defrosting in the pantry. Then Carol called me, and I went back to the kitchen . . .' Now he stopped.

'Okay. What were you feeling at this point?'

'Scared. Scared of what she had found.' He took a deep, slow breath as Lulu had told him to do. 'And now I went back into the kitchen.'

The two of them walked back along the corridor.

'Carol showed me that one of the rings was on, on the cooker. And then I saw the pan – with water in it – and the bag of oatmeal open next to it.' His chest was heaving. Suddenly, he wheeled and stared at the table. 'Three mugs.

Three bowls. Spoons. Carol found . . . she found Isla's toy rabbit.'

Lulu had no real warning. One second, he was upset, yes, but controlled. The next, he was flinging her hand from him and running at the table and gripping its edge, hauling it up and over, overturning it so everything on it slid to the flagstones. Flowers tumbled from a vase, spilling water, and the vase shattered. Cutlery clattered.

And then he was at the worktop, snatching up a mug and hurling it to the flagstones. Shards of china hit Lulu's legs.

'Nick!' She grabbed his arm. 'Nick, stop! *Nick!*'

The face he turned to her was contorted in a snarl, his eyes wild. She dropped his arm and stepped back instinctively. And another face flashed into her head – Paul's face, during that last session, suddenly unrecognisable as the anger had consumed him.

Nick dropped to his knees. 'I'm sorry! Oh God, I'm so sorry!' He reached for a shard of china.

'It's okay, it's fine. Hey, that vase was hideous anyway!'

Nick sat back on his heels and looked up at her. 'What happened, Lulu? What the *hell* happened to them?'

Lulu had found the kitchen at last. She stood with her hand on the smooth, white-painted panels of the Victorian door, calling out to her family. She knew they were in there.

'Mum!' she shouted. 'Dad!'

Silence.

And she couldn't open the door, she realised, as she passed her hand over the ridges and planes of the panels. She couldn't open the door because there was no handle.

But she was here.

Finally, she had found the kitchen.

. . .

THE NEXT MORNING, she woke late and realised that Nick must have decided to let her sleep in after yet another disturbed night. She yawned and sat up, watching the sunlight streaking across the carpet through a gap in the curtains. She felt . . . not good, but not as bad as usual. Last night's session had been a bit of a breakthrough, and she was confident that they were both ready, now, to tackle what needed to be tackled.

They had a late, leisurely breakfast at the picnic table in the rose garden, and when they had finished, Lulu asked Nick for the car keys so she could go for a drive.

He stared at her. 'You want to get away from me? After what I did last night . . . Oh God, Lu, are you frightened of me?'

'Of course not!' She *had* been frightened, but *for* him, not *of* him. 'I just want to go for a drive.'

'I'll come with you.'

She reached across the table and took his hand. 'No. I'm going to go for a drive, and then park up somewhere and call Karla.' She looked at her watch. 'It's eight in the evening in Sydney, so now will be a good time for her.'

'You're going to tell her what I did?'

'Yes, I'll discuss last night's session. But it's completely confidential. Like docs having a confab about a patient. And – well, I'm not going to tell her it's you, because what we're doing . . . it's kind of frowned upon to treat your own family.' If she told Nick it was actually breaking the rules, he would probably refuse to continue. The last thing he'd want would be to get her in trouble. 'And listen, last night, it's nothing to worry about. These feelings coming to the surface – it's all good.'

'Oh yes, it's great.'

'Really, it's all part of the process. It's a good sign. It's progress.' She stood. 'Can I have the car keys?'

'I don't want you going out in the car on your own.'

'Why on earth not?'

'You're not used to driving on these country roads. I am. I've been driving on them since I was thirteen. Michael used to let me take his tractor from one field to the next. Illegally, of course.' He shook his head with a reminiscent smile. 'And that kind of thing still goes on. You come round a corner to find some kid bowling along in a tractor. If you're not used to it –'

'I grew up in the outback! Of course I'm used to country roads!'

'But not single-track ones like these. They can be pretty dangerous, Lu. I wouldn't have a minute's peace all the time you were out.'

'Nick, it'll be fine. Give me the keys.'

'I'm sorry, but no.'

She gaped at him.

He grimaced, apologetically. His mouth quirked. 'Mr Nutter strikes again.'

For once, though, the humour did not disarm her. 'Having PTSD doesn't make you a "nutter".'

'But it helps?' He laughed. 'Don't worry, I'm not going to do a Paul on you.'

It was uncanny, the way he always knew what she was thinking.

She turned away from him. 'That's not *bloody funny*!'

She made the call in the library.

'Karla, I'm sorry to bother you again.'

She could imagine Karla sitting in her stylish modern living room, her bob of tight grey curls pushed behind her ears, poking her glasses up her nose. How many former students did she have who, like Lulu, kept bugging her? She probably spent most of her life on calls like this.

But, 'You're not *bothering* me!' Karla laughed. 'Always good to hear from you.'

When Lulu had told her a week ago that she had a new client she would like advice about, Karla had been enthusiastic, saying this was just what Lulu needed, getting back on the horse and all that. And she'd been encouraging about Lulu's idea of performing the therapy in the client's home, the house from which his mother had disappeared. Lulu had changed the details a bit so Karla wouldn't suspect who her client really was.

When she told Karla about the last session, and her client's anger spilling over into attacking inanimate objects, Karla said, 'Well, it sounds like he's processing what happened. Sounds like things are moving along well.'

Phew!

As Karla continued, Lulu reflected that she already knew everything Karla was telling her, but she still needed to hear it: that people in therapy often appeared to get worse as they started to let the feelings out and the painful memories came to the surface. She needed to hear that this was a sign that the therapy was working, that Nick, at last, was acknowledging the trauma of the past. That they would get through it and come out the other side.

'I've never had a client get physically . . . not violent. What's the word I'm looking for?'

'Destructive? Hey, it was just a vase!'

Lulu smiled. 'But you know, Karla, if I'm honest, the house kind of gives me the heebie-jeebies too.'

'Of course it does. You just can't help yourself, can you?' But Karla's voice was gentle. 'Are you dwelling on it? Bad dreams?'

'Yes, and yes. It's . . . I dream I'm in the house. That I can't find my family.'

For a few minutes, they talked about Lulu's dreams. Karla

confided that she sometimes experienced bad dreams herself when the client's situation was particularly distressing. 'We're not automatons. We can't just switch off at the end of the day. And remember, dreams are useful things. They're the brain's way of –'

'– Processing,' Lulu finished. 'I know. But . . .'

'Doesn't make it any easier. You just have to remember what I always say. The fact that you over-empathise is hard for you, but it's great for your clients. You're able to get right inside their heads in a way other therapists just can't.'

'But I didn't, did I, with Paul?'

'Oh, Lulu.'

'I should have *known*, Karla. I should have known how he was feeling, but I had no inkling. Not a *single one*!'

'And now you don't trust yourself with this new client.'

A long silence. Then, 'No,' Lulu whispered.

'Well, that's a load of bull! No one's infallible. You know how many of my clients have completed suicide? Eight. *Eight*, Lulu! And do I beat myself up about it? You bet! But when all's said and done, you can't make decisions for them. All we can do is hope to help. Their lives are their own, to do with as they will. And we have to accept that.'

The metallic flash of a black vehicle went past the window.

Lulu thanked Karla effusively, ended the call, scurried to the kitchen to wash her face, and put on a smile. As she stepped out of the front door into the sun, Nick almost barged into her, coming the other way.

Yvonne was standing leaning back against a Range Rover, arms folded.

'Let's see what Lulu has to say about it. Lulu, I'm off to have coffee in town and wondered if you'd like to join me.'

This was a surprise. Lulu didn't particularly want to

spend time with Yvonne, but the chance to escape for a couple of hours was too good to pass up.

'Oh, uh, yes, that would be lovely,' Lulu said at the same time as Nick said, 'No, Lu, you can't, remember we –'

'You husband seems to think you have plans,' interrupted Yvonne drily.

'I'm sure it's nothing that can't wait.' Lulu reached out to rub Nick's arm. 'Just let me get my bag and make myself look more presentable, and –'

'We. Have. *Plans*,' Nick said forcefully, catching hold of Lulu's hand and tucking it through his arm.

'Nick,' said Lulu gently. 'I'd really like to go out for coffee with Yvonne. I'm sure we can postpone whatever you had in mind.'

'We're not living in 1860.' Yvonne snorted. 'Stopping your wife leaving the house is against the law. It's called coercive control.'

'Oh, goodness, no.' Lulu laughed. 'Nick's just a little over-protective sometimes.'

Nick was staring at Yvonne, eyes narrowed.

'That's what they all say,' said Yvonne.

After that, of course, Nick could hardly object to the outing. Lulu quickly got ready, but by the time she returned to the hall, Nick had disappeared.

'Off in a sulk,' Yvonne said breezily. 'Climb aboard.'

On the drive to Langholm, Yvonne cracked open the windows to let the fresh and not-so-fresh country smells blow about the car. 'I think we rather got off on the wrong foot,' she said. 'Tell me about yourself, Lulu.'

So Lulu told her about Braemar Station and her parents and brothers, and her rather feral childhood. Yvonne reciprocated with information about the farm and the cheese-making business which now employed three local people full-time.

'And how did you meet Nick?' was Yvonne's next question.

This was a little embarrassing but also hilarious. Lulu launched into the story.

As she'd approached her thirtieth birthday, Lulu had decided it was about time she saw a bit more of the world than Sydney, where she lived, and Leonora, where she spent all her holidays, so one fine day in October she'd got on a plane to Europe. Jenny and Beth had been horrified that Lulu's family were 'letting' her do this on her own, as if Lulu were nine years old, not twenty-nine. It was a standing joke that Lulu couldn't be trusted to go to the grocery store without having some sort of disaster befall her, like locking herself out of the truck or losing her purse or, on one unfortunately memorable occasion, the truck actually exploding in the parking lot while she was in the store – although how was it her fault that some malevolently inclined possum had decided to chew through the wiring?

The terrible thing was, the whole Europe trip *had* been a disaster.

Within two days, she'd managed to lose almost all her belongings. She'd been so seduced by the beauties of Ithaca, by all the smiling faces and friendly shopkeepers, by her charming room at the guest house which was its own little self-contained building in the grounds, with purple bougainvillea round the door, that she'd gone for an evening walk round the harbour and left all her stuff in her room *with the door unlocked*.

When she got back, everything was gone.

Even the red hairbrush she'd left on the bedside table. She'd had that hairbrush since she was eleven. It had been her silent, sympathetic companion through the acne years, when she'd spent hours sitting at her dressing table mirror gazing at herself in horror, but then she'd pick up the brush and swish it through her hair, her glossy, shiny, straight blonde hair, and somehow it wouldn't seem so bad. Ridiculously, she cried over the loss of that hairbrush, imagining the poor thing clutched in the hand of some horrible thief.

All she had left was her phone and the euros in her pocket. And her phone was out of charge. And the charger was gone.

She'd been sitting slumped in the courtyard of a taverna watching the sun set over the Ionian Sea, her remaining notes and coins spread out on the table, wondering whether she could afford a main course and who she could ask to charge her phone, but not really wanting to because then she'd have no excuse for not calling Mum and Dad and admitting what had happened, and groaning, actually groaning out loud, when she'd been conscious of The Beautiful Man – dazzling white shirt, tanned skin, designer sunglasses – passing her table.

She'd seen him around in Kioni and christened him The Beautiful Man and made up a whole life story for him in which he was the son of an earl and was here for a secret assignation with one of the minor royals. She'd even had a brief conversation with him in a shop. She'd been all flustered because the shopkeeper kept nodding and smiling and saying, 'Twenty euro' and trying to put a cheap-looking gold necklace into her hand, no matter how many times she said 'Neh'.

'Uh, you realise that "Neh" means "Yes" in Greek?' Sean Connery's voice had murmured behind her, and she'd turned to find herself looking straight into the gorgeous, long-lashed blue eyes of The Beautiful Man.

'Oh. Really? Oh God, that explains a lot!' she had giggled, and he had thrown back his head and laughed.

She stared at his back as he walked towards the taverna entrance, admiring his lean, muscled body and the way he moved, athletically, like one of the big cats. And then he stopped, and walked back to her table, and took off the sunglasses to reveal those beautiful eyes.

'Are you all right?'

She must have looked a fright. Puffy red eyes from crying. Sweaty T-shirt from frantically running around trying to find a police station like a ditzy heroine in a bad romance. And here was her knight in shining armour.

'Perfectly fine, thanks,' she assured him.

'Hmm,' was all he said.

She glared up at him. He was smiling. And then she was smiling too, grinning, laughing hysterically and telling him the whole sorry story as he took a seat opposite her, long lean legs stretched to the side. 'I was *so sure* I locked the door!'

'I'm sure you did.' And he told her that that guest house was notorious for stuff going mysteriously missing. The owner had a nice little sideline in theft going on. 'I wouldn't feel any compunction in skipping out without settling your bill, if that's what you're worried about.' He was looking at the fifteen euros spread on the table.

Oh God. She hadn't even thought about the guest house bill! She couldn't just leave without paying, even if they had stolen all her stuff. Could she?

'Look, I'm off to Athens in an hour, flying back to London for a few days. If you're at a loose end, I wonder if you'd consider housesitting for me while I'm gone?' He said it diffidently, as if it were Lulu who'd be doing him a favour rather than the other way round. 'I have a little villa up the coast. It would give you a chance to get everything sorted out.'

'But you don't even know me!'

He smiled. 'I'm an excellent judge of character.'

So she had stayed in his 'little villa', which had turned out to be a charming five-bedroom house with a red-tiled roof and a terrace under a pergola with views down a vertiginous drop to a secret turquoise cove. For three days, she had munched through the contents of his fridge and spent her days trekking up and down the steep little path to the private beach and wondering about him, her rescuer, this Nick Clyde who'd been holidaying alone in this private paradise. She had snooped shamelessly, discovering his favourite bands were the Bee Gees and Abba – was he gay? Typical of her luck if he was gay. But the centrepiece of the long console table in the dining room, a broken female torso that was probably not just an antique but an antiquity, and the nude painting of a woman in his bedroom suggested otherwise.

And then he'd come back, and she'd meant to leave that day.

And then the next.

And then the next.

Typical Lulu, as Beth and Jenny had remarked.

Yvonne didn't seem to find any of this particularly funny, but she was a good listener, obviously interested in the story. By the time they'd arrived in Langholm and were sitting down at a table in a cute little café, Lulu was beginning to relax. Yvonne seemed a reasonable person, if a bit humourless and literal. But that just made her virtual abandonment of Nick all the harder to understand.

'Duncan's wife used to own this place,' Yvonne said, picking up a menu. 'Hence the name. Maggie's.'

'Oh!' Lulu looked around her.

'That's her friend Pam behind the counter.' The woman serving was all smiles for the customers. Her hair was very short, almost a crew-cut, but she had the bone structure to carry it off. 'Pam took the place over after Maggie . . . well. After the disappearance.'

Lulu lowered her voice. 'Nick thinks . . . he thinks Maggie . . .'

'Killed them?' Yvonne said at normal volume. 'That's just nonsense.'

'So, what do *you* think happened? Do you think the police were right, that they just up and left?'

'I suppose it's possible. There have been all kinds of theories mooted over the years.'

'Such as what?'

But Pam had approached their table. After they'd ordered, Yvonne didn't answer Lulu's question but came out with, 'Nick's making your life hell, then, is he?'

'No!' Lulu almost laughed. 'No, of course not! He's just . . . being back here is churning a lot of stuff up for him. Actually, that's the reason we're here.' She explained about the therapy she was using to treat his PTSD.

'PTSD?' Yvonne snorted. 'And the "therapy" is working, is it?'

'It's a process. It's too soon to say whether it's working or not, but the fact that he's dealing with what happened, addressing his feelings about it –'

Yvonne shook her head with an expression almost of pity. 'Look, Lulu, you seem like a nice girl. Nick's my flesh and blood, but I'd be the first to admit he's bad news. You need to get out of that relationship, and fast.'

Wow.

Lulu blinked. 'I know he's got issues –'

'Oh yes, he's got those all right.'

Lulu felt herself bristling. 'After what he went through, it's not surprising.'

'Nick's issues are nothing to do with what he "went through". He's always been a little shit. A callous, calculating little shit.'

Wow.

'No,' Lulu said sternly. 'Maybe he was a difficult teenager, but the Nick I know – and I *do* know him, although we've only been together six months – the Nick I know is a lovely man.'

Yvonne snorted.

'He really is! He's always surprising me with fun days out and weekends away. Just before we came up here, he booked a day at one of those adventure places and we were swinging through the trees and zooming down water slides like a pair of kids. I hadn't had so much fun since I *was* a kid! You need to get to know him properly, Yvonne.' She reached across the table and lightly touched the other woman's hand. 'It must have been hard for you, dealing with Duncan and Maggie and Isla disappearing like that, and Nick probably being a handful. There's been a lot of water under the bridge since then, though, and I promise you, when you properly get to know Nick, you're going to like him.'

Would he ever let Yvonne close enough to see the real Nick, though? Lulu pushed away the niggly little worry about how he was going to be when she got back. Would he give her the silent treatment for disloyally going out with Yvonne?

'Lulu –'

'Come to dinner!' The suggestion was out of her mouth before she'd really thought it through. 'You and Michael. Tomorrow night? Why not? Just a dinner?'

Yvonne wasn't looking at Lulu. She was watching Pam collecting crockery from the table opposite. Finally, she met Lulu's eyes. 'Okay, fine. I suppose there are things we need to discuss, about the house.'

'Great! Oh, and another thing I was going to ask you – do you have a phone number for Carol Jardine?'

'Carol? Why do you want to talk to Carol?'

'What you said just now about whether I was sure the therapy was working? When you're dealing with trauma, it's good to get independent confirmation that the person is accessing real memories. People with PTSD are at risk, sometimes, of producing false ones. Carol will be able to tell me if what Nick is apparently remembering is right or not.'

Yvonne plucked her phone from her bag and settled a pair of bright pink-framed reading glasses on her nose. 'I think I have her number, yes. For all the good it'll do.'

When Lulu got back to Sunnyside, she found Nick in the kitchen, washing up at the sink, and as he turned to her, she braced herself for the silent treatment. But he smiled as he dried his hands on the towel and asked, a little sardonically, if she'd had a good time with Yvonne.

'It wasn't as bad as I'd expected.'

'What, so you were expecting it to be an ordeal, but anything was better than staying here with Mr Nutter? No, Lu, I don't blame you! God, I'm such a pain in the arse these days.' He came across the room and took her, very tenderly, in his arms. 'I'm sorry for being such a brute. I've attempted falafels to make up for it – yes, from scratch, and with a lot of creative thinking required as we have none of the right ingredients. Do you think it's acceptable to substitute sweetcorn for chickpeas?'

Lulu gurgled, 'No!'

'Yeah. I don't expect you to eat them. It's the thought that counts, though, yes?'

'Yes.' She reached up to put a hand through his hair.

'Oh, and if you're looking for Nero, forget it. I assassinated him. Drowned him in the loo.'

And the two of them dissolved in saving laughter.

12

Duncan was home!

Maggie had been thinking about asking Yvonne, after all, if she and Isla could stay at the farm, but now there was no need. Nick had worked out that CCTV outside a shop in Hawick could have caught Duncan's car driving past, and sure enough, CCTV had captured a clear image of Duncan in the car, time-stamped 20:38 – and Hawick was half an hour's drive from The Phoenix Centre in Langholm, even if Duncan had taken the most direct route possible. The police had found Dean's body at 20:55, and the time of death had been estimated to be between 20:25 and 20:50. Dean would have died within minutes of being stabbed, so there was no sequence of events that could possibly place Duncan at The Phoenix Centre committing the murder.

The icing on the cake was that several locals had come forward to say that the so-called altercation between Duncan and Dean outside the newsagent had just been Dean kicking off and Duncan trying to calm him down and defend himself.

The authorities had had no option but to release him.

'The hero of the hour!' went Duncan as he dumped his holdall in the hall, throwing an arm round Nick, who went beetroot but insisted, 'The plods would have got there eventually. I just sped the process up a bit.'

'I don't know that they would have. They weren't looking at any alternative scenarios after they found out about that altercation I had with Dean in the street.'

'Well, but they'll have to now, won't they?' Nick looked at Maggie. 'They'll have to start thinking who else, maybe someone with a history of violence, could have been in the vicinity at the relevant time.'

'Well, yes, hopefully they'll find out who did it.' Duncan took Isla from Maggie and lowered his face to hers, breathing her in. 'Ah, it's good to be home!' He beamed at Nick. 'You know what I've really missed? Our early morning runs. How about going for a run with your old man now? I've been hitting the gym while I've been behind bars, I have to warn you.'

'Uh, yeah, but from the look of that belly you've also been hitting the baked goods section of the cafeteria pretty hard.' Nick grinned. 'All right, old man. Back here in five?'

'Oof, give me ten.'

Upstairs in their room, Maggie trailed Duncan from the wardrobe to the chest of drawers to the en suite, as he threw off the clothes he was wearing, had a piss and pulled on shorts and a T-shirt. As he went on about how glad he was to be back, not saying much about what it had been like in prison, Maggie psyched herself up for what she had to tell him. She'd decided not to say anything about what Nick had done, or her suspicions about Dean's death, while he was inside. There was nothing he could do about it other than worry himself to death. But now she needed to speak.

Before she had a chance, as he sat on the bed to tie the

laces of his running shoes, he said, 'I think there's maybe an issue with Nick.'

Hallelujah!

But Maggie made her face serious. 'Aye,' she went, rocking Isla in her arms. 'I think there is.'

'I've been spending too much time with this little one.' He smiled at Isla. 'Irresistible as she is, I think I've maybe been neglecting Nick a bit. Making him feel . . . overlooked? That was the impression I had when he came to visit me in Dumfries. He said it was good to get uninterrupted time with me.' He shook his head. 'What kind of crap father needs to get put inside and made to sit at a table in the visitors' room to spend quality time, as they call it, with his son?'

'That's blethers!' Maggie puffed. 'You've always spent loads of time with Nick.'

'Not since Isla was born.'

'Well, obviously no parent can spend as much time with their first child once a second one comes along. If Nick wasn't so fucking self-centred, he'd realise that and not guilt-trip you about it.'

'He wasn't . . .' Duncan frowned. 'Nick isn't "self-centred"!'

'If only that was all that was wrong with him!' Maggie put Isla down in her cot and sat down next to Duncan on the bed. She turned her right hand over so he could see the burn. 'Nick did this. And my leg's burnt too. He superheated a mug and gave it to me on a tray. Fucking boiling tea tsunami. Missed Isla by inches, and I had to go to A&E. I didn't tell you about it because I didn't want you worrying.'

Duncan took her hand gently and examined it. 'Ouch. That looks painful. But I'm sure Nick didn't mean to give you a mug that was too hot.'

'Of course he did!' She snatched Bunny up from Isla's cot. He'd not been the same since the hot tea had been spilt on him, the soft fur now matted at one side. 'That's where the tea landed,' she hissed, waving the rabbit in front of Duncan's nose. 'That could have been *Isla*! Her delicate wee skin –'

'Maggie –'

'Naw, Duncan. You're going to have to face up to this. There's more. Isla – I only ever left her alone when he wasn't here. I was in the kitchen, and I heard . . .' Jesus, she was choking up all over again! 'I heard Isla screaming on the baby monitor, and then Nick's voice saying, "Don't cry, little sister." By the time I got up here, he'd gone, but Isla was going mental, screaming her head off. And there was a big bruise on her! Aye, it's faded now, but it's still there – see?' Gently, she lifted the sleeping Isla from her cot and turned her so Duncan could see the place.

'What, this?' He pointed to the yellowish mark on the side of her head.

'Aye. I put a cold compress on it right away, so it healed up quick. But that was a bad bruise. He must have hit her, Duncan. He *hit Isla*!' She held Isla close, then laid her back in her cot. 'He must have sneaked out of school, biked back here . . . He threatened me with social services. He'd make out that I did it, if I went to the cops.'

Duncan was staring at her, shaking his head. 'But why on earth would he want to hurt Isla?'

'He's jealous of her! You've obviously picked up on that subconsciously, eh? Which is why you're going on about spending more time with him. He *hates* me and he *hates* Isla.'

'It was probably a voice on the radio you heard, not Nick. Did the school say he'd been AWOL?'

'Naw,' she admitted. 'He was clever about it. He must have sneaked away, as I said. And he . . . I think it was Nick who killed Dean, Duncan. And then tried to set me up for it.'

As she explained what had happened – the phone call that had lured her to The Phoenix Centre, finding Dean's body, realising that the knife was one from Sunnyside –

Duncan put his head in his hands. 'Oh God, Maggie, listen to yourself! This is *ridiculous!* Someone must have broken in here and stolen the knife. Of course it wasn't *Nick!* He was at the rehearsal for the school play the whole time. The police confirmed that. Nick said . . .' He looked at her. 'Nick said you pointed the finger at him, and that's why he was questioned by the police. I didn't believe that for a minute. I thought it was just Nick and his . . . weird ideas about you. I assumed the police must have questioned everyone who could have had access to the keys to The Phoenix Centre. But – did you really do that? You really told the police that Nick could be responsible?'

'Aye, I pointed the finger at Nick! Maybe he didn't do it himself. Maybe he got some other bastard to do the actual murder.'

'Why on earth would Nick . . .' He lifted his head, hair wild. 'No. Maggie . . .' He exhaled slowly. 'This has been a horrendously stressful time for all of us, but this . . . I think maybe you need help.'

'You're in denial!' Maggie shot back at him. 'Go on then, go for your run with golden boy! Never mind that he's probably busy planning his next scheme to get rid of me and Isla!'

'You're letting paranoia get the better of you.'

'*This* isn't *paranoia!*' Maggie shoved her burnt hand in his face. 'And neither is *this!*' She snatched up Isla, who was now yowling, and turned her to show the bruise. 'But you'd rather believe it's all in poor mental Maggie's head than that there's anything wrong with this family!'

Maggie clutched Isla to her and ran from the room.

Straight into Nick, who was standing in his joggers and T-shirt on the landing. 'Oh dear,' he said. 'You really do need help, don't you, Mags? Shame you're not going to get it. And just for the record, I'm not *jealous* of *that.*' He wrinkled his nose at Isla. 'Christ, it stinks to high heaven.'

After Maggie had changed Isla, she put her into the pram and took her out to the lawn. And there they were, Duncan and Nick, running through the field in front of the house towards Billy McLetchie Hill. Nick was laughing, running backwards a few steps, calling back at Duncan, who flopped his arms like he was going *Aye, okay, son, I give up.*

Duncan was never going to accept that Nick was evil.

She looked down at Isla's wee sleeping face, shaded from the sun by the pram hood.

The only way to keep Isla and herself safe was to leave Duncan. Get a divorce. It would break her heart. But if it was the only way . . .

But naw.

That wouldn't work. Duncan would get joint custody of Isla. There was no reason why not. And that would be even worse. Isla would have to spend days at a time here alone with Duncan and Nick, with no Maggie to protect her. Maggie could imagine Duncan putting Isla down in her cot; calling to Nick to mind her while he went out . . .

She wheeled the pram to the garage.

AT MAGGIE'S, she told Pam she needed to have 'a private word' with Liam about his employment and shut the kitchen door behind them. Liam looked from Isla, strapped to Maggie's chest in her baby carrier, to Maggie and back. He must be worried about what this 'word' was, but he was also obviously freaked out by Isla. He probably hadn't had much to do with babies.

Ordinarily she'd have messed with him, asked if he wanted to hold her.

But she came straight out with it. 'This isn't about your employment. You're fine. You're great.'

He relaxed. 'Right?'

'I need your help.'

And now he was grinning all over his face, like he knew fine well she would come round to his way of thinking eventually.

'Not to put a hit on Nick.'

The grin vanished.

'But if you really have the contacts you say you have,' said Maggie, 'I need fake IDs for Isla and me. And I need them fast.'

13

L ulu had laid the table in the dining room and lit candles in the candelabra, but she wasn't fooling anyone that this was fine dining. Neither she nor Nick was a great cook, and Lulu felt embarrassed to be making Michael and Yvonne eat this muck. The potatoes were mush, the beef was so tough you could hardly swallow it, and the cabbage was like rubber too.

But Michael, bless him, had a second helping.

'I'm sorry, I'm not much of a chef,' Lulu apologised, handing him the potatoes. 'You really want more of these?'

'All ends up the same way, doesn't it?' said Michael cheerily.

Yvonne, in contrast, had only eaten a couple of mouthfuls.

'This recovered memory thing,' Michael said, ladling sloppy spuds onto his plate. 'Is the idea to work out what might have happened?'

Yvonne shot him a repressive look.

'Uh, no,' said Lulu, glancing at Nick, who was refilling his own wine glass without offering more to their guests in a very uncharacteristic show of bad manners. 'It's about helping Nick process what he went through.'

Nick took a slug of wine. 'It would be good, though, wouldn't it, if I did happen to remember something important? Something we could take to the cops. But no joy so far.' He took another slug. 'Whatever happened must have happened between my leaving the house in the morning and returning in the evening. It's convenient that the place is so isolated. No one to see what was going on. Apart from you two, maybe. If you were out and about on the farm, in the fields, you might have seen something.'

Michael shook his head. 'I was in the shed most of that day, taking a tractor apart. It was November. Not much call to be out and about on the fields. The ploughing was finished. We were digging drains near the track, but not that day, and there's no view of Sunnyside from there anyway.'

'And I was away,' said Yvonne.

'Oh. Yes,' said Nick. 'So you were. At a conference in . . . was it York?'

'Harrogate.'

'What was it, The International Smelly Cheese Symposium?'

Yvonne pursed her lips. 'It was The Technologies for Small Businesses Conference.'

Nick looked off, his eyes narrowing, and Lulu was sure he had gone back there again, back to the day of the disappearance. She was sure this was the last thing he wanted to talk about, but he seemed to brace himself as he looked back at Yvonne. 'But you left early.'

'Of course. Michael called me the night they went missing, and I drove back.'

Nick nodded slowly. 'I appreciated you doing that.'

'I was worried about my brother, my sister-in-law and my niece,' snapped Yvonne. 'Not everything is about you.'

Lulu's heart sank. She'd hoped that aunt and nephew might move towards a reconciliation tonight, but Nick was having to get drunk to get through it and Yvonne was making zero effort to build bridges.

When they'd finished the main course, Yvonne helped Lulu and Nick clear it. As Nick took another bottle of wine back through to the dining room, Lulu scraped food into the bin and handed the plates to Yvonne, who was stacking the dishwasher as efficiently as, Lulu suspected, she did most things.

'All this *therapy* nonsense isn't going to get you anywhere, you know,' Yvonne said as soon as Nick had left the kitchen. 'You're barking up the wrong tree entirely.'

Lulu handed her another plate wordlessly.

'You don't know what you're dealing with here.' Yvonne slammed the dishwasher closed. 'You need to look at reasons for Nick's behaviour other than that he's a poor traumatised soul. You need to wake up, Lulu.'

Oh God. Not only had this evening failed to bring aunt and nephew closer together, but now the aunt was trying to sabotage his marriage?

'I don't think I'm the one who's not seeing clearly here,' Lulu snapped back.

'Oh, no?' Yvonne strode to the door, but instead of storming out, she slammed it and came back to Lulu and said rapidly, 'You know Michael said they were digging field drains, at the time Duncan, Maggie and Isla disappeared? That meant there was a digger sitting in the field. Michael always puts the key on the back wheel, and Nick knew that. He also knew that Michael was going to be spending all day tinkering with one of the tractors. The coast was clear.'

Lulu gaped at her. 'Just what are you suggesting?'

'How could a sixteen-year-old boy possibly have had anything to do with his family's disappearance? That was the police thinking. That was everyone's thinking. There was no way he could have cold-bloodedly killed the three of them and somehow disposed of their bodies.'

Lulu couldn't believe she was hearing this. 'Yvonne, *no*! Nick would *never ever –*'

'You know him so much better than me, of course, after your two months of marriage.' Yvonne held Lulu's gaze. 'And you've got degrees in psychology. So tell me – is the controlling behaviour Nick is demonstrating a classic sign of a psychopath, or is it not?'

Lulu shook her head. 'He's not "controlling"! He's over-protective, yes, but only because he's so anxious about me. He bends over backwards to accommodate my every whim in all other ways! I can't believe you could think he . . . what? Used the digger to –' She lowered her voice to a whisper. 'To take their bodies to the drain and tip them in? But whoever was digging the drains would have seen them!'

'Not if he back-filled that part of the trench. But no, actually, that's not what I'm suggesting. The police dug up some of the drains and brought in sniffer dogs, and they found nothing. But they didn't even look at the top field, which had just been ploughed and would have been perfect to dig a hole in. Nice, soft, ploughed soil.'

SHE WAS STANDING AGAIN at the door. The white panelled kitchen door with no handle. She needed to get in there. She needed her family to open the door.

'Mum! Dad! Dennis! John!'

She thumped on the door with the thing in her right hand.

Thump thump thump!

It was heavy and made of metal, the thing in her hand. It had a big, wicked-looking hook on one end.

It was a big crowbar.

THE NEXT DAY, very early in the morning, while Nick was closeted in the study making trades, Lulu set off on a walk in a soft drizzle, striding away from the house up the farm track. The fields here were so lush, such a contrast to the parched land at Braemar Station. The air smelt of damp earth and verdant undergrowth. To her left was grazing land, cattle turning lazily to watch her pass by and, beyond them, sheep and the stark hump of the bare hilltop. To the right was a sea of oats, green tinged with yellow ochre, the surface rippling in places as a little breeze got up.

It was hard to imagine that this rural idyll had ever been part of The Debatable Lands, which must have been like some sort of dystopian, sci-fi nightmare. But it had been real. And it had happened here. Nick's ancestors, probably, had been caught up in it all.

She walked up the edge of the oats, up a slope to a little knoll covered in beech trees, and sat on the weathered, bone-grey smoothness of a fallen tree under a sheltering beech canopy, looking back down the fields to the trees that screened Sunnyside from view.

Oh God – was this the 'top field' Yvonne had spoken about?

She jumped to her feet and ran back down the edge of the field, the breath tearing in and out of her lungs. How could Yvonne think that Nick – *Nick* – might have *murdered* his *own family*? She was his aunt. Surely she should know him better than that?

But she didn't, of course, because she'd never taken the trouble.

Oh, Nick! The only blood relative he had left didn't just dislike him, she thought he was some kind of monster.

By the time she got back to Sunnyside, she was sobbing.

The study door came open and Nick was standing there, hair slightly rumpled, eyebrows raised in that gently enquiring way of his, ready to hear all about what was going on with her, ready to provide a sounding board, a shoulder to cry on, an ally against the world who would always be in her corner.

He was so kind, so *empathetic*.

How could Yvonne not see that?

He strode across the hall and swept her into his arms. 'What the hell's happened?'

'Nothing! Nothing.'

He held her away from him, tipping her chin with one finger and contemplating her gravely, just a hint of a tender smile lifting his lips. 'Funny sort of nothing.'

'Yvonne . . . Yvonne said something to me last night, and I can't believe . . . I can't believe your own aunt would think something so terrible.'

'Ah.' He raised his eyebrows.

'She said – she suggested that you . . .'

'Might have killed them?'

And now she was blurting, 'She suggested you could have used the digger that was standing in the field to . . . to dig a hole and –'

He tightened his arms around her. 'Shh. Shh. It's okay. She's been peddling that little rumour for the past twenty years, but I don't think anyone seriously believes it.'

'But why would she do that? She doesn't actually believe that you hurt them?'

He shrugged. 'Possibly. Yvonne has never really "got" me, as they say. Thinks I'm being serious when I say outrageous things. She certainly didn't appreciate the admittedly warped sense of humour I had as a kid.' He suddenly smiled. 'I was a right little horror, it has to be said. This one time, Andy and I spent ages mocking up a severed arm with a bit of old mannequin from the art department at school, and when we were helping out at the farm one weekend, I went running into the kitchen carrying the arm, pretending Andy had fallen into the hay bailer.' He began to gulp with laughter. 'We'd gone crazy with the tomato ketchup. Even put a sleeve on it the same colour as the jumper Andy was wearing.'

'Oh no, *Nick*!' She couldn't help smiling.

'Final confirmation of Yvonne's long-held opinion that I was one sick puppy.' He suddenly sobered. 'And now she thinks I'm an actual psychopath.'

'I'm sure she doesn't, deep down. Not really. She probably feels guilty about not taking you in when you needed her. Convincing herself you're a bad person is her way of coming to terms with what she did.'

He smiled.

She smiled back at him. 'What?'

'You always have to find a reasonable explanation for people, don't you, no matter how abhorrent you might find their behaviour?'

'No, I'm not saying that. I'm not saying that what Yvonne did was reasonable. Because it wasn't. It was the *worst*, Nick. It really was the *worst*.' And she burst into tears all over again at the thought of him, sixteen-year-old Nick, standing in this very spot, maybe, a suitcase in his hand, off to boarding school. And Yvonne . . . Yvonne on the doorstep, jiggling her car keys and looking pointedly at her watch.

THAT AFTERNOON, when Nick had closeted himself in the study again at three o'clock, Lulu slipped out of the house into the now heavy rain and scuttled down the path to the garage. The drive forked halfway along the avenue, an offshoot going to the garage and former stables. Presumably, this dated from when the Victorian owners wanted the horses and their smell kept well away from the grand residence. The study faced the other way, so Nick wouldn't see the car leave. Or hear it, hopefully.

She felt really bad about sneaking out behind his back, but when she'd broached the subject of the car in bed last night, after they'd made love – usually a good time to broach anything controversial – he had sighed and said he would drive her anywhere she wanted to go.

He could have driven her to Carol Jardine's house.

Lulu could have told him why she wanted to speak to Carol. But that would have implied that she was checking up on him, that she thought he might, as Yvonne had suggested, be pulling the wool over her eyes, when nothing could be further from the truth. The problem was that people with PTSD sometimes presented with a mix of real and false memories, and it was important for the therapist to determine which was which.

The key to the garage door was kept in a safe fixed to the side of the building, but Lulu knew the combination. Nick had kept going on about how ridiculous it was that Yvonne had chosen the date the house was built – 1889. Presumably, this made it easy for the guests in case they forgot it, because the year 1889 was carved in a stone panel above the front door.

Lulu twiddled the combination lock to 1889, opened the safe and removed the key. She unlocked the garage door and slipped inside. Then she rootled around in the inner compartment of her bag for the spare car key. She'd remembered last night, as she'd lain in bed trying to sleep, that one of the random keys in her bag was the spare one for the Audi, which she'd started carrying around after locking herself out of the car for the second time.

The engine starting sounded horribly loud. Wincing, she

eased the Audi out of the garage and crept to the fork in the drive. Then she cut the engine and coasted down the avenue to the public road.

Carol and Steven Jardine lived in a modern bungalow in a little hamlet by the River Esk, one of a scattering of houses amongst tree-lined fields. The bungalow was set in a large garden that had probably once been a field too and was given over mainly to lawn. Carol, a solid woman in jeans and a floral top, seemed delighted that Lulu had looked her up, and kept staring at her and saying, 'Nick's wife! You're *gorgeous*! You must make *such* a handsome couple!'

They sat in the conservatory watching sheet after sheet of rain sweep across the garden, sipping tea and demolishing an amazing gingerbread cake that one of Carol's daughters had made, as Carol talked about Kathleen, Nick's mother, who had been her best friend.

'I still miss her.' She sighed. 'Even though she's been gone over twenty years. We used to have such a good time together. Kathleen used to joke that it was a shame shopping wasn't an Olympic sport because the two of us would be definite contenders. We used to haunt the local auction houses for fixtures and fittings for Sunnyside, and all the sales in the posh interiors shops in Edinburgh.'

'Sunnyside is a beautiful house,' Lulu felt obliged to contribute.

Carol beamed. 'Isn't it? In a terrible run-down condition, though, when they bought it. Duncan's elderly uncle had been living there and really let it go. Renovating the place stretched Duncan and Kathleen's budget to breaking point. A real money pit. I didn't like to ask, because maybe the truth was that they couldn't have any more kids, but I used to wonder if maybe that was the reason Nick was an only. Early in their marriage, they were – what's the phrase? Asset rich, cash poor. They maybe felt more kids wasn't an option finan-

cially, especially given all the money they spent giving Nick
the best of everything – activities, holidays . . .' She sighed
again. 'Kathleen used to say she worried Duncan spoilt him,
but Nick was a great kid. I'm so glad he's made a good life for
himself.' And she smiled, but rather sadly, at Lulu.

'He has, but he's never really got past what happened. It's
still affecting him quite badly, to be honest.'

'Of course it is.' Carol's eyes filled with tears. 'That poor
boy.'

Lulu had already told Carol on the phone about the
PTSD therapy she was using with Nick, and now, when she
started to list the things he had said he remembered about
the kitchen, Carol nodded. 'That's right. One of the rings on
the hob was on. There were three mugs of half-drunk tea on
the table, and three bowls and three spoons – no one knows
why there were three of everything and not two, but I don't
suppose it's important. Isla's rabbit was on the floor.'

Lulu sighed in relief. 'So the memories he's accessing are
real. Sometimes they're not.'

Carol cupped her hands round her mug. 'You know, it's
silly, but I still think about that little rabbit. About what
happened to it. It's probably sealed in a police evidence bag
somewhere, forgotten in the archives.'

'What do *you* think happened to them? To Duncan and
Maggie and Isla?'

'Oh, goodness.'

Lulu waited.

'The police think they went off somewhere, voluntarily,'
Carol said carefully.

'But you don't believe that?'

Silence. Then: 'No. I don't. Duncan would never have gone
off like that and left Nick. And Isla's rabbit . . . If they'd decided
for some reason that they needed to disappear, they wouldn't

have left Isla's favourite bunny behind. They doted on that child. My husband thinks it was one of the young offenders Duncan used to mentor – which would explain the third mug and bowl and spoon. He thinks they invited one of them for lunch and the yob went psycho. Or maybe it was one of Dean Reid's relatives. The boy who was murdered? Has Nick told you about that?'

'Um . . . no?'

There had been mention of a murder in that YouTube clip, Lulu remembered.

'A few weeks before the disappearance, one of the boys on Duncan's programme, Dean Reid, was murdered at The Phoenix Centre. There was a big mix-up and Duncan was arrested for it and charged, but evidence soon came to light clearing him. My husband thinks one of Dean Reid's relatives might have thought Duncan got away with the murder and took revenge.'

'But you don't think that?'

Carol took a sip of tea. 'No. I'm afraid I've always thought *Maggie* must have . . . I don't know. Had one of her mad turns. A murder-suicide is what I suspect. Maggie was a troubled soul. Could even be quite – violent. Nick was always sure that *she* murdered Dean Reid too.'

'But why would he think that?'

'Dean was a real little tearaway. Had been giving Duncan grief. Making things up about him, like Duncan had hit him. Even tried to blackmail him for a thousand pounds. Nick thought Maggie flipped and killed him.'

'And do you think she could have? I mean, she was tiny, wasn't she?'

'*Though she be but little, she is fierce.*' Carol grimaced. 'Oh, you wouldn't have wanted to pick a fight with Maggie.'

Really? Lulu thought of the petite woman in that wedding photo, sunnily smiling.

'Wouldn't she have been incapable, physically, of – well, of disposing of Duncan's body?'

'She probably had help from one of her delinquent friends. Maggie had mixed with all sorts. She probably called one of them and got him to take Duncan's body away and deal with it.'

A man with a van.

It was so surreal, sitting here talking to this nice woman in her nice conservatory about body disposal options.

'So how did Maggie seem, that morning, when you picked Nick up?'

'Oh, I didn't see her. I picked Nick up from the end of the drive as usual. There was a little sort of hut there where he used to wait for the school bus. A lot of country properties have them.'

As Carol walked Lulu to the Audi, sheltering them both under a huge red and yellow golf umbrella, another vehicle appeared, snaking along the driveway towards them between the lawns.

'Here's my son, Andy.'

The car came to a halt, and a giant of a man unfolded himself from the driver's seat. He must have been six-five at least and was very well built. He gave Lulu a shy smile. He had a scar running through his mouth that pulled one side of his face down.

'Andy, this is Nick's wife, Lulu,' said Carol, with the air of presenting him with a wonderful surprise.

But Andy gaped at Lulu as if he'd just seen an alien jump from her stomach.

'Nick's back!' Carol burbled on. 'Well, for a couple of weeks, anyway. I was thinking, Lulu, it would be lovely if you and Nick had time to come round for dinner, and you can join us, Andy. We can have a proper reunion!'

Andy was still standing with his mouth open, rain

pouring down his face, and Lulu remembered, now, that Nick had suggested that Andy maybe wasn't playing with a full set. Lulu gave him a warm smile and told Carol that would be lovely.

She'd just got back to Sunnyside and secreted the Audi back in the garage when her phone chirped. Michael.

'Lulu, it's Yvonne. I think she's in trouble.'

14

MAGGIE - OCTOBER 1997

At the back door, Maggie handed Duncan a pair of gardening gloves. 'Here you go. And here's the repellent.' He was going to be clipping the yew trees at the bottom of the garden, and they were always full of midgies, apparently. Midgies couldn't get enough of Duncan.

'You think of everything!' He put an arm round her, leaning over to nuzzle Isla in the baby carrier on Maggie's chest. He hadn't said anything about the fact that Maggie was now taking Isla with her wherever she went. It was the October holidays, and Nick was at home all the time, so no way was Maggie trusting Isla out her sight.

Maybe Duncan had decided to humour her.

'I think that baby monitor we have could be buggered,' she said. 'You know you thought maybe the voice I heard on it, the voice I thought was Nick, was the radio? The radio definitely wasn't on, but Pam was saying a woman told her she started picking up weird stuff on her monitor, deep voices effing and blinding, like her baby was possessed. Turned out it was tuned to the frequency a local security firm used on their walkie-talkie thingmies. I was wondering if maybe ours has been picking up some other bastard's monitor.'

Aye, right.

There were no near neighbours apart from Yvonne and Michael, so it didn't make sense, but Duncan was nodding along. Any explanation for what had been going on in this family, other than *Nick is a psycho* or *Maggie is a loony*, would float his boat.

'We should replace it, then,' he said.

'I was thinking I might go into town and get one from that baby shop. Will be expensive, mind. Can I take some cash from the drawer?'

'Of course you can.'

Maggie would take maybe a hundred quid and add it to her stash. By the time Liam had Maggie and Isla's new identities sorted, she'd hopefully have a few thousand to start their new lives with. Duncan would never notice if the baby monitor was a new one or not, the big lummock.

She watched him wheel the barrow down the drive with that athletic, springy walk of his. He was wearing manky, worn old trousers and a stained shirt. Maggie had tried to get the stains out, but he'd laughed at her. 'It's my bloody gardening shirt! It's meant to look like shit. I don't think it's even been washed for about a year.'

It would break her heart to leave him.

And his, when she and Isla just disappeared one day. Vanished in a puff of smoke.

But it was his own *fucking fault*! If he would only believe her about Nick, she wouldn't have to do any of this. He would understand that Isla had to come first.

Maggie pulled the crocheted cap down more snuggly over Isla's fragile wee skull.

No way was she risking Nick hurting Isla again.

That was the bottom line.

Walking along the passage to the kitchen, she saw there was a tiny piece of yellow plastic by the skirting board. A piece of her measuring spoons. She bent to pick it up and put it in her pocket.

Mrs Greenlees. The first person who had believed in her.

At first, she had hated those Home Ec classes because all the other lassies had laughed at her for not recognising flour and not knowing how to use an oven. But then Mrs Greenlees had told them to shut their geggies. Mrs Greenlees wasn't all prim and proper like the other Home Ec teachers. She was big and loud and told it like it was. The next week, she'd asked Maggie if she'd like some extra lessons on how to cook, one-to-one, so she could get up to speed with the basics.

Maggie hadn't wanted the humiliation of extra lessons, but then Mrs Greenlees had said she could take home the results, and she'd imagined herself showing Ma what she'd made, the aroma wafting off it filling the flat, and Ma saying, 'That's pure amazing,' and the two of them sitting on the settee eating it.

Of course, that had never happened. After the lessons, she'd take the food into the janitor's shed and sit on a bucket and scowf the lot, whatever it was – scones or traybakes or lukewarm lasagne or bread and butter pudding.

She hadn't taken it home because she knew Ma would turn it round on her somehow. There'd be something not right about it, it would taste 'bowfing' or be 'foreign muck'. Or maybe it would be the simple fact that Maggie had accepted 'charity', or Ma would get it in her head that Maggie was trying to show her up. Maggie could never predict what was going to set her off, but there would be something about that bread and butter pudding or those scones that would warrant a battering.

They had been magic, though, those lessons, and Maggie had really got into the process of turning stuff you couldn't even eat, like flour and yeast and raw eggs, into a finished product that was dead tasty and 'full of goodness', as Mrs Greenlees used to say. Sometimes what Maggie produced was so tempting that Mrs Greenlees couldn't resist, and she'd say, 'Ooh, can I have a wee taste?' and Mrs Greenlees and Maggie, and sometimes another teacher if anyone was there working late, would polish off the lot, sitting there in the brightness of that Home Ec room while the winter darkness fell outside. And while they ate, Mrs Greenlees would talk about funny things, like the 'shenanigans' of her two grown-up sons and their pals, and she'd ask Maggie about herself and her plans, and the two of them would go off into a fantasy land where Maggie had a fancy restaurant somewhere on the west coast and cooked amazing seafood and got her own TV programme.

When she'd left school with her one O Grade, Mrs Greenlees had given her those spoons. It had been the first time Maggie had received a present, and she'd been made up. All the way home, she'd held the spoons and fanned them out and put them back in place, smiling at how each one was just so much smaller than the one behind that it fitted snuggly against the curve of its bowl. But best of all, she'd known that every time she used them she'd think of Mrs Greenlees and how she'd almost been like a ma.

WHEN THEY GOT BACK from their trip to Langholm, Maggie put Isla in her pram with Bunny and pushed her round and round the garden. There was a breeze, and Isla loved watching the tops of the trees swaying above her. Maggie was talking daft nonsense about how the trees were waving at them when a piercing sound split the air.

The fucking fire alarm.

Probably just Nick or Duncan burning toast, but she'd

best check. She parked Isla at the front door and got in there pronto. She could smell burning, the reek of it making her cough. That wasn't just toast. There was smoke billowing from the kitchen doorway. Putting her sleeve over her nose, she peeked inside.

The smoke was coming from the cooker.

From a pan on the hob.

It had boiled dry and triggered the alarm.

Thank God it was nothing worse. She used a tea towel to push the pan away from the ring and turned it off. Then she opened the windows and got up on a chair to switch off the alarm.

Nick.

Probably hoping she'd take hold of the handle and burn herself again.

She left the hot pan steaming in the sink and ran back out through the hall, out through the front door.

The pram had gone.

No.

No no no!

'Duncan!' she yelled. '*Duncan!*'

She ran through the garden, along the paths, across the lawn, behind the greenhouse. As she charged round the side of the house, she was just in time to see the pram hurtling down the drive, bouncing and swaying but going so fast that the bumps in the tarmac weren't enough to deflect it from its course as it shot in and out of the shadows cast by the trees. Streaming out behind it came Isla's wail.

Nick stood at the top of the drive watching, just the trace of a smile lifting his lips.

Maggie was running, running faster than she'd ever run in her life, flying down the drive after the pram as she became aware of another sound, a rumbling sound that she knew, the sound of one of the massive timber lorries coming along the road.

'*Duncaaaaan!*'

She wasn't going to catch the pram.

He'd timed it.

He'd probably practised, when he was alone in the house. Timed the pram's descent. Timed the lorries from when he could first hear them to when they passed the bottom of the drive.

Too slow!

Maggie was too slow.

The pram was moving too fast.

And then Duncan appeared, running out of the trees, right into the path of the pram, staggering backwards as he flung his arms around the hood and stopped its onward rush just as the first of the timber lorries thundered past, the vortex it made pulling at his hair and shirt.

Sobbing, gasping, Maggie snatched a red-faced, yowling Isla up out of the pram and pressed her to her body. 'It's okay, you're okay, my wee darling.'

Duncan was still hugging the pram, his face stiff, chest heaving.

'He did it! *Nick did it!*' Maggie wailed, clutching Isla, although she knew Duncan wouldn't believe her. 'He must have waited for the lorries and then pushed the pram –'

But Duncan's face was white. 'Yes,' he said. 'I saw him. I saw him do it.'

15

'I t's just so strange,' said Michael. 'Yvonne always takes her phone with her on her walks.'

He'd told Lulu and Nick that he'd become worried when Yvonne hadn't returned from her walk at the usual time. He had driven around, checking out the various places she liked to walk, until he'd found her car. Now they were standing in the rain, the three of them, in the small, informal parking area at the entrance to a forest track at a place called Craibstone Wood, waiting for the police to arrive. Yvonne's phone was visible on the passenger seat of her car.

Lulu was trying to stay upbeat. 'Typical, isn't it? The one time she doesn't take her phone, she twists her ankle or something and can't summon help. But she can't have gone far. We'll find her. Should Nick and I start looking while you wait here for the police?'

'Yes. Thanks. Yes.'

As she and Nick headed off up the track, Nick grumbled, 'Stupid bloody woman. Who goes walking in the rain on slick forest paths without their phone?'

As they trudged along, calling Yvonne's name, Lulu

looked around her at the sodden trees and imagined Yvonne, huddled somewhere out here, soaked through, cold, maybe in pain, maybe not able to call out for help . . .

They did a full circuit of the main track, returning to the parking area to find that the police had arrived. Michael came hurrying towards them. 'They've sent for a dog. They said I should go home, and I will, but only to fetch our dogs. I'm going to help with the search.'

'We will too,' said Lulu at once.

As Michael hurried off towards a policewoman in a yellow tabard, Nick shook himself like a dog, sending drips flying off his jacket. 'What did you have to say that for? We're soaked through already.'

She stared at him. 'Nick! Yvonne's probably lying out there *hurt*! The more people searching, the sooner we'll find her.'

'The cops will have drones and what have you. We'll just be getting in the way, enthusiastic amateurs getting themselves lost.'

She touched his damp arm. 'I know this must be hard.' It was bound to be triggering, yet another member of his family going missing.

He snatched his arm away. 'Of course it's *hard*!'

Lulu took a step back.

Then he sort of froze, staring off at the trees so intently that Lulu turned to see what he was looking at. Then she realised that his eyes were unfocused. What he was seeing wasn't in the here and now.

He made a sort of wordless sound, almost a whimper.

'Oh, Nick.' She put both arms around him and pulled him into a soggy hug.

THEY DIDN'T FIND HER.

They searched for five hours, until the light began to go and the police called a halt. Lulu suggested that Michael come to Sunnyside with them, but he said he wanted to go back to the farm, 'Just in case she calls the landline. Or comes home.'

And thank goodness Michael hadn't come with them, because as soon as they'd stepped into the hall Nick doubled up, as if in pain, and then Lulu was cradling him like a baby while he sobbed.

'It just takes a heartbeat,' he gulped, clutching her shoulder. 'And you're gone. Snuffed out. The end of it all.' And suddenly he was roaring in her face: 'Why is life such a *fucking bastard*?' And he was half-laughing, half-crying, and gently Lulu was guiding him through the hall and into the big, airy drawing room, where they'd forgotten to shut two of the windows and the room was filled with the fragrant, earthy scents of summer rain.

In the dusk, the room was cool and shadowed and calming, she hoped. She eased him onto the big chintzy sofa and sat with him, rocking him. 'We don't know that any harm has come to Yvonne.'

'Oh yeah?' He barked a laugh. 'Of course *harm* has *come* to her! God, Lulu. How do any of us keep going, how do we keep functioning in a world where one misstep, one split second of inattention, one stupid mistake of trusting the wrong person can bring it all tumbling down, and that's your nice, safe, normal, everyday existence *fucked forever*?'

'Nick –'

'At the wood, it was like I was back in that day, back telling the cops what had happened, and they were looking at me the way they looked at Michael, like they were thinking *poor bloody idiot*. The cops, they *know*. They *know* how fucking dangerous it is, the world out there, and they know that most of us are living in blissful ignorance of the fact until some-thing like this happens.'

Gently, she turned him to face her. 'But the world can be a wonderful place, too. Look at us. Look at how we found each other. I mean, what are the chances? If I'd chosen another island . . . if I hadn't had my stuff stolen . . .'

'You're the only good thing in my life,' he groaned.

'Oh, Nick, that's not true.'

And it was terrible, but a little surge of impatience went through Lulu as a reprehensible thought surfaced – that she missed the old, stoical, humorous Nick. The Nick who was so scathing about people 'getting in touch with their feelings'.

Where had that come from?

She was a therapist, for God's sake.

She should be glad that the barriers were finally coming down.

Maybe it was because the old Nick reminded her a bit of her dad, whose summation of Lulu's whole client base was 'load of whingers'. She knew there was a theory that some women used their father as a template for what a man should be and subconsciously chose the same type for their partner.

But it was more than that.

There was something about Nick's extravagant emoting that was repelling her.

Nick took a deep breath and covered his face with his hands. 'Are you regretting it?' he muttered through them. 'Encouraging me to let it all out?' Sometimes it really was as if he could read her mind.

'No, of course not!'

Karla used to warn her students that the natural human reaction to someone breaking down and letting out their emotions wasn't necessarily to comfort, but to avoid. 'It's part of the self-preservation instinct,' Karla had explained. 'To put distance between yourself and someone in trouble. People with mental health problems are often isolated not only because they withdraw, but because those around them instinctively do so too. You need to acknowledge that you're part of the human race with the same pre-programmed survival instincts, and it's normal to want to avoid your clients.' She had grinned round at the class. 'But you need to let the rational part of the brain get on top of the amygdala and the primitive, instinctual response it's trying to produce.'

Lulu, at the time, had smugly reflected that that advice wasn't aimed at *her*, someone Karla had singled out as being worryingly empathetic. *She* had never felt repulsed by anyone letting out their emotions.

Until now.

Oh God!

What did that say about her? How could she feel nothing but sympathy when it was a virtual stranger pouring their heart out, but not when it was Nick, her own, beloved husband?

Maybe it was because this was so much more personal. Maybe her amygdala was dominating her rational brain because it was important, in the dim distant past of human evolution, for a woman to have a partner who was strong, who could protect her and provide for her. Evidence to the contrary could prompt her to shrink away from him.

She had to repress that primitive response.

She didn't need Nick to protect her. She'd been raised on Braemar Station, for crying out loud, and she was one tough cookie. Mum and Dad had always instilled in her the belief that she could do anything she put her mind to. 'The only limits are the limits you put on yourself,' Dad used to say.

But what if Nick's problems were a challenge too far?

No.

She could do this.

She could help him get through it.

And then maybe the old Nick will come back, said her treacherous amygdala.

Nick heaved in another breath. 'I'm sorry.' He took his hands from his face. 'Didn't mean to throw such a pity party.'

'You don't need to apologise, silly!'

'What do you think's happened to Yvonne?' he said quietly.

'I – I don't know.'

Oh God, Yvonne!

Yvonne, lying out there in the dark, somewhere in that forest. Surely the police would find her tomorrow?

AT DAWN, Lulu and Nick returned to Craibstone Wood to help with the search. Lulu felt like a zombie after a night of sleeplessness and fractured dreams she couldn't now remember, and Nick insisted that Lulu mustn't ever be out of his sight – the latest in a new, long list of rules he'd started laying down that morning at breakfast.

'Lu, please, you must promise. You mustn't leave the house without telling me. You must always keep your phone on you, charged up and switched on, even when you're in the loo. If Yvonne had had her phone with her . . .'

'Okay,' she had reassured him. 'I promise.'

There was, she had to admit, something reassuring about Nick being right next to her as they walked through the gloom of the forest. Her throat was raw with calling Yvonne's name, and it was much more tiring than you'd think, tramping through a forest where your feet were always slipping into holes or through rotten fallen wood, where you were always having to skirt round obstacles and duck under low branches.

They proceeded in a line, like on a TV drama, all dressed in yellow tabards. There was a huge turnout of local people, which was a surprise, as Lulu couldn't imagine Yvonne being very popular. Carol Jardine was there. She caught Nick in a tight hug and introduced her husband, Steve, to Lulu, a bearded man in a waxed jacket.

'Andy's here somewhere, Nick.'

They met back at the car park for sandwiches and tea provided by one of the other farmers, a brisk woman who served everyone from the back of a pickup. As Lulu joined Nick in the Audi, her phone beeped. A London number she didn't recognise.

'Hello? This is Lulu Clyde?'

'Mrs Clyde, good morning. This is DC Tariq Akhtar from the Met. I'm one of the team investigating Paul Montgomery's death.'

'Oh, right, yes. Hello.'

'Would you have time to answer a couple of quick questions?'

Her heart plummeted. 'Okay. Yes.'

'Can I just ask you . . . did you take anything away from the scene?'

'No. I don't think so. I – I went into the kitchen and found him there, found him . . . hanging from the ceiling. I got up on the chair and tried to –' Her throat closed up.

Lulu really didn't want to be thinking about this.

And suddenly she was angry.

'I tried to hold him up, and then the police arrived and got me to go outside. I had Milo in my arms. So, no. Of course I didn't take anything away! Why would I? Oh my God, are you accusing me of *stealing something from the house*?'

'No, no, *no*, definitely not.' A long breath. 'I'm sorry, I've been very clumsy about this. Absolutely not. It's just that there's a strange anomaly we're trying to clear up. Mr Montgomery used blue nylon twine to um, to –'

'Hang himself,' Lulu snapped.

'Yes. Uh. Yes. Well, some very small pieces of the blue nylon material – we're talking under a millimetre in size – were found on the kitchen floor, presumably falling there when the twine was cut. But no ball of twine, or any other lengths of it, were present anywhere in the property. It's possible that Mr Montgomery cut the twine to size earlier and disposed of the twine he wasn't going to use somewhere outside the property, but it doesn't seem likely. It's, uh . . . well, it's literally a loose end.'

'Does it matter when Paul cut the twine and what he did with the rest of it? I mean, *really*?' She rolled her eyes at Nick, who was staring at her fixedly, the pungent egg sandwich in its greaseproof paper untouched on his lap. 'I've got rather more important things to worry about here. My husband's aunt is missing and we're helping with the search. I have to go.'

She ended the call and puffed out a breath. 'Unbelievable.'

She told Nick what the policeman had said.

Nick heard her out without speaking. Then he said, slowly and clearly, as if to a child, 'Why would the police ask *you* if you'd taken anything from Paul's house?'

'Well, because I was in shock, I suppose, and might have shoved the twine into my pocket without thinking.'

'But he wasn't just asking about the twine, was he? Did you take *anything*. It's the sort of question he might ask some-one's partner, someone who was familiar with the house, not someone who'd only been there once.'

'He *was* just asking about the twine.'

'No,' he said patiently. 'You said he said "anything".'

'Meaning the twine. Obviously.'

'Oh. It's *obvious*, is it, and I'm too thick to get it?'

Lulu shook her head in confusion.

'Had you been to Paul's house before?'

'What? No! What exactly are you accusing me of?' She felt suddenly shaky and weird, as if the world had tipped on its axis.

'You and Paul were very friendly, weren't you? Hugging and kissing.'

'Nick, don't be *ridiculous*! We never *kissed*! Oh my God! You can't seriously be thinking there was anything going on between me and *Paul*?'

She recoiled as he suddenly thrust his face into hers. 'You tell me, Lulu.'

And then he was gone, out of the car, striding off to rejoin the search, walking straight past Andy – who was standing gaping at him – without acknowledging the giant of a man or even seeming to see him.

Lulu moved on autopilot through the forest with the others, Nick's implicit accusation going round and round her head. He was just two people down the line from her, but whenever she looked over at him, he studiously ignored her.

She told herself that it was enough to make anyone lose it, lash out at the person closest to them – yet another member of his family disappearing. What must that be doing to him?

When they'd finished searching the area they'd been assigned and were walking back along the track, Nick walking ahead of Lulu with Carol Jardine, a quiet voice said, 'Lulu?'

Andy was at her side. He didn't return her smile.

'I need to talk to you,' he said in a rapid whisper.

'Yes, of course.'

'Not here. Not now. Can you meet me, tomorrow morning? It's important.'

'Well, I –'

'You can't tell Nick. Mum said you told her he works early in the morning, yes? From seven till nine? You could meet me at, say, seven-thirty? But it can't be in public. There's an aban-

doned little farmhouse about quarter of a mile west of
Sunnyside, up a track on the right. I'll meet you there. And
don't tell Nick. You mustn't tell him, okay? Or anyone?'

And before she could respond, he had run off ahead of
everyone down the track, arms hanging, rather ape-like, by
his sides.

Lulu sighed inwardly. Presumably Carol had told Andy
that she was a therapist, and he had issues he wanted to talk
through. Searching for Yvonne was inevitably going to be
tough on everyone who knew her, not just Nick. Anyone with
an underlying vulnerability, such as she sensed in Andy, was
going to be particularly at risk of a negative impact. She could
meet him tomorrow, she guessed, and let him talk.

Back in the car park, as she and Nick were changing out
of their walking boots in a tense silence, one of the police officers, a small, neat woman with her hair in a bun, approached
them. 'Mr and Mrs Clyde? I'm PC Melissa Jackson. I wonder
if it would be possible for myself and a colleague to speak to
you about Ms Moncrieff? Can we meet you, back at your
property?'

16

'But *why* did he do it?' went Duncan.

Maggie and Duncan were sitting side by side on the bed, Isla safe in her cot next to them.

'I've told you,' she said, making her voice gentle. 'He hates Isla. He hates the fact that she's taking your attention away from him.'

'But that's not a *reason* to try to *kill* her!'

It was half an hour since Nick had been carted off. Duncan himself had called the police, and he and Maggie had both made statements, and Nick had been arrested for attempted murder and taken to Langholm police station for questioning. Maggie had also told the cops that she suspected Nick may have killed Dean Reid, and they should look again at his alibi. The cops had asked whether Duncan or Maggie wanted to accompany Nick, as he had the right to have an appropriate adult present when questioned.

'No!' Maggie had snapped. 'How is it *appropriate* for a parent of the baby he just tried to *murder* to sit in his corner?'

Duncan had just shaken his head.

She didn't know how Duncan had got through it.

'He tried to *kill* Isla,' he kept repeating.

And now he took her hand in his. 'Tell me. All the things you tried to tell me before about Nick, about what he was doing to you and Isla.' He sucked in a breath. 'I'm so sorry. I'm so sorry I didn't listen.'

Maggie took him through everything Nick had done since her arrival at Sunnyside.

'He's clever,' Maggie finished. 'Apart from that time when he didn't know Yvonne was in the room, there was no evidence I could bring you of what he was doing.'

'But I should have listened to you.'

'Aye, well, ideally. But you thought it was my old problems coming back to bite me, making me paranoid. So . . .' She shrugged.

'The day you heard him on the baby monitor,' said Duncan slowly. 'The school said he'd been there all day, but I wonder if that's true? What day was it? What day of the week?'

Maggie frowned. 'I think it was a Tuesday.'

'Okay. Tuesday. Nick has a double period of PE just before lunch on a Tuesday, and sometimes they do cross-country running. He could have –' He stopped. Closed his eyes. 'God, I can't believe I'm saying this. Nick. *Nick!*'

'Started the run with the rest of them, taking off ahead of everyone else as usual,' Maggie filled in for him. 'Doubled back to the pavilion, biked it back here, maybe, or got a taxi, eh? When the other kids and the teacher got back to the pavilion, they'd have thought Nick had already showered and gone to lunch. And then after lunch, he'd have been back at school for his first lesson like he'd never been off the premises.'

Duncan just nodded. And then, after a long silence: 'But

Dean . . . what you're suggesting is so cold-blooded – that Nick *killed* that boy to get you banged up for murder?'

'And it wasn't *cold-blooded* the way he came back here from school to hurt Isla? Set himself up with an alibi for that too, didn't he? Took some planning. As did pushing her pram into the path of a *fucking lorry!*' Maggie got up from the bed as the anger washed through her. She paced to a window. 'This hasn't come out of nowhere, Duncan. No way. No way can Nick have been the wee paragon you've been making him out to be. I don't buy it. Didn't you used to call him King of the Wild Things when he was a kid? Must have been a reason for that.'

Duncan lifted his arms in a helpless gesture, and just for a moment, Maggie felt her anger turn on him. *The stupid bastard!* Yvonne was right. Duncan wanted to be Nick's friend, so discipline had evidently gone out the window. Maybe if he'd laid down the law to the wee shit more often, they wouldn't be in this mess.

Nick had wanted to come on the honeymoon cruise with them – and, unbelievably, Duncan had wanted that too. He'd broached the subject while they were at the booking stage. 'Nick's keen to come along,' Duncan had muttered, not looking at her, as they sat side by side in the travel agent's.

'Aw Jesus no,' had been out her mouth before she could stop it.

She'd expected Duncan to try to persuade her to let Nick come along, because she'd known that Nick had been a daddy's boy even before Kathleen's death. Duncan had told her that, as a toddler, Nick had always wanted to go with Duncan when he left for work, and once he'd managed it by hiding in the back of the car. Kathleen had been going mental looking for him. It wasn't until Duncan had arrived in Langholm that wee Nick had pounced on him from his hiding place in the footwell of the back seat, wrapping his arms round Duncan's neck and saying, 'We're going to work!' And Duncan hadn't had the heart to take him back home, and had phoned Kathleen to say Nick could stay with him for the day.

So she'd been surprised and secretly delighted when Duncan had grimaced, and pulled another brochure towards them, and said, 'But he'll be absolutely fine staying with Yvonne and Michael for two weeks,' making out like this had been the plan all along, when Maggie knew fine well that he'd only decided this after seeing her reaction.

'There must have been problems,' she insisted now.

'Nick was a . . . *challenging* little boy, yes. Very boisterous.'

'In other words, a fucking nightmare.'

'No! He could be so sweet, so funny. He just . . . he's always had problems fitting in with his peers. Playing nicely.'

'You mean he went for the other kids.'

Duncan closed his eyes, breathed deeply, opened them again. 'I suppose so. He was banned from the local nursery group for hitting and biting, and didn't get invited to birthday parties because he was too "disruptive". Kathleen wanted to take him to a child psychologist, but I – I thought people were just overreacting to normal, boisterous little boy behaviour.' He swallowed. 'I thought he was just frustrated because the other kids were so far behind him, developmentally, and . . . and I didn't agree to it. I talked Kathleen out of it. I accused her of being too hard on him. Oh Christ, Maggie, this is *all my fault.*'

Aye, maybe it was. She wasn't going to say it wasn't.

'No point playing the blame game now,' was the furthest she was prepared to go to make him feel better.

'When he was twelve, thirteen . . . he used to go wandering up the road, and this couple who lived up there, they used to complain that he was hurting their cat. Squeezing it and making it yelp. Nick said he was just hugging it. But then the cat was found dead. Stabbed in the throat. The guy came round here in tears with the cat's body, accusing Nick . . . accusing him of having killed it. I sent him off with a flea in his ear.' He got up and came to where Maggie was standing. 'And there were other incidents. That scar Andy's got . . . Nick did that. They were eight years old. Somehow they got into the tool shed and started messing about with an adze. I'm not sure what happened, but Andy came running into the house, blood streaming, and Nick was running after him and he was *laughing*. "His mouth's split in two! Look!" he said, as if this was some amazing phenomenon I was going to be fascinated by. He must have been in shock. People sometimes laugh inappropriately when they're in shock, don't they?' Duncan stared at Maggie, like he was begging her to agree that aye, that was probably the explanation.

'So he was completely unrepentant? In fact, he enjoyed the whole thing?'

Duncan said nothing.

Isla started to grizzle, and Maggie went to her.

'Can I . . .' Duncan reached out his arms for Isla, but Maggie couldn't do it, she couldn't pretend it was all okay now that Duncan had seen the error of his ways.

'She almost *fucking died*!' she hissed at him. She grabbed Isla up and left the room.

MAGGIE HAD BEEN SHUT in one of the guest rooms with Isla all the next morning when there was a tap on the door, and Yvonne came in.

'Nick?' Maggie said at once. 'Has he been charged?'

'Not as far as I know. We haven't heard anything from the police yet.'

They could keep Nick in custody for forty-eight hours before either charging or releasing him.

Yvonne looked down at Isla in her cot. 'Duncan's in pieces,' she said quietly.

'Oh, boo-hoo.'

A sigh. 'Look, Maggie, I can totally understand why you're furious. I'm pretty furious with him myself. But think about it – what sort of parent is going to turn against their own child without pretty strong evidence of their wrongdoing? What would you do if someone tried to tell you Isla was an evil monster?'

Maggie snorted. 'That would never happen!'

'Wouldn't it? She's Nick's sister. She might have a genetic propensity –'

'Of course she fucking doesn't!' Maggie was up off the bed, fists clenched.

Yvonne nodded. 'There you go. That's how Duncan's been feeling. And now he's feeling a hundred, a *thousand* times worse because he's had to accept that his son, the son he's loved for sixteen years, *is* a monster.'

Maggie felt the fight go out of her. 'Aye. Aye, right enough.'

They moved Isla back to Maggie and Duncan's room, where the baby monitor was, and then the two women went downstairs to the drawing room, where Michael and Duncan were seated on either side of the cold hearth. Somehow, this formal room seemed right for what they had to talk about.

'Okay,' said Yvonne, as Duncan shot a wee look at Maggie. 'Who wants a drink?'

'I'm sorry,' went Maggie and Duncan at the exact same time, and this at least raised smiles, as Duncan got up and pulled her into his arms. 'I'm so sorry, Maggie.'

'Aye, well, Yvonne here has read me the riot act. Of course

you couldn't get your head round Nick being . . . well. The way he is. It was only natural.'

'*You* knew,' said Duncan, turning to Yvonne, who was handing round brandies. 'I thought your coldness towards Nick was just down to your not liking kids. But you saw . . . you saw . . .'

'No. I was in denial too, Dunc.' Yvonne flopped into a chair. 'When he was a little kid, I kept thinking he'd grow out of it. Most kids are cruel little buggers, aren't they, given half the chance? And you were so soft with him.'

Duncan sat back down, and Maggie perched on the arm of his chair.

'He's obsessed with you, you know,' Yvonne went on. 'In his eyes, anyone who gets close to you is a threat to the father-son bond. Maggie, Isla. Maybe even Kathleen.'

Duncan's face was pure white.

Yvonne leant forward and eyeballed her brother. 'I've never told anyone this, and I never thought I would, but . . . a few weeks before her death, Kathleen confessed to me that she was sometimes scared of Nick. *Her own son.* She made me promise to say nothing to you. After she died, I told the police, in confidence, what she'd said, but I'm not sure they believed me. They certainly didn't follow it up.'

'Oh, no,' said Duncan. 'Yvonne. *No.*'

Maggie put a hand on Duncan's shoulder. 'Where was Nick when Kathleen died?'

'He said he was in his room,' said Duncan in a flat voice. 'He found her body. Called 999. Forensics indicated she'd been dead a couple of hours by that time.'

Silence filled the room as, Maggie was sure, each one of them played out an alternative scenario – Nick pushing Kathleen over the bannisters, watching her plummet to the tiles, standing there watching the blood pool under her . . . and

going back up to his room for two hours before calling the
police.

Now Duncan was up on his feet. He strode to the door
and left the room but then he was back, pacing to the bay
window, to the fireplace, like he didn't know what to do with
himself. 'I used to think Kathleen was so hard on him. I used
to think she was all wrong, that he responded better to – to a
more positive approach.' He clutched at the hair on either
side of his head. 'How could I have got it all so wrong! It's my
job to rehabilitate troubled youngsters, to spot signs of
trouble –'

'It's completely different when it's your own kid,' said
Yvonne. 'It's not your fault. People like Nick are born that
way.'

'People like Nick?' Duncan choked. 'You're saying – what?
That he's . . . got some kind of – syndrome? Some kind of –'

For the first time, Michael spoke. 'Yvonne means he's a
psychopath.'

Duncan's face collapsed.

Maggie stood; went to him. There was nothing she could
say to make it better, so she just put her arms round him and
held him while he cried.

MICHAEL AND YVONNE left after midnight. Duncan had been
hitting the brandy hard and had eventually fallen asleep in
his chair, so Maggie showed them out. As they stood on the
gravel by Michael's Land Rover, no one speaking, Yvonne, to
Maggie's surprise, pulled her into a brief hug.

'They're surely not going to give him bail,' Yvonne said.
'He'll be remanded in custody, and then he'll be put away for
murdering that boy; for trying to murder Isla. You don't have
to worry about Nick any more.'

As Maggie slowly made her way back to the front door,

she looked in at the lighted windows of the drawing room, at the scene that might have come straight out a period drama – a handsome man sleeping in a big fancy chair in a posh room. Just went to show you never could tell. A couple of lines came into her head from somewhere, maybe something she'd learned at school or more likely seen on telly:

For sweetest things turn sourest by their deeds;
Lilies that fester smell far worse than weeds.

17

PCs Melissa Jackson and Iain Mair refused Lulu's offer of tea or coffee and got straight down to business, sitting at the kitchen table, the two of them opposite Nick and Lulu. PC Jackson took out her phone and asked if they minded if she recorded the conversation, while PC Mair, an older, jowly man with cropped grey hair, got out a notebook.

'When was the last time you actually saw Ms Moncrieff?' he asked.

Lulu didn't have to think about that one. 'Three days before she disappeared. She and Michael were over for dinner on Tuesday night. That was the last time we saw her. Unless you . . .?' She turned to Nick.

'No, I didn't see her after that.' He was frowning at PC Mair. 'I'm not quite sure why you're wasting your time with this. What's the relevance of Yvonne's movements in the days leading up to . . .' He swallowed. 'To her disappearance? I mean, her car was there at the wood. It's obvious she's gone for a walk and got into trouble. Yvonne's a great walker. She could have gone miles from the car. You need to extend the search.'

'We've extended it as far as she could reasonably have walked in the time. We're now exploring other avenues.'

'What other "avenues" can there possibly be?'

'We're just checking people's movements on the day in question,' said PC Jackson, completely unruffled. 'I understand that Mr Moncrieff called you, Mrs Clyde, to let you know that his wife was missing?'

'Yes. Well, we didn't know she was missing at that stage. She hadn't returned from her walk, and we thought she'd maybe slipped on the wet path and hurt herself.'

'Where were you when you got the call?'

'We were here. I –' Oh God. She was going to have to admit to having taken the car out secretly to go and see Carol. 'I had just got back from visiting Carol Jardine.' She shot a look at Nick, expecting him to be staring at her in horror, to be angry, but he didn't react. He was looking down at the table, as if his mind was on other things.

'And at what time would you have left here to make your visit?'

'About three o'clock? Yes, it would have been around three o'clock because that's when Nick closets himself in the study to work every afternoon, and I was at a loose end, so . . . so I decided to take the car and visit Carol,' she ended lamely.

'And you, Mr Clyde?'

'As my wife says, I was working. I'm a City trader. We're sort of on holiday, but I still have to clock in at certain times to keep things ticking over. I was making trades and speaking to clients from three to four-thirty.'

PC Mair looked at Nick for a moment. 'And that can be corroborated, I suppose?'

Lulu's heart did a little flip.

They hadn't asked her for corroboration of *her* movements, so why were they asking Nick? They thought Nick might have something to do with Yvonne's disappearance? Thank goodness he had a watertight alibi.

'Yes, of course it can be corroborated,' Nick said impatiently. 'Why? You think one of us – what? Lured Yvonne into the forest and bumped her off?' He gave a short laugh. 'Ten out of ten for thinking outside the box, but really, I think your time would be better spent searching said forest. But I suppose sitting on your arses in people's kitchens is a rather more pleasant way of spending an evening. We had intended going back out searching now ourselves, but if we're *suspects*, maybe that's not permitted?'

'No one's a suspect, sir,' said PC Jackson smoothly. 'We're just, as I said, getting an idea of everyone's movements.'

Nick raised his eyebrows. 'I'd forgotten just how weird and wonderful policing is up here. My family had some very . . . shall we say *interesting* experiences with the force a few years back. Very creative thinking outside the box on your part, to the extent that my father and then myself were arrested, on no evidence whatsoever. Nothing much has changed, I see.'

'Just trying to do our jobs, sir.'

'Hmm. Yes. Could try a little harder, I feel.'

Lulu showed them out, and when she returned to the kitchen she found Nick leaning back against the worktop, arms folded.

'What on earth was all that about?' she said. 'Why would they think either of us –'

'Oh, okay, let's see. While I've been shut away in the study working, you've been sneaking off here, there and everywhere, listening to all the local gossips. Carol Jardine. Was Andy there? He's been bad-mouthing me, no doubt? And you've been stirring him up, telling him all about me and my *anger management issues*. Andy's touched in the head. He's probably told the police I've done something to Yvonne.' He unfolded his arms and came across the kitchen towards her. 'You. Are. My. *Wife*. You're supposed to be on *my side*.'

Lulu just shook her head. Her mouth was suddenly dry, and she felt weak, insubstantial, as if all her muscles had lost their strength.

'I *am* on your side,' she got out.

He kept walking towards her, and she found herself moving back.

'I put a tracking app on your phone,' he said, smiling a little, but his eyes on her were completely without expression. 'I already knew you were at Carol's.' And suddenly she had nowhere to go. Her back was pressed against the door to the passage and his face was so close she could see a tiny piece of stubble in the little hollow under his mouth.

'I thought I could trust you!' he spat at her.

Lulu took a big breath. 'If you thought that, why did you put a tracker on my phone?'

He took hold of her, his hands grasping the flesh of her upper arms, and then he was slamming her back against the door, her head ricocheting off it painfully.

She didn't cry out.

He didn't say a word.

For a long moment, they stared into each other's eyes.

Then his face crumpled. 'Oh God, Lulu! I'm sorry!'

She felt herself caught into a hug, pressed against the muscles of his chest as he kept repeating how sorry he was, how much he loved her. She felt his hand stroking her hair over the place where her head had hit the door and made herself not flinch from it. Made herself hug him back.

'It's okay.'

He held her in front of him, his gaze running up and down her body. 'Did I hurt you? Lulu, tell me I didn't hurt you!'

No. She wasn't going to let him off that lightly. 'You banged my head.'

And then he was weeping, choking that the tracker was for her protection, that of course he trusted her, but after what had happened to Yvonne, surely she could see now that it made sense to be ultra-careful?

It took all Lulu had to step outside herself in that moment and be objective. Re-examining his traumatic memories had been fuelling his paranoia. She'd always known that things would get worse before they got better. And now, with Yvonne gone, it was no wonder he was freaking out.

'It's okay. I understand.'

He shut his eyes. 'I don't deserve you!'

'Let's take some time out, and then we'll go for a walk and talk this over. Okay?'

'Okay.' It was a whisper.

They walked round the garden and along the road a little way, and Nick talked quietly, apologising over and over again and admitting that Yvonne's disappearance was churning up all sorts of emotions.

'So talk to me about them,' Lulu said quietly, taking his hand. 'I'm your wife. That's what I'm here for.'

'I'm sorry,' he said again. 'You're an angel. You're my angel, Lulu, and you have no idea how much I love you.'

'I think I maybe have some idea,' she whispered with a little smile, taking him into her arms.

18

Maggie was dozing in the summerhouse with Isla when Duncan opened the door, came in and sat down on one of the wicker chairs.

'They've released Nick without charge. Michael's gone to pick him up from the police station. He's going to bring him here.'

Fuck.

'I'm sorry, but – Yvonne won't have him at the farm, and where else can he go?' His voice broke. 'He's still my son, Maggie. He's still my Nick.'

'Of course he is,' she made herself say. 'But how could they possibly not be charging him?' She reached out to touch the pram.

Duncan just lifted his shoulders.

19

The track was so overgrown that in places Lulu was pushing her way past prickly gorse bushes and brambles, and her trainers were soon soaked from walking through the wet grass and wild flowers growing in the middle of the track. It had rained overnight, but the sky was now cloudless and the fields of pasture that surrounded her were gently steaming. The smells of early summer were intense – pollen and wet grass and warm soil. The sun danced on all the millions of water droplets on the gorse and the nettles and the blades of grass.

She was late. It was already 7:40.

She'd underestimated how long it would take her to walk here from Sunnyside. She would have to be careful to be back before Nick left the study at the end of the trading period or he'd freak out, wondering where she was. She hadn't brought her phone, leaving it in the pocket of her other coat, which was hanging up in the boot room.

Where had Andy parked? He surely couldn't have brought a vehicle up here.

The little house came into view, its slate roof sagging, the sash windows silvery with age but retaining their panes of glass. No vandals, she supposed, way out here.

An expensive-looking bike was propped against the wall, a bright yellow helmet slung on one handlebar.

She could just imagine Beth and Jenny's reactions to what she was doing, meeting a man she didn't know, someone Nick described as 'touched in the head', in a lonely place like this. She didn't even want to think what Nick would say.

'Hello?' she called tentatively, walking round the side of the house to an old courtyard of tumbledown outbuildings full of waist-high weeds. Someone, though, had recently trampled a path through them, and Lulu followed this through the courtyard, the wet vegetation soaking her jeans below the knees. The path led to an open doorway in one of the outbuildings.

She peered into the gloom of the interior. The floor was cobbled, the walls glistening wet and green with algae. This outbuilding looked much older than the house. Maybe it had been here for centuries, maybe right back to the time of The Debatable Lands, when the people who lived here could have locked their enemies up in this dank –

'Lulu,' said a voice behind her.

She gasped, a hand going instinctively to her breastbone, and wheeled round.

Andy Jardine was giving her his lopsided smile. 'Wet out here. We can get into the house through the back door.'

Wildlife had been making itself at home inside the house. There were pigeon droppings everywhere, a thick crust on the floor, and Andy identified the pungent smell as fox. 'Must have a den under the floorboards.'

It was a sad old place, with peeling layers of flowery wallpaper making Lulu think of all the people who had called it home through the years.

Andy went to one of the windows, so filmed with grime it

was hard to see through it. 'You're sure Nick can't have followed you?'

She supposed he wouldn't want his friend to know about whatever issues he was having.

'Yes. He was shut up in the study when I left.'

There were a couple of old wooden chairs in what would have been the kitchen, set companionably in front of the remains of the old black range built into a recess. Andy dusted them off with a tissue and they sat down.

'Is Nick abusing you?'

Oh my God!

'*No*, of course not!'

'Sexually or physically?'

'No!' Where on earth was this coming from?

'At Craibstone Wood, I saw him. I saw how angry he was with you.'

She remembered, then, that Andy had witnessed Nick storming off, after she'd got the phone call from the police about Paul. 'That was a silly misunderstanding.'

'You're saying he's never hurt you?'

'Never! For goodness' sake, Andy!' Lulu didn't want to talk about her marriage with this man. But she made her expression sympathetic. 'Yvonne going missing is hard on him, as I'm sure it is on everyone. Have you been finding it hard? Is that why you wanted to talk to me?'

'No. I want to talk to you about Nick.'

Andy, she suspected, was on the spectrum. If so, he would find people's behaviour hard to understand. Seeing Nick angry like that, on top of the upset over Yvonne, could have been frightening for him. 'You and Nick were good friends when you were young, weren't you? Best friends?'

Andy stared at her.

She left a silence.

Eventually: 'He terrorised me, Lulu. From when we were

little kids. In fact, I can't remember a time in my childhood when Nick wasn't terrorising me. He hit me, he bit me, he cut me. But he soon learned that those things leave marks that have to be explained. So he would pull my hair. Give me Chinese burns. Make me eat sand. Do you know how painful it is to pass sand out of your arse?'

Completely inappropriately, laughter bubbled up in Lulu. She suppressed it, schooling her face. She knew, from growing up with two younger brothers, how horrendous small boys could be to one another. Andy probably hadn't been diagnosed with Asperger's as a child – had he been diagnosed, even now? – so the adults around him wouldn't have known that he would find the normal rough and tumble of kids' interactions extremely challenging. And the other kids, of course, would hardly have given him an easy ride. Quite the opposite. 'That must have been awful. Did you tell your mum and dad?'

'When you're really young, three, four, five, you just go along with the status quo, don't you? I did try to tell Mum, but Nick was always so convincing. *Oh no, Andy fell over. I was trying to catch him, not push him. Andy ripped his arm on a nail – I don't know why he's saying I cut it.* And Nick did this.' He touched the scar running through his mouth. 'With an adze from Duncan's shed.'

Oh God.

'As we got older, the physical abuse stopped, but he started messing with me in other ways – like he'd steal things from other kids and put them in my locker and get me in trouble. He said if I told anyone about it, he'd kill me. And I believed him. I still believe that he was serious. He *would* have killed me, and enjoyed doing it. But that was his plan B. He didn't want me dead because I was useful to him. I don't know how many times I provided him with an alibi; said he was with me.'

'Andy, I'm sure Nick was only joking when he said he would kill you.'

'No.' Andy shook his head vigorously. 'No, Lulu. He meant it.'

How awful, for teenage Andy, that he had thought his best friend was genuinely threatening to kill him. How awful that he still believed it. But how to reassure him? 'I've got two brothers,' she tried. 'They were real tearaways when they were children. Dennis has a scar too, on his leg. It was ripped open on a broken twig when John pushed him out of a tree. And they were always coming up with terrible ideas of how they might kill one another. But they didn't mean it. They were only joking.'

'Nick wasn't *joking!*' Andy suddenly shouted at her.

'Okay.' She kept her voice calm. 'It was very wrong of him to say it, whether he was joking or not.'

'He wasn't *joking* when he murdered Dean Reid!'

Oh my goodness. Had she heard that right?

Andy was looking down at his hands, clutched in fists on his lap. 'You know who Dean Reid was? One of the disadvantaged youngsters Duncan mentored at The Phoenix Centre in Langholm? Nick set the whole thing up in an attempt to frame Maggie. He had it timed to the second. He'd texted Dean, pretending to be Duncan, saying he'd pay him the money Dean was trying to blackmail out of him and telling him to be at The Phoenix Centre at eight-thirty on Thursday night and wait till he got there. We had a rehearsal for the school play that night. In the interval, Nick used my bike to get to The Phoenix Centre, stabbed Dean, got back to the school in time to be back on stage. When the police questioned me, I said I'd been with him for part of the interval. That meant there was no time for him to have got to The Phoenix Centre and back. Rock solid alibi. He used a knife from Sunnyside with Maggie's fingerprints on it to frame her.

He called her from a phone box on his way back to the school from the Centre, pretending to be a concerned neighbour worried about what was going on in there. Then he called the police. Maggie hot-footed it over there, presumably. But she was streetwise. Former young offender. She must have found Dean dead, realised what Nick was trying to do, and legged it before the police turned up. There were no fingerprints on the knife, so she must have wiped it.' He looked up at her at last, focusing somewhere around her left shoulder. 'Oh, Nick was not happy about that *at all*. Particularly when Duncan was arrested for the murder. Duncan was charged, but then it turned out there was CCTV footage proving he was miles away at the time.'

The poor, poor guy.

All these years, he had really been convinced that this had all happened, that Nick had committed a murder? Could she make him see that he was wrong, that what he was saying didn't add up? If he'd really thought Nick had murdered someone, would he have continued hanging out with him? The day the family had disappeared, Nick had been returning from a nice day out in Edinburgh with Andy and Carol. At some level, the teenage Andy must have known it was all nonsense, Nick's wind-up about the murder of this boy.

She had to tap into that part of his brain now.

'So you lied to the police to give Nick an alibi, even though you knew he'd done it?'

'I'm not proud of it.'

'Isn't it possible, Andy, that that's what you told the police because you really *were* with Nick?'

'No! I wasn't! But Nick said if I didn't give him an alibi, he'd tell the cops *I* did it. He said –' Andy suddenly leapt from the chair as something crashed through the doorway behind Lulu, and Lulu was up on her feet too as a pigeon flapped around the room before exiting into the back hall and out through the half-open door.

Andy was breathing fast. 'I'm just going to check, okay? Check there's no one out there. Stay here.'

When he came back, he didn't sit down. 'I need to make this quick. I don't like it, being here, so close to Sunnyside.' He went to stand by the window and stayed there looking out as he spoke. 'So – Nick told me he'd dob me in to the cops for Dean's murder if I didn't cooperate. He said the tyre tracks on the muddy path leading to the back door of The Phoenix Centre would confirm that my bike was at the scene of the crime. He threatened to tell the cops *I* had made *him* give *me* an alibi. He had it all worked out. He even engineered an altercation between me and Dean a week or so earlier. Dean was always on a short fuse, so that wasn't difficult. He made sure there were witnesses. Ironically, a similar incident between Dean and Duncan was what pointed the cops in Duncan's direction.'

Lulu felt suddenly very conscious of the wet material of her jeans leaching the warmth from her shins, her calves.

'Andy,' she said slowly. 'Obviously, I didn't know Nick then, but I know him now. I know he could never have done what you think he did. He must have been winding you up. Nick admits himself that he was a real wind-up merchant as a teenager. Like the prank with the severed arm at the farm? It's pretty sick, but he was obviously pretending that he'd killed this boy and seeing if he could get you to believe him.'

'He did kill Dean. And he killed Duncan and Maggie and Isla. And now probably Yvonne. Yvonne was onto him. She never liked him. Maybe he was worried she might know too much? Maybe he decided to take the opportunity to eliminate that risk while he was up here.'

Lulu's heart sank. This wasn't just mild Asperger's – this was some sort of paranoid disorder. Maybe with an element of delusion. Far beyond what she was qualified to deal with. Had Andy ever seen a psychiatrist? Surely his family, his mother and father, must have realised something was wrong and got help for him?

How much of what he'd told her about Nick claiming to have murdered that boy was even true? After the police had questioned Andy, had Andy constructed a whole scenario in which Nick sped about the town on his bike with murderous intent? And Andy had been at Sunnyside a few weeks later when they'd discovered that Nick's family had gone. Had that triggered a fresh bout of delusion? And now Yvonne's disappearance had churned it all up again?

'You're in danger too,' said Andy.

There was no point in trying to challenge any of this now. She needed to speak to Carol. How much did Carol know about what was going on with her son? Often the family were the last to realise something was amiss or downplayed the extent of the issue.

'I can see that you're very concerned about Nick,' she said carefully. 'And worried about me. Thank you for that. I really appreciate it. I –'

'You need to be very, very careful.'

'I will be.'

'Okay, I'm going now,' said Andy. 'You obviously shouldn't tell Nick you talked to me.'

And without saying goodbye, he walked out of the room.

20

Maggie, clutching Isla, stood in the bay window of the drawing room and watched Michael's Land Rover roll to a halt. The passenger door flew open, and Nick jumped down and went striding to where Duncan stood, giving it, 'How could you do it, Dad? How could you *shop me to the cops*? When I've done *nothing wrong*?'

No.

Oh, no. This wasn't happening. She wasn't going to let him get in Duncan's head, plant a seed of doubt, make Duncan start to think he'd got it all wrong after all.

She hurried outside.

'*She* left Isla alone!' Nick was raging. He pointed a shaking finger at Maggie. 'Oh yes, I put the cops straight about what happened. I told them all about you, Mags. All about how you've had the baby blues and haven't been coping. You left her alone –'

'Because you triggered the fire alarm by leaving a pan on the hob and I had to stop the fucking house burning down! I wasn't going to take Isla into a fucking inferno, was I?'

'I didn't leave anything on the hob! Really, Dad, I didn't! I found Isla all alone, and she was crying, so I pushed her round the house in the pram, talking to her, trying to get her to calm down. Then on the drive, I tripped . . . I let go the pram . . .' His lips wobbled as he stared at his father. 'I let go the pram! I feel terrible about it, but it was an accident! I can't understand how you could think I would do it deliberately! I *love* Isla! I would *never* hurt her! She's my *little sister!*'

'Of course it was deliberate!' Maggie growled, pulling at the soft yellow blanket to shield Isla's face. She didn't even want him *looking* at her.

'The cops believe me, so why can't you?' Nick was crying now, arms dangling, not trying to stop the tears, standing pathetically in front of Duncan like he was waiting to be hugged.

Duncan didn't move towards him. 'Because I saw you do it. I saw you push the pram. That was no accident.'

'It *was!*' Nick clutched at Duncan's arm, but Duncan shook him off.

'*Tell the truth for once!*' Duncan suddenly shouted at him.

Nick covered his face with his hands, and the three of them stood like they were frozen there, with Michael in the background skulking by the Land Rover, obviously not wanting to intrude but not feeling he could just leave either.

Then Nick raised his head and whispered, 'I didn't mean her any harm. That *is* the truth.' He was staring at Duncan like he was drowning and Duncan was the only one who could save him. 'I just thought it would be a laugh to push the pram down the drive. I didn't think! I'm *so sorry!* I didn't know there was a lorry coming! I didn't even think about the road!'

'Yes, you did.' Duncan's face was blank. 'You knew those lorries were coming. That's why you pushed the pram.'

21

A fter searching the forest all afternoon and into the evening, Lulu suggested that she and Nick accompany Michael back to the farmhouse. 'This isn't maybe a very attractive offer, but we could cook for you. You probably don't feel much like bothering.'

He looked from her to Nick. 'Thanks, Lulu. That would be great.'

The big farmhouse kitchen into which Michael ushered them was as spick and span as Lulu had expected, but cosy and obviously the heart of the home, with a long pine table and an Aga, in front of which were two dog beds, one plain red and one white with black bones printed all over it. The two collies ignored these, though, and positioned themselves in front of a cupboard, sitting staring at it until Michael, with a smile, opened the cupboard door to reveal tins and bags of dog food.

He opened a tin and combined the foul-smelling contents with dry mix in two bowls. Then he pressed a button on the phone and a recorded voice filled the kitchen. 'Hi, Michael, just wondering if there's any news on Yvonne. I've got the kids to put her all over social media, and they're getting their pals to do the same.' The voice cracked. 'Anyway, we're thinking about you. Let us know if there's anything more we can do.' The next message was similar. Michael cut it off and glanced at Lulu.

'People are being very kind.' He sighed, watching the dogs inhale their food. 'You don't realise, do you, how much a person is valued until something like this happens.' He collapsed onto a chair. 'Yvonne's done a hell of a lot for people in this community.'

'It's obvious she's very well liked.' Lulu had been realising this from talking to the other searchers. It seemed Yvonne's gruff exterior concealed a very good heart.

'Larder's through here,' said Nick, and when they were alone in there, picking out a packet of pasta and tins of tomatoes and tuna, he hissed, 'God, Saint Yvonne!'

'Well, people do seem to be rallying round –'

'Because they're a load of ghouls, not because they liked her!'

'I don't think that's true, Nick.'

When they returned to the kitchen, Lulu asked Michael what veg he had, and Michael straightened from petting the dogs. 'We've a vegetable plot round the side of the steading.'

'This is the girl from Leonora you're talking to,' said Nick. 'Lulu doesn't know what a steading is.'

'Big old stone farm building,' Michael translated. 'Come and I'll show you, Lulu.'

While Nick made a start on the meal, Lulu went with Michael through the farmyard to the neat vegetable patch. There was a grid system of gravel paths between the beds and netting draped over posts shrouding the strawberry plants and raspberry canes.

'I grew up on a farm in Western Australia,' Lulu told him.

'Mum has a veggie plot, but she fights a losing battle with the drought.'

'Not a problem we have here.'

As they picked some spinach leaves, he suddenly said, 'Lulu, you need to know . . . I've been to the police. I've told them I think Nick might have . . . done something to Yvonne.'

Lulu froze.

'*What?*'

He grimaced at her apologetically.

'But – Michael! That's ridiculous! I know they didn't get on, but going to the *police*? Accusing *Nick*? Why would you do that?' Her legs were suddenly shaky. She sat down abruptly on the edge of a raised bed.

Michael looked back off towards the farmhouse, his ruddy, usually cheery farmer's face drawn and ill-looking. 'Yvonne sussed him long ago. She was convinced he killed Kathleen.'

For a moment, Lulu couldn't think who Kathleen was – a dog or a cat maybe? – until it hit her like a sledgehammer.

Kathleen was Nick's mother.

'Oh my God.'

'I'm dubious about that myself, but what I do know is that he tried to kill Isla. His baby sister. Pushed her pram down the drive towards the road when a timber lorry was passing. Duncan happened to be there and was able to grab the pram before it got to the road, but it was a near thing. He got off with it, of course. Pretended he tripped.'

'But – surely he did! He wouldn't have –'

'I heard him myself, admitting to Duncan and Maggie that he'd pushed the pram – but only after Duncan remained firm in his conviction that he'd seen Nick do it. Nick changed his story, tried to claim he was just messing around and didn't realise the danger.'

'But that must have been true! Teenagers often aren't aware of danger –'

'Oh, he was aware of it, all right. There was also suspicion he could have killed one of the delinquent kids at The Phoenix Centre, where Duncan worked. But he had a cast-iron alibi, supplied by his friend Andy.' He lowered his voice to an urgent whisper, eyes darting, as if expecting Nick to suddenly spring out at them from behind the beans. 'And it seems he's set himself up with an alibi again, for Yvonne. The police say they've "looked into" the possibility of Nick's "involvement" and are satisfied he was working at the crucial time. They checked with the City firm he works for, and apparently he was trading and calling clients from just after Yvonne set out for her walk at quarter to three until four-thirty. She was already overdue back by then, and I went out looking for her not long afterwards and found her car – so that's him covered, apparently.' Eyes bright with tears, he shook his head, as if angry with himself for not holding it together.

'It's true,' Lulu said urgently. 'He was working in the study. I got the call from you as I arrived home, and he was there. You've got it all wrong, Michael. How could you think that Nick . . . I mean, my God!'

'But what if he wasn't in the study at the crucial time? What if he was on the move and trading on his phone rather than a laptop in the study or whatever? I've told the police they should check the movements of his phone, but I doubt that they will. They think I've lost it.'

'Nick would never hurt Yvonne,' Lulu insisted.

Michael was crushing the spinach in his hand. 'I wish I was wrong, Lulu. I really wish I was, and Yvonne's maybe just taken a tumble and is wandering, disorientated, out there somewhere. But I know that's not what's happened. Nick arrives back here for the first time in over ten years, and a week later Yvonne disappears. Don't tell me that's a coincidence.' His voice cracked. 'You need to get away from him.' He grabbed her arm. 'You need to get far, *far* away from him. Go back to your farm in Australia. Back where there are people who can protect you.'

'Michael, this is all nonsense.' She tried to make her voice calm and gentle, but she was disturbed to find that she couldn't, that it was high and squeaky and breathless. 'You're talking like Nick –'

'Like he's a psychopath? That's because he is.' He took the leaves she'd picked from her hand. 'And you know, it's more than I can stomach, breaking bread with him. Please just go. Take Nick and go.'

BACK AT SUNNYSIDE, Lulu kept building herself up to tell Nick what Michael had said, but she couldn't do it to him, just as she couldn't tell him about Andy's accusations. Had Andy and Yvonne been feeding off each other's paranoia about Nick? And now Michael had been sucked into the ridiculous conspiracy theories they'd dreamt up?

She'd told Nick that Michael was tired and wasn't hungry and they needed to leave.

As she lay, sleepless as usual, in bed, she was very conscious of the warmth of Nick's body next to her. How long would it be before Michael flung his accusations at Nick himself? Just how much more could Nick take?

Well, but maybe there was a way to make Michael see sense.

She eased out of bed and crept to the door.

Downstairs, she flicked on the light in the study, wincing at the sudden brightness. Their phones were charging in here on the windowsill. She hesitated only a moment before picking Nick's up and tapping in his code – the year and month of their marriage – and opening up the trading app he had once shown her. It took a while to find the history log, which showed the dates and times of trades made from the phone, but once she was in the right place, it took seconds to find that no trades had been made from this phone on the day of Yvonne's disappearance. That meant he'd been using his laptop.

This was proof positive that Michael's suspicion that Nick could have used his phone to make trades on the afternoon of Yvonne's disappearance, in between whatever Michael thought he'd been doing to Yvonne, was completely baseless. She picked up her own phone, switched it on and waited impatiently for it to boot up. Then she took a photo of Nick's screen showing trades a couple of weeks ago, but nothing since.

Hopefully, this would set Michael's mind at rest.

She was turning Nick's phone off when a text came in from someone called Ben Sinclair.

Sorry to hassle, I know you're on holiday, but need to sell half my holdings in DGK when the LSE opens tomorrow first thing. Not sure if this is the right number for you – will try the other one too. Thanks, Nick.

Feeling guilty for reading the text, she was turning off the phone when there was another ping. But not from the phone in her hand. It seemed to have come from the cupboard under the windowsill.

She opened it.

It was full of printer paper and random cables. There was also a small cardboard box that seemed illuminated from within. Lulu peered inside. Under a tangle of more cables, she could see a screen lit up.

It was another smartphone.

Heart bumping, she pushed aside the cables and pulled it out. There was another text message from Ben Sinclair showing on the screen.

*Nick, trying you on your new number too. Could you sell
half my DGK holdings when LSE opens? First thing.
Please let me know when done. Thanks!*

Lulu felt her insides plummet. She stared at the phone in her hand, and then, as if of their own accord, her thumbs were navigating to the call history.

There were only three calls in it.

All from the afternoon of Yvonne's disappearance.

She let the phone drop to the windowsill. Why would Nick have used a second, secret phone to make calls on that particular afternoon?

There was only one possible explanation.

Lulu sank to her knees, as if in prayer.

No no no, God, no!

He must have left his own phone here, switched on so the police would be able to ascertain that it never left Sunnyside during the crucial period. He had taken the other phone with him, a phone presumably not registered to him, and used it to make trades and calls to his clients, including this Ben Sinclair, so they could give him an alibi and confirm he was working when Yvonne disappeared.

Andy and Yvonne and Michael had been right.

Lulu had been so, so wrong.

Nick had killed Yvonne.

Because Yvonne knew he had killed his family.

Nick.

Nick?

Nick was some sort of psychopath?

But this was madness! Psychopaths were callous. They

didn't feel empathy. They didn't love people, because they couldn't. And Lulu knew, without a shadow of doubt, that Nick loved her – too much, if anything. And he'd loved his dad. The idea of Nick being capable of hurting anyone, let alone his family, his beloved father . . .

But she had the proof right here. The proof that he'd set himself up with an alibi for Yvonne's murder, just as Andy had told her he'd set himself up with one for the murder of the delinquent boy.

How could she have been so stupid, thinking Andy and Yvonne had somehow been feeding off each other's paranoia? Why hadn't she *listened to them*?

Nick – her Nick, her darling Nick –

He had killed all those people.

Yvonne had been trying to tell her that his problems weren't those of a poor, traumatised soul. Controlling behaviour and rages could be symptoms of PTSD, but they could also be psychopathic traits. Psychopaths were often charming and plausible. They were manipulative. Nick had been playing a part, all this time.

And sucked Lulu right in.

Controlled her.

She grabbed both phones and got shakily to her feet. She had to go to the police with these. They could look at the call histories and see that he was using the second phone on the afternoon of Yvonne's disappearance. No doubt his plan was to dispose of it and, if the police ever got round to checking the actual phone records and queried the lack of calls on his own phone – which had never left Sunnyside – at the crucial time, he'd have said he used a different phone, an old one, one he had since chucked out.

Oh, he'd have some plausible answer.

She stared at herself in the darkened window, stared into

her own eyes, as if this was someone apart from herself, some woman who had been so, so stupid and gullible and –

Behind the reflected Lulu, there was movement.

She wheeled round.

Nick, wearing nothing but a pair of boxer shorts, raised his eyebrows at her.

She looked down at the phones in her hand. 'I – I heard a ping,' she blurted.

'Couldn't you sleep?'

She shook her head.

'Oh, darling. How about a cup of hot chocolate?'

She couldn't move, she couldn't say anything as he crossed the room and put an arm around her shoulders, his hand gripping her upper arm just a little too tightly. He gave her a gentle shake. 'You okay?'

'Yes,' she croaked.

He took the phones from her hand and laid them down, side by side, on the windowsill.

'Come on then, let's get you sorted.'

It was like she'd stepped into one of her nightmares. This couldn't actually be happening, could it? Numbly, she walked at his side, feeling the heat of his body against hers, willing him not to challenge her, not to ask her anything about the phones. She just had to go along with him, with anything he suggested, pretend she didn't suspect anything.

And hope she got a chance to run.

22

MAGGIE - NOVEMBER 1997

They sat round Michael and Yvonne's big kitchen table, the four of them, to have what Yvonne called a 'crisis meeting' while Nick was at school. Maggie had put Isla down in one of the spare bedrooms, and the baby monitor sat on the worktop behind her. It was a grey, misty, gloomy morning, and Yvonne had put on all the wee lights under the high-level cupboards as well as the overhead ones.

'We locked ourselves in the bedroom last night,' went Duncan, looking down into his mug of coffee. 'Locked ourselves away from *Nick*.'

'Well, you're the only one here who finds anything strange in that,' said Yvonne briskly. 'Thank God Maggie had the sense to buy a bolt for the door.'

'But ...' Duncan was hanging on by a thread. 'What were we thinking he'd do? Come in while we slept and ... what?'

'Hurt Isla, maybe,' said Yvonne. 'Who knows what he's capable of? For God's sake, Duncan, he *tried to kill your baby*! You have to keep remembering that. Remembering what you saw. Nick pushing the pram into the path of that timber lorry. He wants her *dead*.'

As if on cue, a mewing sound came from the monitor, then stopped.

Maggie jumped up.

She'd become dead paranoid about Isla. She was up those stairs in record time, grabbing her up from her carry cot, hugging her close as she grizzled. 'Come on, then, wee one. Come on and join the party. Bunny can come too.'

She took her down to the kitchen, and Duncan went back for the carry cot and set it up between him and Maggie. They settled her back in it, but Maggie kept a hold of Bunny, smoothing his matted fur, while they talked.

'You can't go on living like this,' said Michael.

Michael, Maggie was discovering, was one of those folk who, ninety per cent of the time, bored the pants off of you, but in a crisis he had the knack of hitting the nail on the head.

Thank God he'd saved her from saying it herself.

'You're right,' she agreed. 'But going to the authorities won't get us anywhere.'

'So trying to get him sectioned or something . . .' Michael grimaced. 'You don't think that's an option?'

'Look what happened when we took him to that psychiatrist, supposedly eminent in his field,' went Duncan in a tight voice. 'Nothing to worry about, we were told.'

'And he's bamboozled the police too.' Yvonne nodded. 'Oh, he's clever, all right.'

Making out like she really didn't want to have to reveal this, Maggie told them about the fake identities she'd asked Liam to get for her and Isla. 'I didn't *want* to leave you.' She blinked at Duncan. 'But you just weren't listening to me.'

'Oh God.' He shook his head. 'I'm sorry, Maggie. I'm so sorry you had to go through that alone. I'm such an *idiot*.' He slapped a hand down on the table, making the plate of biscuits jump.

Maggie took a deep breath. This was a wee bit of a risky strategy, but surely Duncan wouldn't agree to what she was about to suggest? She made her voice weak and scared. 'If he gets what he wants, that'll be the problem solved. If I go away with Isla, using Liam's fake identities, so Nick will never find us –'

'No!' went Duncan, at the same time as Yvonne puffed, 'We can't let him win!'

'What other option do we have, eh? I can rent a flat somewhere, open another coffee shop.'

'Absolutely not.' Duncan's voice rang round the kitchen. It was his parade ground voice, as Yvonne called it, full of authority, the voice Maggie remembered from the programme when he was wrangling all those hard nuts, but she'd never heard him use it at home before. 'I may be a pushover when it comes to Nick, but I'm not having that. Why should you and Isla suffer just because I've – I've let my son grow up to be . . .'

'A cold-blooded killer,' finished Yvonne.

Duncan nodded, almost calmly. 'Who's to say he wouldn't track you and Isla down, despite the fake IDs, and try to hurt you, or worse?' He turned to face Maggie. 'There's no way I'm having you going off on your own. You and Isla need me. I'm not going to let you down again. No way.'

Thank Christ for that.

'But what are we going to do, then?' she whispered.

Come on, come on.

She could almost see the cogs turning in Duncan's brain. This couldn't come from Maggie herself.

'You all have to go,' said Yvonne at last.

Maggie shook her head, like she was all confused. 'What do you mean?'

'You *all* have to disappear, and fast.' Yvonne sat up straight. 'You need to get a fake identity for Duncan too, and then the three of you can take off, set up new lives for yourselves far away. As completely different people.'

'But if we disappear, we'll be all over the news as missing persons,' Maggie protested. 'We'd be recognised.'

'If the police think you've just taken off because you want to get away from Nick – and they will assume that's what's happened, after everything that's gone on – they're not going to launch an appeal. And you could change your appearances easily enough. Maggie, you could cut your hair short. You'd suit it better like that anyway. Duncan, you could shave your head. You could lie low for a few months in a rental somewhere, an isolated cottage in Cumbria or Wales or wherever.'

Thank God for Yvonne, whose mind seemed to run along the same lines as Maggie's.

'I suppose that would work,' went Maggie slowly. 'But what about Nick?'

Yvonne snorted. 'What about him? We can pack him off to boarding school, let someone who's being paid for it deal with him. Then he's off to uni. He'll probably end up a professor of psychology or something, with a spot of serial killing on the side.'

'Yvonne!' groaned Duncan.

'Sorry, but really. Nick should be the least of your concerns.'

'He's my *son*.' Duncan was staring at Maggie. 'I suppose, once we've got our new lives established, I could come back and try to sort him out. Get him the help he needs.'

The only *help* Nick needed was a bullet to the head, but Maggie nodded. 'Aye, you could, right enough. But you'd have to be careful not to let on to him where we were.'

'Of course.'

No way was that happening. No way was Duncan coming

back here once they'd left. She could talk him out of it, if and when the time came. Maggie looked across the table at Yvonne, who raised her eyebrows, just a wee bit, to telegraph that the two women were on the same page here.

Once they were gone, they were gone.

23

L ulu had the crowbar in her hand. Dad was standing in front of her saying something, but she wasn't listening, she was too angry, she needed to stop him, she needed to *shut him up*, and now she was doing it, she was hitting him over the head and he was grimacing.

'Ow,' he was saying, his mouth twisting. 'That hurts. That really hurts, love.'

And now he was falling, there was blood everywhere and Lulu was holding the crowbar and staring down at him and wailing, screaming –

SHE OPENED HER EYES.

Her mouth was sticky. She had to push her tongue between her lips to unseal them. When she sat up the room spun, and she felt woozy, a bit like she did when she woke after taking zolpidem, but much, much worse. The light filtering through the curtain, dim as it was, was too bright.

So it was morning?

There was no sound in the room apart from the pattering of rain on the window.

So she was alone?

Fractured images began chasing themselves across her memory.

Drinking the hot chocolate Nick made for her in the kitchen, trying to act normal. Waiting for her opportunity to escape.

She had to escape.

From Nick.

Nick, who was a killer.

A completely different person from the man she thought he was.

She pushed aside the covers and forced herself upright, but she swayed and overbalanced and sat back down heavily on the bed. A suspicion began to form in her mind, and she reached out to pull open the bedside drawer.

Her pack of zolpidem was there. She hadn't taken any since she'd arrived at Sunnyside, so there should be what – twenty-three tablets left? With shaking hands, she opened the packet and pulled out the blister strips.

Twenty.

And now she remembered. Last night, he'd left her in the kitchen for a couple of minutes while the kettle boiled. She'd run to the back door, but it had been locked and she couldn't find the key. And then he was back, his arm round her again, guiding her to a chair at the table. She'd sat there stupidly as he stood with his back to her at the worktop, making her hot chocolate.

He had drugged her.

He knew.

He knew that she had finally, belatedly, realised what he'd done. What he was. So he had drugged her. Given her three times her usual dose to make sure. By rights, she should still be zonked out, but the noise of the rain on the window must have woken her. Or maybe her amygdala, the part of the brain responsible for the fight or flight response, had fought the zolpidem, had fought through it to wake her.

Her heart was pounding in her ears. Killers often drugged their victims, didn't they, before they . . .

What was he going to do to her now?

24

MAGGIE - NOVEMBER 1997

Maggie left the farmhouse kitchen to make the phone call to Liam.

'Maggie, I was just going to call you,' his chirpy voice came down the phone at her. 'I've got the goods you were wanting, and they are the cat's pyjamas, let me tell you.'

'Good. That's great, Liam. Actually, I'm needing more from you. I'm needing the same again for Duncan. Pronto. I mean *yesterday*. Can I meet you in town after lunch, and I'll get you the photos and details you need?'

'Phew. Aye, okay then, Maggie. How about I meet you in the churchyard?'

Duncan insisted on coming with her.

Liam was standing in the shelter of the massive church doorway, smoking a joint. When he saw Duncan was with Maggie, he looked down at the joint in his hand and then all around for somewhere to hide it. Then he dropped it and stood on it.

'Old habits die hard, eh?' went Duncan, shaking rain off their umbrella.

'Uh,' went Liam, not making eye contact.

'Thanks for doing this, Liam. It's a big ask, I know, making you revive contacts you'd rather not have to see again.'

'No problemo.' Liam took an envelope from his pocket and handed it to Maggie. 'Your name's now Teresa Black. There's a passport with the baby on it too – she's still Isla – plus birth certificates and NI number. And a refund. Mates' rates.'

'You keep it,' said Maggie, opening the envelope and handing Liam the notes.

'Uh-uh. You're going to need all the cash you can get. Once you're gone, you can't access your bank accounts. There can't be a money trail.'

'We're leaving our savings in place for Nick, anyway,' went Maggie quickly.

Duncan handed Liam the envelope with the passport photos in it and his date of birth and other details that Liam's contacts would need to match him to his new identity.

'The two of you will have different surnames.' Liam pocketed the envelope. 'You could marry down the line, or not. Up to you, but best not. You need to, like, stay under the radar.'

Duncan nodded. 'We really appreciate this, Liam. As I said, I'm really sorry to have to ask you to –'

'Hey, Duncan, it's my pleasure, you know? If it wasn't for the two of you, fuck knows where I'd be now. Probably lying rotting in an underpass in Niddry with foxes gnawing my belly, you know?' He chuckled. 'Naw. I'm just sorry I can't do more.' And he eyeballed Maggie.

She shook her head at him, under cover of saying, 'You pulled yourself up all by yourself, son. We're dead proud of you. You keep on the straight and narrow, aye?'

If it was just down to her, she'd say go for it, take Nick out. The world would be a better place without Nick Clyde in it, no question. But she couldn't do it to Duncan. He'd be devastated if Nick turned up murdered. He still loved the fucker, and Maggie loved him for it. Duncan was the sort of man who was decent through and through, and loyal, and he couldn't just turn his feelings for his son off, no matter what he'd done.

'How long do you think it will take?' went Duncan.

Liam shrugged. 'Couple of weeks? You can't rush this stuff. This is the rest of your lives we're talking about, you know?'

BACK AT YVONNE and Michael's, the crisis meeting resumed with an eye on the clock – Nick would be back from school at four-thirty.

'We'll have dinner as usual.' Maggie turned to Duncan. 'I'll be giving him the cold shoulder, but you'll act as if you've accepted his version of events, that he was just messing around with the pram. Do you think you can pull that off?'

Duncan nodded. 'Then we lock ourselves in the bedroom overnight.' He was in military campaign mode now, Maggie was glad to see. 'Tomorrow he'll be in Edinburgh with Carol and Andy all day. That will be our chance. As soon as he's gone, we leave.'

'We don't want the police tracing the car,' said Maggie quickly. 'We can't count on them not launching a massive missing person search. We'll have to leave the car at Sunnyside. Maybe hire one, although –'

'No, no,' went Yvonne. 'I'll drive you. Come here on foot, via the track, and I'll drive you to Wales. Tell Nick that I've gone to a conference or something. There's bound to be one going on somewhere that would be relevant to the business. I'll take you to a hotel, or maybe a holiday rental would be better. I'll phone around tonight, see what I can arrange.

Then you can wait there, under Maggie's new name, until Liam can get Duncan's new documents to us.'

'We can't withdraw money from our account, even before we leave. It could be traced when we spend it,' said Maggie. 'They sometimes keep a record of the numbers on banknotes.'

And Yvonne stepped up, as Maggie had hoped she would. 'I'll give you money from the business. It would be suspicious if a large amount of cash left our personal accounts – I suppose the police might try tracing those notes if we did – but I'm paying out to suppliers all the time from the business account.'

Duncan sighed. 'Thanks, Yvonne. We'll pay you back when we can.'

'No need for that. The business is doing well. The money's just sitting there. You may as well make use of it.'

'Well, we'll see. This way, though, Nick will have all our savings, and the house. You'll make sure he's okay, won't you?' Duncan swallowed.

'No way is he living with us, but yes, we'll arrange the boarding school and make sure he's comfortable financially.'

'But you'll have him for the holidays?'

'That's a lot to ask,' Maggie put in.

'But we can't just . . . turn him loose. Without anyone.'

'Okay.' Yvonne sighed. 'He can come here for the holidays.'

Maggie wouldn't be surprised if she had her fingers crossed under the table.

As they got up to go, Maggie turned away to hide a triumphant smile. This was all going even better than she could have expected. None of them, not even Yvonne, had rumbled her plan.

L ulu managed to stand up, straining her ears.

Nothing.

He couldn't have left her alone in the house, surely? He must be downstairs.

Stupid stupid stupid!

How could she have been so stupid, marrying a man she barely knew? Telling herself he was her soulmate, when all the time he was just being what he had worked out she wanted him to be.

Typical Lulu.

Gets herself married to a psychopath.

Her stomach roiled, and she only just made it to the loo in time, staggering along the corridor in her bare feet, throwing up into the toilet, trying to do it as quietly as possible.

She needed a phone.

But there was no landline here because it was just a holiday let. And now he would have all three phones, his own and the burner and Lulu's, either on him or hidden away. He wasn't stupid.

She peed, quickly washed her face and tiptoed back to

the bedroom. Then she pulled on clothes at random and her trainers. Slung her bag across her body and opened the bedroom door.

She still couldn't hear him.

Maybe he was in the kitchen. She ran lightly down the stairs and across the hall. Carefully, she turned the knob on the library door and eased it open; eased it shut behind her. The room was shadowed. Torrential rain was now being flung against the windows and it was as dark as dusk out there, huge black clouds blocking the light.

There was a bureau desk with cubby holes full of stationery for the use of the holiday let guests. She flicked on the little desk lamp to examine what was there. She remembered watching a programme on TV in which a reformed burglar revealed the tricks of the trade, and one of them was to stick parcel tape all over a windowpane before breaking it to reduce the noise and the risk of injuring yourself.

Was there parcel tape?

She rifled through the cubby holes, through the little drawers under them. Paperclips, marker pens, paper, scissors ...

She couldn't see any.

But there was Sellotape. She picked up the roll and the scissors and crossed the room to the far window facing the front of the house, the one furthest from the kitchen. Her heart was going into overdrive, pumping away, and she could hardly get her fingers to work. The breath sobbed in her throat as she fumbled with the first length of tape and it all stuck to itself. She balled it up and threw it down.

The ripping sound the tape made as she pulled another length from the roll seemed to reverberate through the room. She fumbled with the scissors. Finally she had a length of Sellotape in her hands. The huge size of the Victorian window meant just one half of the lower sash would be plenty big enough for her to get through. She pressed the tape to the lower right-hand pane, diagonally, and then another piece the other way, like she'd seen in old wartime films. The pane of glass, streaming with rain, was cold to the touch. She stuck more tape across it horizontally and vertically.

That would have to do.

There was a tweedy throw across the sofa.

She balled her hand up in it and, turning her face away, punched at the window.

The old glass, thankfully, was thin. It shattered, but the tape held most of the shards in place. Lulu punched again with the throw wrapped round her hand. The pieces of glass fell out to the gravel below and rain came flying in at her.

She pushed the remaining jagged shards out of the frame and spread the throw over the bottom edge of it. Then she clambered out into the wet and ran across the sodden lawn to the path that led to the garage, her feet splashing through big puddles.

She still had the spare set of car keys in her bag.

By the time she got to the garage, she was soaked through, water running from her scalp into her eyes. She got the key from the safe and let herself in, unlocked the car and got inside, pushing her hands through her hair and then rubbing them on the upholstery of the passenger seat to dry them.

She started the engine.

Inching slowly out of the garage and along to the fork in the drive, wipers going madly in an attempt to clear the windscreen, it occurred to her that she was safe – that it didn't matter, now, if he heard the car. Something defiant in her made her gun the engine, roar down the drive and onto the road.

She would go straight to the police. Was there a police station in Langholm?

She was halfway there, splashing through flooded areas of the road, having to keep her speed down because visibility was so bad, when it occurred to her.

What proof did she have that Nick had done anything wrong? The police weren't going to arrest him because his wife thought he might have put sleeping tablets in her hot chocolate. She had no proof of that. The zolpidem would probably be out of her system by the time they could get round to testing her, if they even bothered.

And she didn't have the burner phone. She could tell them that Nick's phone had no calls in the crucial period, when he'd said he was calling clients, and they could check the phone records and confirm that, but Nick would explain that away. She had no proof of anything.

So not the police. Not yet.

London.

She could get her passport and then fly home to Leonora and decide what to do when she was safely away from him. She supposed that Yvonne's suggestion, that he could have disposed of the family's bodies using the digger, was possible. But it would still have been very risky, if he'd done it in broad daylight. Michael or Yvonne could have appeared at any moment. Unless he killed them either the night before they supposedly disappeared or very early that morning and disposed of the bodies under cover of darkness? It had been November, so the nights would have been long. Carol had said she hadn't seen Duncan or Maggie or Isla on the morning of their disappearance. She'd picked Nick up from the end of the drive, as usual.

Yes.

For someone as clever as Nick, it would have been possible.

Maybe she and Michael and Andy, together, could persuade the police to take radar machinery to those fields, like archaeologists used, that told you what was under the ground. If the bodies were found, the police would have to launch a murder investigation. They'd have to seriously consider the possibility that Nick had killed not only Duncan, Maggie and Isla but Yvonne too. Nick's sleight of hand with the phones would be exposed, maybe, if people who were experts in that kind of thing got onto it. Maybe they could determine that a phone active at Craibstone Wood that afternoon had also been active at Sunnyside, even if Nick had now disposed of it.

What was Nick thinking, now? He had probably realised that she'd gone. Would he try to come after her, to London? To intercept her? Or was part of him, maybe a tiny little part, glad that she'd got away?

Her hands were shaking so much she was having difficulty steering, veering wildly round a sharp corner, almost over onto the other side of the road.

She slowed the car.

No.

All that angst Nick had shown, all that emotion when Lulu had been taking him through the events of that night, the night his family had disappeared . . . he'd been play-acting. The whole Nick persona was an act, designed specifically to appeal to Lulu.

Why?

If he really was a psychopath, why did he want her at all? Why, in London, had he been so obsessed with her safety? Psychopaths were controlling, but only in as far as other people were pawns, to be moved dispassionately about the board. They didn't *care* about anyone but themselves. Yes, they often had partners, but only to service their needs, not because they believed in any such thing as a soulmate. Psychopaths didn't have souls.

'People don't fit neatly into boxes,' Karla used to say. 'No two people with the same condition will present in the same way.'

She'd been talking about people with conditions like PTSD, anxiety disorders, depression . . . but maybe that also applied to psychopathy? Maybe some psychopaths *could* feel things for other people, become attached to them, obsessed with them?

She pressed her shaking foot to the accelerator.

He'd been obsessed with his father. And killed him.

The third mug, the third bowl and spoon on the table had been there because *Nick* had been there.

Because Nick had killed them all.

26

MAGGIE - NOVEMBER 1997

Maggie was scared shitless that Duncan was going to give the game away. So when Nick got back from school, after he'd disappeared up to his room, she suggested that Duncan have a nice long bath while she made dinner.

'But I want to spend time with Nick. This could be . . . could be the last time . . .' Tears filled his eyes.

'Course it's not!' Maggie puffed, jiggling Isla in her carrier. 'Once we're settled, you'll be back to sort him out.' *Would he ever!* 'We need to act like everything's normal. If you go mooning around after him, he's going to suspect something's up. Go and have a bath.'

When Duncan was safely shut away in the en suite, Maggie picked Bunny up from Isla's cot, took him downstairs and pushed him to the back of one of the kitchen cupboards, the one with cleaning products which neither Duncan nor Nick was ever likely to open.

· · ·

ON THE MORNING OF D-DAY, as Maggie was thinking of it, they ate a late breakfast together, during which Duncan sat gazing across the table at Nick like a big numpty. Hopefully Nick was putting Duncan's strange behaviour down to his new, conflicted feelings about his son after the little bastard had tried to kill Isla.

But Nick was putting on the charm, jumping up helpfully to get milk from the fridge or cereal from the cupboard, smiling at Maggie, acting like nothing had happened.

Or not quite. He was acting like he was turning over a new leaf.

It was almost like he knew.

It was almost like he was showing Duncan there was no reason to leave. That Nick had seen the error of his ways and was reformable, like all those kids at The Phoenix Centre. Like Maggie herself.

Maggie was washing the breakfast dishes at the sink with Marigolds on her hands. She planned to leave all the clean dishes from yesterday in the dishwasher, so it would look like no one had had a chance to unload it before disaster struck.

As Nick finished his cornflakes and brought his bowl and mug to the sink, he gave Duncan a sad smile. 'Can I just say again how sorry I am? I know what I did was really, really silly and dangerous. I know I need to address some . . . some troubling behaviour.' He gave Maggie a wee grimace. *Oh aye, he was good.* 'I was thinking. You know you use that horse therapy thing, Dad, with some of the kids in the programme?'

This was a new initiative where the yob was given responsibility for a horse at a local stable and had to clean out its stall, look after its tack, groom it and feed it. The results had been promising, apparently, with one of them even talking about becoming a stable lad.

'Maybe I could do that,' went Nick. 'I think you're right

and I'm not dealing with Mum's death too well. I think it could help me.'

'Okay,' said Duncan heavily, not meeting Nick's eye.

'We can talk about it tonight,' said Maggie, sneaking Nick's unwashed mug into the empty sink along with hers and Duncan's. 'We don't have time for this now. Carol will be here in ten minutes to pick you up, Nick.' Fifteen, actually, but she needed Nick out of here, and not just because of the effect he was having on Duncan. It was important that Carol didn't set eyes on Maggie, Duncan or Isla. 'She's picking you up from the bottom of the drive, aye?'

She was, because Maggie had made sure of it. She'd called Carol last night to tell her Nick would be waiting there as usual.

Nick turned to her. 'Are you worried I'll go psycho with the horses, Mags? Like those sickos who go round at night maiming animals in fields?'

Ha!

He just couldn't help himself.

'Naw,' went Maggie, looking right at Duncan. 'You'd have to be a right mental bastard to even think about it.'

WHEN NICK HAD GONE, Maggie told Duncan to go upstairs with Isla while she made sure everything was 'shipshape' down here.

'We don't want to leave the place in a mess,' she said, wiping a cloth along the worktop. 'Yvonne's doing enough for us as it is.'

Duncan got up from the table like his limbs were made of lead.

Maggie grabbed him with one yellow-gloved hand. 'We have to do this. I know it's *fucking hard*, but we have to do this for Isla.'

He nodded and turned away to the door.

Right.

Now to stage the scene.

She dried and put away the breakfast stuff, apart from the three mugs. She took some chicken from the freezer and left it defrosting in the pantry, like she'd taken it out last night or very early this morning, so it would be ready to cook up today. She filled a pan with water and opened a bag of oatmeal next to it, like they'd been in the middle of making porridge for breakfast when it had happened. She put three bowls and spoons on the table and poured a wee bit more tea and milk into the three mugs and set them on the table as well, like they'd all been drinking tea.

Then she took off the gloves, got a knife from the block and went through to the drawing room. She pulled the blade across her thumb. She would tell Duncan she'd cut it while emptying the dishwasher. But she wasn't going to empty the dishwasher.

Squatting on the floor, she squeezed drops of blood out and watched them drip onto the cream pile of the carpet. Nick maybe first attacked her in here. She ran outside, but he caught her. Maybe there'd be more blood in the hall? She squeezed some more onto the tiles, thinking suddenly of Kathleen. That poor woman.

She looked down at the wee spots of blood on the tiles, then up at the landing.

There were benefits, right enough, to being a delinquent.

She smiled to herself as she opened the kitchen cupboard where she'd hidden Bunny last night.

'Sorry, Bunny,' she went as she chucked him down on the kitchen floor.

They maybe hadn't left voluntarily. That was what she was hoping it would look like. The cops already knew Nick was a psycho, even if they couldn't prove it. Hopefully, all this would plant a wee suspicion that Nick could have had something to do with their disappearance. Maybe he'd killed the lot of them very early this morning, at a pre-dawn breakfast, giving him time to dispose of their bodies under cover of darkness – Nick was a bright lad, he'd have thought this through – before turning up at the foot of the drive for his day out as if nothing had happened, like the callous wee bastard he was.

It would have been tight, to be there for Carol to pick him up as arranged, so he didn't have time to clear up in the kitchen, to clear away the evidence of breakfast having been interrupted. Or maybe incriminating housework details just hadn't crossed his mind.

Of course, circumstantial evidence like this wouldn't even be enough to arrest him on, let alone charge or convict him, but he'd be questioned, and, given what had been going on, the business with the pram and Dean's murder, she was hoping at least some of the cops would maybe be thinking the wee fucker had done this, even if nothing could be proved.

And that would be Nick on their radar.

He needed watching, they'd maybe be thinking.

And maybe next time he killed someone, or tried to – because there *would* be a next time – he wouldn't walk free.

Well, she'd done all she could.

There had always been the possibility that Duncan or Yvonne or Michael would scupper it all by querying why, for example, they needed to leave the car at the house. She'd gone on about why this was necessary, saying that the police might trace it and find them, but she'd just been waiting for someone to go, 'Maggie, you're talking shite.' Because there were plenty ways round that one – keeping to the back roads that wouldn't have cameras. Changing the number plate.

Dumping it somewhere and buying a new second-hand car with cash.

But none of them had the criminal mindset. They hadn't stopped to think that maybe Maggie was setting it up to look like they hadn't left at all – or at least, not of their own accord.

And they hadn't stopped to think why it should be a no-no to withdraw money from their accounts before they left. The idea that the bank would have recorded the numbers on the banknotes was mental. But they'd bought that as well. None of them had rumbled Maggie's real motivation – that there should be nothing to suggest that their vanishing was premeditated.

Once Nick came under suspicion, of course, there was the risk that Yvonne and Michael would leap to his defence and tell the cops what had really happened. But they hated Nick. They'd surely be happy enough to let him sweat.

She shut the kitchen door behind her and called up the stairs to Duncan: 'Okay, we'd best get going.'

She'd already persuaded him they should take nothing with them because she wanted 'a completely fresh start' with no reminders of their old lives. Duncan had bought that too, so there would be no missing clothes or suitcases to suggest they'd packed up and gone, skipping off into the fucking sunset.

Duncan came downstairs, holding Isla and weeping.

'What's Nick going to think? When he comes back to find us gone? He's going to be so bewildered! So upset!'

So angry.

'He'll be fine.' Maggie put her arms around him. 'Yvonne and Michael will look after him.'

'Yvonne has never liked Nick! Oh God! What sort of a father abandons his child? He loves me, I know he does, and I love him, despite everything he's done. How can I do this to him?'

Fuck.

Maggie took a step back so she could look him in the eye. 'If he really loved you, would he have tried to kill Isla? Would he have hurt me? He doesn't care if you're happy or not, as long as he has you all to himself.'

Isla, as if on cue, looked up at Duncan and smiled, one arm waving about like she was trying to grab his hair. Duncan took her little hand in his and began sobbing again.

Ruthlessly, Maggie said, 'Nick pushed her pram into the path of a timber lorry. If you hadn't happened to be there, she would have been crushed to death under its wheels.'

Duncan swiped at his eyes.

'Our first priority is this wee one. Look at her. *Look at her, Duncan.* She is *completely* helpless. She can't protect herself, so we have to do it for her. Nick's sixteen. He's technically an adult. We have to make ourselves safe, *make Isla safe*, and then we can think about what to do about Nick.'

After a long moment, he nodded.

Thank God, he nodded.

THEY LEFT the front door unlocked but shut, and walked off across the gravel to the track that led through the trees to the fields. The sun was out, and the air smelt dead nice, all earthy and clean. Where the trees began, Duncan turned and looked back at the house.

'It's not forever,' said Maggie.

Aye, right.

She touched Duncan's arm and adjusted Isla, who was strapped to her front in the new baby carrier she'd secretly bought, identical to the old one, which she'd left in a cupboard upstairs. There had been no need to bring the car seat, as Duncan, in his typical over-the-top way when it came to Isla, had bought an extra one for Yvonne's car, 'Just in case of emergencies'. She wasn't sure who, apart from Michael and Yvonne, knew about that. Hopefully no one, so when the car seat was found in place in their car, that would be another reason for suspicion that they hadn't left voluntarily.

As they entered the wood, Maggie's heart started to hammer and she found herself looking back every few steps. She kept expecting Nick to suddenly appear at her shoulder in that creepy, silent way he had.

But when they reached the fields, she began to relax a bit.

Michael had given his farmhands the day off, pretending that with Yvonne away at the conference he wouldn't know what to do with himself and wanted to keep busy, so would do their jobs himself. There should be no one in the fields. No one in the farmyard to see them as they got into Yvonne's car.

She was thinking about that, about their escape, about what would happen next, when a figure stepped from the shadow of an oak tree.

27

LULU - JUNE 2019

In Langholm, as she approached the garage on the High Street, Lulu decided to pull in and get petrol and something to eat and drink. Maybe the shaking would stop if she had something inside her. And she'd need a full tank of petrol for the drive south. As she stood by the car filling up, she noticed that everything seemed different: the noise of the traffic slowing for some hold-up ahead was drilling through her head, loud and aggressive-seeming; a child that suddenly ran after its mother on the pavement made her heart jump in her chest; the rain on her hair, on the sleeve of her sweatshirt, was somehow malevolent, as if deliberately targeting her, making her, ridiculously, want to cry.

Oh God.

She had to hold it together.

She consciously slowed her breathing, taking a long breath in and then letting it out gradually, gazing across the street at the buildings opposite.

Something, some part of her subconscious, must have kicked in, because suddenly she was focusing on the face of one of the drivers. The man in the small silver car a few vehicles down from the one opposite her . . .

It was Nick.

It was Nick!

If he turned his head just fractionally, he would see her!

But no.

It *wasn't* Nick. This man had grey hair in a crew cut, and he was at least thirty years older. But she knew him. She knew his face. It was the face on the wall of the apartment.

It was Nick's dad.

It was Duncan Clyde!

And the woman sitting next to him, the woman with short greying hair – was that Maggie? Her face was fuller, but it was the woman in the wedding photograph, wasn't it?

Nick's stepmother.

They were alive.

They hadn't been murdered.

She didn't stop to think about it. She dropped the pump, not even bothering to put it back in the holder, and jumped into the car. She would come back later and pay. Her feet slipped on the pedals, and the car kangarooed forwards as she steered to the exit and out into the queue of traffic.

Was it really them?

But how could it be?

As the traffic started to move, she was focusing so hard on the small silver car that she almost went into the back of the vehicle directly in front of her.

Duncan and Maggie. Could it be Duncan and Maggie, or was it just her drugged, battered brain playing tricks?

Wanting to be wrong about Nick?

Ahead of her, the silver car's indicator flashed, and it turned off the High Street onto the bridge. Onto the road to Sunnyside. As she followed them out of the town, one crazy scenario after another chased through her head. They had been living in Langholm all this time . . . They had come back and murdered Yvonne for some reason . . . They had heard Nick was under suspicion and were here to make amends . . .

But soon they turned off the road, onto one Lulu didn't know. She drove on autopilot, hardly conscious of the twists and turns of the road as they travelled through dank forests and fields and crossed bridges over muddy torrents. She was hypnotised by the red taillights of the car in front.

Eventually it slowed and indicated right, and turned onto a track signposted *Rose Cottage* with *4* Holiday Home* underneath.

Lulu drove on past and parked as soon as she could, in the gateway to a field. Then she ran back in the soaking rain to the track entrance. It was a well-maintained track, more of a driveway, really, which wound slightly uphill amongst big old beeches and sycamores. Soon, she could see the cottage, a long, low, whitewashed building with a slate roof, the windows glowing a welcoming yellow, a wisp of smoke rising into the rain from a chimney. There was a pretty garden in front, a lawn and flowerbeds and some apple trees. To one side was parked a Land Rover, and the silver car was manoeuvring in next to it.

Lulu ducked down in the shelter of a sopping wet rhododendron as the door of the cottage opened and Michael appeared, hurrying along the path towards the two people who had got out of the car – a small, elfin woman with short grey hair and a strong nose, and a tall, older man with a salt-and-pepper crewcut in smart chinos and shirt, loping along behind her.

'Maggie!' exclaimed Michael, catching the woman in a hug before shaking the man's hand, the emotion on their faces plain to see, even from this distance, as 'Oh, Michael!' the woman cried out.

Nick's family.

It was Nick's long-lost family.
Alive and well.

28

MAGGIE - JUNE 2019

'Come on in to the fire,' went Michael, leading them along the path and into the cottage, and then footering about getting tea, the three of them rummaging in the kitchen for cutlery and mugs.

Maggie had forwarded Michael the details of Rose Cottage after they'd managed to get a last-minute booking, and he had come over here ahead of them and opened up and got the fire going.

Duncan had wanted to come straight back as soon as they'd heard Yvonne was missing, but Maggie had persuaded him against it. Then Michael had called in a terrible state, saying he'd had enough, he was going to confront Nick. They'd talked the stupid bugger down and made him promise not to do anything until they got there.

Once the decision to come back had been made, Maggie had wanted to get going pronto. They'd left their small-holding in Wales at mad o'clock, and Maggie was feeling like death warmed up. It felt like the right thing, though, being here. Maybe Duncan had been right and they should have come back as soon as Yvonne went missing, but what could they have done?

Yvonne was likely dead.

Nick had likely killed her.

But they owed it to Michael, to Yvonne, to be here. Yvonne had had their backs all these years, eh? Not that Maggie had always appreciated it. That fateful day they'd left Sunnyside, and Yvonne had appeared on the track in front of them, Maggie had yelled at her: 'You daft cow! You scared the shit out of me!'

Yvonne had apologised and said she had to come and make sure they were okay, that she'd had the horrible thought of what might be happening if Nick had rumbled them.

And that was Yvonne all over.

Duncan had hardly slept since he'd heard she was missing, and Maggie was finding it hard too. Over the years, she and Yvonne had become pals. Most summers, they met up abroad, all five of them, for a week or two in the sun. Isla loved her Auntie Yvonne to bits and the big shocker was that Yvonne returned the sentiment. When Isla was wee they had this game they used to play, 'naughty horsie' – Isla would jump on Yvonne's back and Yvonne would trot round the room neighing and pretending to try to buck Isla off, the two of them laughing their heads off.

Maybe Maggie was wrong about Yvonne being dead.

God, she hoped she was wrong.

She never thought she'd be back here again. Knowing that Nick was at Sunnyside, just a few miles away, was giving her goose pimples.

Back when they'd disappeared, Yvonne and Michael had kept them up to speed with the police investigation. The cops had only questioned Nick once, as a witness, not a suspect, and concluded that there was nothing suspicious about the

Clydes vanishing. Yvonne had said that one of the officers had let it slip to her that the theory was that Nick was the teenager from hell and Duncan and Maggie had finally flipped and legged it with Isla to get away from him, leaving the hob on in their flustered state. The extra crockery could be explained in any number of ways.

The cops weren't as daft as folk thought.

They all sat round the wood-burner while Michael poured out everything that had happened, starting with Yvonne's disappearance and then jumping back and forward in time so it was hard to work out what had happened when. But it seemed Nick and his new wife had come to stay at Sunnyside for a couple of weeks, supposedly so the wife – who sounded like a right silly bitch – could 'help him heal'. And a few days later, Yvonne had gone missing.

Michael kept running his hands through his hair, making it stand on end. If Yvonne had been here, she'd have tutted and smoothed it down. Maggie swallowed.

'He's killed her, hasn't he?' went Michael. 'I know he's killed her.'

'Why would he do that?' Duncan was sitting with his face in shadow in an armchair in the corner.

'Yvonne was trying to get Lulu to leave him,' said Michael. 'That alone would be cause enough, for that psycho.'

'Nick couldn't have found out what Yvonne did, could he?' went Maggie self-centredly. 'That she helped us get away?' Worst-case scenario was that he had forced Yvonne to give away their new identities and location.

Michael lifted his shoulders. 'Aw, Maggie, I don't know.'

'Teresa,' Maggie corrected him automatically. 'We're Teresa and Peter now.' Although they made mistakes so often that they'd had to tell everyone that Maggie and Duncan were their middle names and they sort of chopped and changed. And, when Isla was thirteen, they had told her the truth about everything, having come to a decision that she was safer knowing than not, just in case Nick did ever manage to trace them. They'd impressed on her that it was dead important she tell no one, for the safety of all of them. If Isla had been a different, less mature kind of thirteen-year-old, maybe they'd have waited, but it had been a massive relief, coming clean to her and being able to explain all the odd wee things they did, like why her old fogie parents refused to go anywhere near social media.

'Sorry,' went Michael. '*Teresa.* Maybe he has found out she helped you. But he's always hated Yvonne. That's why I wouldn't have him in the house, after he left school. I was scared of what he might do to her. When he came back here, I should have taken Yvonne away, off on holiday, until he'd gone. *Why didn't I do that?*'

'You don't know that Nick's done anything to Yvonne,' Duncan kept on.

Maggie snorted. 'What, it's just a coincidence that he comes back here after twenty-odd years, and a few days later Yvonne disappears?'

'But it doesn't make sense,' Duncan insisted. 'At the time Yvonne disappeared, Michael, you said Lulu had taken the car – without Nick's knowledge – to visit Carol. So he had no transport.'

Michael grimaced. 'There are bikes, for the holiday let folk, at Sunnyside.'

'But how could he have transported Yvonne on a *bike*?'

Maggie bit back an impatient sigh. 'You know what an opportunist Nick is. Maybe he saw Lulu leaving, took his chance to lure Yvonne to Sunnyside, did . . . whatever he did to her, took her somewhere in her own car with a bike in the boot, left her there, took her car to Craibstone Wood, cycled back to Sunnyside. Stopping now and then to make trades on his phone to give himself an alibi.'

'So you think he disposed of her body somewhere else and then left the car at the wood so we'd think she'd gone for a walk and got into difficulties? She's dead, isn't she?' Michael moaned.

'We don't know that,' said Maggie. 'He might be keeping her somewhere. Trying to make her reveal our location.' As soon as it was out her mouth, she knew that wasn't helping.

And sure enough, Michael choked up. 'Torturing her, you mean?'

Duncan wasn't liking this one bit. He went, 'There's no reason to think that.'

Maggie made herself breathe. 'What exactly did the police say, Michael, after you told them you thought Nick might be responsible for Yvonne going missing?'

'They were sceptical. I mean, Nick's hardly spoken to her for twenty years. They obviously feel he couldn't have much of a motive, even after I told them about Yvonne helping you disappear. And then he's got this supposed alibi.'

Maggie got up. 'You need to put pressure on them to look at tracking data for his phone. If he was on the move while making the trades, the tracking data will show the phone wasn't at Sunnyside.'

'Oh, he'll have got round that too somehow, won't he?' Michael was hunched over in his chair.

'But it's worth a try. Come on now, Michael. You give them a call, aye?'

Phone in hand, Michael stared stupidly at the screen.

'You tell them they've got to look at the tracking data for Nick's phone because you're sure he's involved in whatever's happened to Yvonne.'

'All this is pure speculation!' went Duncan. 'We have no idea what's happened. Nick could be completely innocent!'

'Well,' said Maggie dryly, 'not completely.'

She and, she suspected, Michael were one hundred per

cent sure that Nick had done something to Yvonne, but Duncan didn't want to believe it. In the last twenty-two years, he'd had regular mad turns when he'd had doubts about Nick's guilt and wanted to contact him.

At first it had been fine. In those early months of their new life in Wales, Duncan had never even mentioned Nick. He'd spent all his time fussing round Isla, his wee princess. Eventually, though, he'd started wondering aloud how Nick was getting on. They had always said it wouldn't be forever, that Duncan would go back sometime and try to help him. Maggie had had to play the 'Isla and I need you more' card, and point out that Duncan didn't know how Nick would react if he turned up again in his life – and if anything happened to Duncan, what would become of Maggie and wee Isla? Duncan loved the two of them to pieces, so this argument had always won the day. Maggie had also played on the fact that Nick, according to Yvonne and Michael, was doing well. It wasn't healthy for him to have Duncan in his life. 'He's better off without the warped obsession he has with you, eh?'

Duncan hadn't needed too much persuading.

But, from time to time, she'd find him going through an old album Yvonne had given him, smiling over the photos of Nick as a toddler and young child.

'So full of life and fun,' he would sigh.

Maggie could see what he was thinking: *Could Nick really be such a monster? Have we made a massive mistake and done him a horrendous injustice?*

And she'd have to get in his face, remind him of everything Nick had done, get him back in that moment when he'd stopped the pram. 'Isla would have been *killed* if you'd been a *second* later!'

Now, she could see she was going to have to get the wee boy Duncan had left behind out his head and get psycho Nick back front and centre.

She went, 'Are you conveniently forgetting what he did to Isla?'

Duncan sighed.

While Michael made his call, Maggie put the kettle back on and brought them all more tea. Then, as Michael sat back in his chair, Duncan said, 'Well?'

'The DC said they've already looked at the tracking data for Nick's phone. The phone was in the house, in Sunnyside, the whole time.'

'The clever bastard,' went Maggie.

Michael nodded. 'He must have left his own phone there and used a burner to make those trades.'

Maggie sat down, straight-backed, like a chairperson taking a meeting. 'Right, so the bottom line is, we've got nothing to take to the police but suspicions.'

'So what do we do?' Michael was looking at her like a wee rumpled kitten, and she wanted to reach out and smooth his hair for him.

And then, suddenly, Michael was up, making for the door, muttering about how he wasn't having this, he was going to go and see Nick and –

'No!' Maggie rapped out. 'Michael, get back here! You are *not* going to confront him. What good will that do? Best case, he'll laugh in your face. Worst case, you'll end up like Yvonne. Michael! Come and sit down, eh? Aye, he's a clever bastard, so we're going to have to be clever about this too.'

L ulu sobbed as she drove. She sobbed until she could hardly see, blinking in time with the wipers, as if the whole world consisted of layers and layers of tears.

Nick.

Her darling.

How could she have suspected him of something so terrible? *Of murdering his entire family?* And how could *they* have done it? His stepmother and his *own dad*, the father Nick adored? They'd left him behind; left him to think they were dead, that psycho Maggie had maybe killed Duncan and Isla and then either killed herself or disappeared.

Why?

And where the hell had they been?

Was Yvonne's disappearance connected to their reappearance?

None of it made any sense.

It was going to be such a shock for Nick to find out that they were alive after all. A wonderful shock, but still a shock.

At last, she turned off the road up the drive to Sunnyside.

She didn't return the car to the garage. She continued round to the front door. There was glass on the gravel from the window she'd smashed. How could the discovery of that second phone have sent her into such a ridiculous spiral of paranoia, just like Andy, picking up on one little thing and constructing a nightmare around it in which Nick was some sort of psycho? There was obviously an innocent explanation for the phone stuff. Maybe he'd started using a new phone and then realised it would look bad that this happened to coincide with Yvonne's disappearance. So he had hidden it. If there really was anything sinister about it, he'd have disposed of it, wouldn't he, not just shoved it in a cupboard?

Last night, he must have seen how agitated she was and decided to slip some zolpidem into her hot chocolate to make sure she got a good night's sleep – which was not acceptable, but the idea that there was a sinister intention behind it was laughable. If he'd intended to harm her, he could have done so at any time.

What must he be thinking? He must be sick with worry.

Had those people any *idea* what they'd done to him?

'*I'm sorry, I'm sorry, I'm sorry,*' she was already saying as she ran through the rain to the door, expecting to find it locked, but it came open when she turned the big brass doorknob.

She opened the door, but she didn't step inside.

What was she going to say to him?

She would have to explain how sorry she was for ever even countenancing Andy's stories and Yvonne's dark hints that Nick had murdered his family. Andy was obviously disturbed. And as for Yvonne – she just didn't like Nick, pure and simple. What kind of a shock would it have been for Michael when Duncan and Maggie contacted him out of the blue?

Or maybe Yvonne and Michael had been in touch with

them all this time. Maybe Yvonne and Michael had described what an emotional mess Nick was and the therapy Lulu was trying with him. Maybe that had pricked their consciences, and that explained why they were back?

Lulu hoped so.

But why did they just up and go like that? Did Maggie turn Duncan against Nick and somehow persuade him to abandon his own son? Did she think Nick really had intended to hurt Isla when the pram got away from him? That would be a powerful reason for a mother to want to take her child and run. Especially for someone like Maggie who already had mental health issues.

And now they realised they'd made a terrible mistake?

Just like Lulu had.

She stepped inside the house.

'Nick?' Her voice came out small and weak, hardly carrying to the far reaches of the hall. 'Nick?'

She was sopping wet. She stood there, dripping onto the tiles, as the kitchen door came open and Nick came striding towards her.

'My God, Lulu! Where have you been? What's happened?'

'I just . . . I needed to get out for a while.' She couldn't, when it came to it, tell him about her suspicions. It would destroy him if he knew she could think that of him.

'You *broke a fucking window*! You just went off without telling me! You took the car! *I didn't know where the fuck you were!*' He grabbed her arms. 'I was about to call the *police*!'

'Oh, Nick, I'm sorry! I needed to get out, to be on my own for a bit, and I didn't think you'd let me, so . . . But that's not important. I've got something really wonderful to tell you, but – it's going to be a really big shock.' She took his hands in hers.

A soft light came into his eyes. 'You're pregnant?' he whispered. 'Your period is late, isn't it?'

'It's a little late, but no.' Lulu was on the pill. She couldn't be pregnant. She was sure it was just the stress messing with her cycle. 'Come in and sit down, Nick.'

She took his hand and led him into the drawing room, and they sat side by side on the sofa. A wave of love, of pity for him swept through her, so powerful that a little sob came out of her mouth.

'What is it?' Nick squeezed her hand and put his other hand to her forehead. 'You're soaked.'

'I – I went for a drive into Langholm. I stopped for petrol, and while I was filling up, I was watching the cars going by and I saw . . . Nick, this is going to knock you for six.' She squeezed his hand back. 'I saw *Maggie and Duncan*! At least, I thought I did. I followed the car to this place called Rose Cottage, a holiday let, and Michael was there. He called the woman Maggie. It's definitely them! They're *alive*! Presumably, Isla too, I mean, it's –'

Nick shook his head. 'That's not possible.'

'I couldn't believe it either, but it was definitely them.' Her voice was shaking, emotion rushing through her at what this meant for him. 'I recognised them from the photos. Nick, *they're alive!*'

'What were you doing in Langholm?'

'What?'

'Why were you filling up with petrol? There was still half a tank left.'

'I was just driving at random,' Lulu improvised. 'I was hungry, and thought I'd stop at the garage shop and fill up while I was there. But that's not important. Did you hear what I said? *Your dad is alive!*'

'No!' he suddenly shouted, grabbing her by the shoulders and shaking her like a doll. 'You're lying! Why are you lying to me? Dad can't be alive. He would never have gone off with that woman and that brat and left me! He would never have done it!'

'Nick, you're hurting me.'

He didn't let her go or even slacken his grip.

'I'm not lying to you.' Lulu tried to keep her voice level and calm. 'It was definitely your dad. And it was Maggie. I've seen photos of her online.'

'When?' he growled. 'When did you go snooping about online?'

'I – I was obviously curious to see –'

'Why the fuck would you want to go looking at photos of that evil bitch?'

'But she's *not*!' Lulu wriggled in his grip, making herself hold his angry gaze. 'Duncan was there too! He's fine, Nick! Your dad's *alive and well*. Maggie didn't do anything to him!'

Nick threw her from him, got up precipitously and strode out of the room. Lulu hurried after him, across the hall to the kitchen.

'Nick,' she said, her voice breaking. '*They're alive.*'

Standing in the middle of the kitchen, Nick suddenly turned and looked at her. 'Liar.'

Lulu made herself breathe. She sucked saliva into her dry mouth and said in what she hoped approximated her therapist's voice, 'I'm *not lying*. Why would I? Let's go to the cottage, the cottage where they are, and you can see for yourself.'

For a long, long moment, he stared at her.

And then he nodded.

M aggie took the whisky bottle from Duncan. 'No more. We need to keep clear heads.'

Duncan drained his glass before nodding.

'But what can we do?' Michael slumped further down in his chair. 'As usual, he's thought of all the angles. Yvonne's dead. She must be dead.'

Maggie fixed him with one of the hard looks she used to give Isla, the odd time she misbehaved as a kid. 'Let's have a bit less defeatism, aye? What if she's alive? What if she's alive, and you're sitting here going, "It's hopeless, let's just give up now"?' She frowned. 'What we need Nick to do is give away what he's done to Yvonne. Where she is.'

'*If* Nick has done anything to Yvonne, he's hardly going to admit it,' said Duncan.

'I'm just thinking out loud here!' Maggie snapped. She took a breath. *Calm, calm, she needed to be calm.* 'Of course he's not going to admit it. But what if he thought the police had a lead? What if he thought some bastard had seen him on his way to or from wherever Yvonne is? If she's alive, he'd have to get there pronto and move her. And when he makes a move, we follow him.'

Michael suddenly sat up straight. 'Yes!'

Aye. This could work. 'So the important thing is not to alert him that we're onto him. Michael, this is going to depend on you. You're going to have to go to him and tell him the cops have let you know there's a promising lead involving a local witness. They told you not to tell anyone, and specifically not to tell Nick, but you can't see any reason not to. Nick's going to put two and two together. He'll be shitting himself that this lead from the local witness involves him – involves someone who knows him and saw him going to or from where he's got Yvonne.'

Michael nodded. 'Yes. I can do that. Maybe you could write it down, what I've to say? I'll memorise it.'

Maggie bit back a sigh. She was moving around the room, opening drawers, looking for paper and a pen, when there was a crash from the hall.

Nick hurtled into the room.

Duncan and Michael leapt to their feet, and Michael said something in a strangled voice, but Nick ignored him.

He hurtled straight at Duncan.

And pulled him into a hug.

'Dad! Oh God, *Dad!*' He was crying, hysterically.

Duncan stood rigid for one, two seconds, and then he was hugging Nick back, tears streaming down his face.

Fuck!

How the fuck had Nick found them? Had he been tracking Michael?

The adult Nick was taller even than Duncan and very athletically built. He seemed to fill the room, to suck the air out of it so she had to gasp for breath. She was making for the door to the hall, thinking she'd find a weapon in the kitchen, but then a woman was in the doorway in front of her. A bonnie young blonde woman, staring at Maggie and then looking past her to the other people in the room.

This was Lulu, Nick's wife?

Aye, this would be Nick's wife. Just the type he would go for, a trophy wife, an airhead he could dominate. She looked like a right nugget, standing with her mouth hanging open, looking at Nick and Duncan, who were still holding each other and sobbing like babies. As Maggie watched the woman, she half-collapsed, a wee sound coming out her mouth.

'Where's Isla?' Nick sobbed. 'Is she here?'

It was like he'd put a cold hand to her throat.

Thank God Isla was well out the way in Sweden. She and a group of friends had gone camping for a month in Skuleskogen National Park to celebrate the end of their exams at uni.

'No,' said Duncan, and, before he could blurt out where she was, Maggie cut in with, 'Of course she's not here!'

Nick's wife suddenly raised her voice over Maggie's. 'How could you do it? How could you have done it to him? Abandoned him like that? *He was sixteen years old!* All this time . . .' She breathed in on a sob. 'All this time, he thought *you* were dead.' She turned to Duncan. 'And that *you* had killed his dad and Isla. Have you . . . have you *any idea* what that's done to him?'

'Oh Christ,' Duncan wailed.

Nick finally released him and stepped back, and Duncan stumbled forward and then collapsed back into his chair, looking up at Nick like he was seeing him for the first time, realising what he'd done to his son for the first time.

Fuck.

Nick looked down at him. 'People do crazy things. I get that. It's okay.'

'It's not *okay!*' Duncan got out.

'No, really, Dad, I don't blame you. I was a right little brat. You probably thought you had good reasons for what you did. You thought I was trying to hurt Isla. I get it. I wasn't, you know, I was just a silly kid with no concept of danger, but . . . I get it. I'm just glad you're all right.' His voice broke convincingly on the last word.

'Nick,' choked Duncan. '*Nick. Oh God, Nick. I'm so sorry.*'

'Dad.' And finally, the timing just right, Nick smiled. Sadly. The brave wee soldier. 'God, I can't believe it. I really thought you were dead. This is like . . . it's like it's a wonderful dream and any second I'm going to wake up and you'll still be gone. You've no idea how many times I've dreamed stuff like this. Finding you in a bar or on a street or once . . .' He attempted a shaky laugh. 'On top of the Eiffel Tower.'

'I'm so sorry we just – we just *left* you. To cope all alone.'

Nick shook his head. 'You know what? Doesn't matter. None of it matters now. All that matters is that –' He gave another shaky little laugh. 'I still can't get my head round it! All that matters is that you're *alive*. I hope . . .' He looked, then, for the first time, at Maggie, his gaze dropping to her hands, which were clenched in fists, his eyebrows quirking. 'I was going to say I hope we can move forward now, but looks like Maggie may have other ideas.'

Maggie was struck dumb.

What could she possibly say?

'It must have been hell for you,' Duncan got out. 'We've put you through hell.'

'Actually, it's worked out fine for me. Uncle Michael here and Auntie Yvonne made sure I was provided for. And I've made a good life for myself. A great life, in fact. I'm a City trader, what you might call a high-flier. Penthouse apartment at Chelsea Harbour, villas in Italy and Greece.' He turned to his wife and gave her a wee smile. 'And this beautiful girl has made me the luckiest man alive.' His face suddenly crumpled, and he stepped blindly across the room and into her arms.

The lassie held him, her chest heaving with sobs.

With a soppy look, Nick put up a hand to her face. 'I'm sorry I accused you of lying. I'm sorry I lost it. But when you told me they were alive . . .' *She* had told him? But how had she known? Maybe not such an airhead after all. 'It was such a shock, I just . . . I thought you were lying to me, I thought you'd turned against me like everyone always does . . .' He looked round at Duncan. 'I know it was Maggie. She poisoned you against me.' He stepped away from the lassie, turning his back to her, to Duncan, to give Maggie a cold, cold stare, the hatred suddenly naked in his face.

'No,' went Michael. 'You did that all by yourself.'

Nick took a visible breath. 'Okay. Look, emotions are running high, unsurprisingly. Can we meet up tomorrow, maybe, on neutral ground, and talk properly when everyone's had a chance to calm down and get their heads round this?'

'Yes.' The word left Duncan's mouth in a sort of sigh. 'Okay. Let's do that.'

'Michael's got my number,' said Nick. 'Think about it and let us know.'

And then he was leaving.

And he and the lassie had gone.

Had that really happened?

Nick had just been here?

Maggie's head was spinning.

'God,' groaned Duncan. 'Oh *God.*'

Maggie turned on him. 'Are you out your mind? You're buying that sob story?'

Duncan just lifted his shoulders.

For a long time, the three of them sat or, in Maggie's case, stood frozen. Then Michael got up from his chair and went to stand over Duncan. 'He's playing you. Maggie's right. You can't let him mess with your head all over again.'

'Aye, he's playing us,' said Maggie slowly. 'But let's us just go along with it, make him think we're buying it. This could work in our favour. We arrange to meet him and Lulu tomorrow in a café some place, and Michael, you pretend to get a call from the police and say your piece about a lead. Then if Nick makes an excuse to leave without Lulu, we follow him. We can hire another car so he won't recognise it.'

Michael nodded. 'Good thinking.'

Duncan made a wordless sound of protest. 'That boy hasn't done anything to Yvonne! He's not the person we thought he was. Isn't that obvious? He's a successful City trader, he's married to that nice girl . . . Oh, God.' He put his head in his hands. 'We've wronged him – *I've* wronged him so badly!'

31

'It's been quite a day,' said Nick, shovelling pasta into his mouth. 'Come on, Lu, eat up. You'll feel better with some food inside you.'

But Lulu couldn't eat a mouthful. She pushed the plate away.

'I can't believe that Dad . . .' Nick chewed, looking off. '*Dad's alive!* It's like all this time I've been struggling along with a huge weight pressing down on me, the thought of what must have happened to him and Isla . . . and all the time *he was alive!*'

'It's only natural if you feel anger towards him.'

Nick shook his head. 'But that's the thing – I don't. I really don't. It was Maggie, you see? All along, it's been that bitch Maggie, getting inside his head, dripping poison. It's not Dad's fault.' He sighed. 'But that's in the past. The important thing is that he's okay, and now we have years and years to make up for lost time.'

'Maybe Maggie . . .' She took a deep breath. 'Maybe she thought she had her reasons.'

He stopped mid-chew. Swallowed. Raised his eyebrows. 'What do you mean?'

Lulu backtracked hurriedly: 'Just that she was a new mum. Any threat – any *perceived* threat to her baby would have sent her into protective overdrive.'

'The bitch was paranoid! *She* was the nutter, not me! I know, I know.' His mouth quirked in a smile. 'There's no such thing as a *nutter*. But once you get to know Maggie – because unfortunately she and Dad come as a package – you might find you change your mind on that one. Christ, she was furious, wasn't she, when Dad and I were hugging? This must be her worst nightmare, the two of us being reconciled.' He nodded. 'I wouldn't put it past her to try something. We need to get that window fixed. Pity there's no alarm system. Maybe we should leave in the morning, book into a hotel, somewhere safer . . .'

After dinner, Nick made them both cocoa and rooted out a packet of chocolate ginger biscuits from the larder. 'Shall we adjourn to the drawing room?'

As they sat side by side on the sofa, Lulu's first sip of the cocoa told her it was drugged. It had a strange taint which the stronger taste of the hot chocolate last night must have masked.

She should challenge him. Tell him she knew he'd put zolpidem in the drink.

Again.

But somehow the words wouldn't come.

It wasn't the right time. He had been through too much today. Tomorrow morning, she would tackle him about it. Wouldn't she?

Suddenly, sickeningly, all her fears from last night, this morning, about Nick came flooding back.

Why was he drugging her? Was he just worried about her not sleeping, or –

Or what?

She knew he couldn't be intending to harm her in any way. Why would he? Nick loved her. She should never have doubted that, not even for a second. Tomorrow, she would tell him she knew he had tried to drug her.

She made herself keep sipping the cocoa.

'I'm beat,' she yawned, after she had drunk less than half the mugful. 'I think I'll have a shower and go to bed.'

'You haven't finished your cocoa.'

So she smiled, and drank the rest of it down.

'Goodnight, darling.' She kissed his mouth. 'It's been quite a day, as you say. A wonderful day, but I feel like I could sleep for a week!'

'Me too. I'll be up soon. Goodnight, my darling Lu.' He kissed her again, more lingeringly.

She would have to be quick.

But she made herself not run up the stairs. She trudged wearily, and only when she was safely locked in the bathroom did she step it up a gear, rushing to the shower and turning it on to provide a covering wall of noise as she stuck her fingers down her throat and vomited into the toilet bowl.

After a sketchy shower, she undressed and got into bed. Had she got the zolpidem out of her system soon enough? She felt so tired, so drained of energy. She wanted to close her eyes and sink down into sleep.

But the question *Why is he drugging me?* kept going round in her head, effectively keeping her awake until the bedroom door opened quietly. She closed her eyes and made herself breathe slowly and deeply. She heard his footsteps approach the bed and then stop. She couldn't help her breath catching for a second. To disguise it, she moved a little, as if in her sleep, and gave a tiny snort.

It seemed like forever before the footsteps moved away again and the door clicked softly shut. She heard his steps receding down the corridor and got quickly out of bed and went to the door. Very gently, she opened it, just a crack, in time to see him disappear from view on the landing. She heard him jog downstairs, and then his steps on the tiles, crossing the hall. The front door opened and shut, and there was a scraping noise – the key turning in the lock.

She was standing irresolute when she heard the car engine. Going to the window, she watched the Audi coming round the side of the house. In the long summer twilight, she could make Nick out clearly in the driver's seat.

Where was he going, at eleven o'clock at night?

A sudden image of Maggie's face came into her head – the way she'd looked at Nick with naked terror. Lulu had seen that look before, on the faces of clients who had been victims of domestic abuse.

Maggie was genuinely scared of Nick.

She thought back over what everyone – Yvonne, Andy, Michael, even Harry – had told her. She thought of how she'd felt this morning, breaking a window to get out of the house. His controlling behaviour in the days and weeks and months before that. She heard Ruth and Jenny chorusing in her head: *Typical Lulu*.

Oh God.

Oh fuck!

Last night, he had drugged her because she'd found the extra phone and he needed to keep her from telling anyone about it until he could work out how to spin it to her. How to dupe silly, trusting Lulu. He must really have panicked, though, when he'd found her gone in the morning, found that smashed window! He must have realised that she'd rumbled him. But then silly, trusting Lulu had come back after discovering that Maggie and Duncan were alive and well, and he must have worked out her thought process, that she'd convinced herself that he was innocent after all and there was an innocent explanation for that extra phone. He always had been able to read her mind.

Tonight, he had drugged her so she could provide him with an alibi, assure the police that she was such a light sleeper that she would have known if he'd been absent from their bed for any length of time.

Silly, trusting Lulu.

Quickly, she dressed in jeans, a navy hoodie and trainers, and ran downstairs. She needed to warn Duncan and Maggie that Nick could be on his way.

Nick hated Maggie so much.

What might he be intending to do?

She needed to call the police. .

She ran into the study. But there were no phones charging on the windowsill.

No phone in the cupboard underneath.

And there was no landline. She went frantically round the house looking for the phones, but he must have hidden them well. She'd have to go to the farm, rouse Michael, get him to call the police. But by the time she'd done that and the police had come from wherever they were stationed – in a rural area like this, that could be some distance away – Nick would have arrived at Rose Cottage, if that really was where he was going.

She ran back upstairs to the bedroom and slung her bag over her shoulders.

Inside was the can of pepper spray Nick made her carry.

And in the garage were the electric bikes that were supplied for the use of the holiday let guests. It was what – three miles to the cottage? She could be there in fifteen minutes.

32

Duncan had gone to bed, but Maggie was sitting up in the living room with her laptop, messaging Isla's friends, telling them she needed to get in touch with Isla urgently. She'd tried calling and texting and emailing Isla, and leaving messages on her social media pages telling her to call her mum pronto. But the group were camping in the wilds of Sweden, where there was often no phone signal and no Wi-Fi.

She needed Isla to change her plans, to go someplace else, just in case Nick had found out their new names, maybe through the people who let Rose Cottage. Just in case he went after Isla. Isla had posted all about the Swedish trip on social media, so it wouldn't be hard for him to track her down.

Maggie and Duncan didn't do social media as they didn't want their photographs out there, even under their new names, but when Isla had turned thirteen they had made the decision that it wasn't fair to ban her from using it, so had allowed her to have accounts as long as she let them have her passwords and never posted photographs of Maggie or Duncan.

Maggie kept thinking of Isla, in her cut-off jeans and favourite faded green T-shirt, innocently blethering to her friends as they strolled along a forest path in dappled sunlight, and Nick jumping out at her – Isla giving him her friendly, open smile, and then realising.

Realising who he was.

Maybe they should fly to Sweden themselves, Maggie and Duncan, and whisk her off somewhere, ban her from social media for the foreseeable future. Maggie's heart was pumping as she navigated to Erin's Instagram account. Erin was one of the group in Sweden, a girl Isla had known since school.

Using Isla's account, Maggie was adding a comment to one of Erin's posts, asking her to tell Isla to get in touch urgently, when she was aware of a movement. She turned, expecting to see Duncan in the doorway, but there was no one there.

The movement was outside.

On the other side of the patio doors.

She just had time to register the tall shape looming there before the glass shattered.

And now she was up out her chair, yelling, running for the door to the back hall that led to their bedroom. But she could already sense him behind her, smell the night air off him as he grabbed her.

He pushed her to the floor.

Kicked her, hard, in the stomach. In the head.

She kept shouting, she put up her hands to try to ward off the kicks. She could see his hands, glowing ghostly white in the dim light, and she realised it was because he was wearing surgical gloves.

Then nothing.

Then voices.

Shouting voices.

She must only have been out for a second because she could see Nick's legs, his long legs in black jeans, his feet moving past her and she could hear Duncan, and as she heaved herself upright she saw him, Duncan, she saw him launching himself through the doorway at Nick.

The two men collided.

Maggie dragged herself to a chair, forced herself upright, looked for something to use as a weapon.

There was a big book on the coffee table.

She grabbed it, and it flapped open, but she managed to slam it closed again and stagger to where they were, to whack at Nick's head, but the book glanced off him as he moved back.

As he pulled a knife from Duncan's belly.

'*No!*' she yelled.

She tried to hit him again, but he kicked out at her, hardly even bothering to look round, and she was flung against the back of the couch and could only watch as he stabbed Duncan again, in the chest . . . could only watch as Duncan collapsed to his knees, his eyes wide with shock, his hands pressed to his belly where blood was blooming crimson on his white T-shirt.

'Okay there, *Dad*?' Nick shouted, pulling out the knife and peering at the chest wound. 'That looks *nasty!*'

Duncan keeled over onto his side and Maggie scrambled across the carpet to him, she reached for him, but before she could get there Nick was grabbing at her, and she fought him, she thrashed and spat and she tried to bite him, but he was too strong. He lifted her like she was a child, and as she screamed, as she yelled Duncan's name, Nick slammed her to the floor and all the air went out her lungs.

She lay there, gasping like a landed fish, as Nick calmly tied her wrists behind her back with something. And then her ankles, and now she could see he was using blue twine.

Then all her attention was back on Duncan.

'Help him,' she got out, looking straight into Nick's eyes, searching there for something she knew she wouldn't find. 'He'll *die*. You need to – call – an *ambulance*.'

'Oh, right,' went Nick, standing back up, hands on hips, looking from Maggie to Duncan like he was surveying his handiwork. 'Is that what I need to do? Call an ambulance so they can save Dad's life?' He crossed the room in a couple of bounds and brought his face down next to Duncan's with a sickly smile. 'What do you think your life's worth to me now, *Dad*?' He spat the word at Duncan's grey face. Duncan, gasping for breath, stared back at Nick, and he tried to say something but just a gurgling came from his mouth and then he was coughing, coughing blood, and Nick jumped back.

'Ugh.'

'*Help him!*' Maggie wailed.

'You know, it's strange, isn't it, the difference twenty-two years make? Twenty-two years of being all alone because your dear daddy has buggered off and left you – left you to think he was *dead*? Weird, the difference that makes. Up until then, yeah, sure, if you'd been injured I'd have called an ambulance *pronto*, as you'd say, Mags. I'd have done everything I possibly could to save you. *I'd have died for you!*' The words came out on a sob.

Again, Duncan tried to say something.

'I thought you'd do the same for me – but no, turns out I was wrong about that. Turns out you don't love me at all.'

Duncan groaned.

'If you loved me, you wouldn't have *abandoned me*! Who does that? Who goes off and abandons their kid and makes it look like he killed them?'

'That wasn't Duncan!' went Maggie. 'That was me! He didn't know I'd set the place up . . . to look as if we'd not left voluntarily. To look as if you might have killed us.'

Nick turned to her. 'Really, Mags? Granted, the plods aren't the sharpest pencils in the box, but *really*? I was out all day with witnesses. I know you set it up to look like I'd done it while we were having breakfast, but a very early breakfast it would have to have been, to give me time to dispose of the bodies. And what sort of monster would kill his whole family and then go off for a nice day out in Edinburgh? Yes, the plods questioned me, but they never seriously suspected me. Weirdly, there were no fingerprints on that third mug, because I'm not a total idiot. I knew we'd cleared up the breakfast stuff. I thought you'd killed Dad and taken off with Isla and set those mugs up to try to implicate me – so I wiped my mug clean before the cops got there.'

Maggie must have grimaced, because he smiled.

'Their theory – and the irony is that *I* didn't accept it, you fooled *me* good and proper – was that you'd up and gone to get away from me, after what I did, or at least, from the plods' point of view, what *you thought I did* to Isla. They never bought your assertion that what happened with the pram was deliberate. But they reasoned you'd both got it in your heads that I was a danger to Isla and were shit-scared of what I might do next. They thought I'd caused your disappearance, but indirectly. What a turn-up that they were right.'

'Please, Nick,' Maggie begged. 'He always meant to come back for you! I know you still love him! If you've got *any feelings left* for him, you'll call an ambulance *now*!'

'Hmm.' Nick tapped a finger to his mouth. 'Let me think about that.' *Tap, tap, tap*, as Duncan's breathing became more and more laboured.

'*Please*,' Maggie sobbed, looking not at Nick now but at Duncan, capturing his unfocused gaze, willing him to hold on.

'Okay. I've thought. And the answer is . . .!' He made the words perky, like a game show host. '*No!* Whatever feelings I once had for you, Dad? *You've ripped them out and stamped all over them and kicked them to death!* So don't look at me like that. You've only yourself to blame. Now hurry up and die, because I don't want to have to stab you again. It's not like I'm a psychopath or something, eh, Mags?' He chuckled.

There was no hope.

None.

Of course there wasn't.

Maggie tuned Nick out. She concentrated only on Duncan, and as the blood left his body and he faded in front of her eyes, she lifted her voice and spoke only to him. 'That walk we did on Saturday up the hill, when we saw that wee frog in the grass, and the branches of the trees were all dancing away in the breeze – mind that? And I finally identified a dunnock disguised as a sparrow, and you said all I needed was the Fair Isle jumper and clipboard to make me a proper bird watcher, you cheeky bugger? And we had ourselves a wee paddle in the stream. And all the time I was wanting to say it but that's not me, I'm not a heart-on-her-sleeve kind of girl, am I? I was wanting to say you've given me a life. You've made me that happy, Duncan Clyde, and I think I'm not being too big-headed if I say I think I've made you happy too? Me and Isla. Oh aye, we've had a good life, you and me, and nothing's forever, eh? But we've had it good. We've had it so, so good, and I don't have to say it because you know you're the love of my life and I wouldn't change a thing.'

But he was gone.

He had gone, before he could hear her say it.

Now Nick was saying something. He was moving towards her. She made herself breathe, slow and even. She closed her eyes, and she took herself off on that walk up the hill with Duncan, to the wee frog and the dunnock and the stream flowing by.

. . .

BUT IT DIDN'T HAPPEN.

Nick said, 'How very touching,' and then he was pressing something into her palm, and when Maggie opened her eyes she saw it was the handle of the knife, the knife he had used to stab Duncan. She tried to pull her hand away but his hand was round hers, forcing her to grip the handle.

'Perfect,' he said cheerily, walking away from her and looking down at Duncan, head on one side. 'Just . . . here, I think.' He dropped the knife. 'And there would be a bit more stuff knocked around, I feel. You made it too easy for me, Mags.' He grabbed a shelf unit and pulled it over, books and ornaments tipping out onto the carpet. Then he pushed over a chair.

'A tragic sequence of events. Duncan wanted to reconcile with me, but evil stepmother Mags wouldn't let him. Things got a bit heated. You've always been so fucking *volatile*, Mags! You've always hated me for no reason and resented my closeness to Dad – so much so that you made out I was some kind of nutter and persuaded him to abandon me all those years ago. When you found him texting me, you smashed his phone. Where's Dad's phone?'

Dad. The word was all wrong on his lips.

'Never mind, I'm sure I can find it. In the bedroom charging?'

He was back in less than a minute with Duncan's phone, holding it by the edges. He bent to Duncan's body and took Duncan's hand in his gloved one.

'Ooh, goody, fingerprint recognition. Dad always did like a gadget.' He straightened; strolled to the couch. 'Okay. Let's see. I've left my phone in the house, switched on, so it should get this pronto, eh, Mags? *Nick. So sorry for everything. Can we talk tomorrow just us two?* Dad's old-school. Would spell out the "two". *Maggie went apeshit.* Or no, Dad doesn't swear. *Maggie went ballistic after you left. Don't come back here. I've locked myself in the loo. She was scaring me TBH. Going to try to calm her down. Let me know time and place if you want to meet. Dad.* Would he add a kiss? Probably, in the circumstances. Right. Perfect. Off it goes. It'll flash up on my screen, and there'll be nothing to say whether I was there to read it or not. The wonders of modern technology.'

He came back round the couch and dropped the phone on the floor, then picked up a chunky vase and brought it down hard on the screen.

'He tried to restrain you, to fight you off, which is when you hit your head on the door frame.'

He came back to where Maggie was lying and picked her up, quite gently, in his arms. He carried her to the door, and then he suddenly spun, whacking her head on the wooden frame.

Maggie's vision blurred as he carried her back across the room and dumped her down by the couch.

'You went for him. Killed him with the knife. Enter stage right the anxious stepson, having hot-footed it here after receiving a worrying text message from dear old Dad. I'm extremely concerned for his safety. And rightly so, as it turns out.' He picked up the vase, grimaced, and smashed it into his own face.

'Oof!'

Then he stooped to force Maggie's hand round the base of the vase. 'You went for me too, of course. Fortunately, that was an unequal contest! I had to restrain you and call an ambulance and then the cops. You don't mind if I use your phone, do you?'

He left the room and returned with her phone. 'I'll maybe leave it a while. Would take me what, fifteen, twenty minutes between receiving the text message and getting here and calling the emergency services?' He squatted down next to her. 'What kind of mother are you, killing Isla's dad and getting yourself banged up for murder, leaving her with no one?' He smiled into her eyes. 'No one but her big brother.'

'No,' went Maggie, her voice all hoarse. 'You leave Isla alone! What has she ever done to you?'

Nick seemed to consider the point. 'Get herself born?'

He stood, and walked to the smashed French doors.

Isla.

What would become of Isla? She would have no one now. No one but Nick, going up to her at the funeral, maybe, to explain everything in his convincing way.

He had thought it all through. That text message – oh aye, he'd planned it all. And there were witnesses to how over-joyed he and Duncan had been to be reunited. Michael might not cooperate, but the wife, Lulu, would tell the police how made-up dear Nick had been to see his da again. Probably give him an alibi too.

A few feet away from Nick was the coffee table with Maggie's laptop on it. He had only to open it, guess her pass-word – why the fuck had she gone for Isla1997? – and there would be Isla's life laid out in front of him. Her network of friends, all those posts about uni, about Sweden ...

'Yvonne.' She had to stop him thinking about Isla. 'What have you done to her?'

'Oh, Yvonne made a *very* silly mistake. At the time of your disappearance, she was supposedly at the Agricultural Marketing UK Conference. But when she came to dinner a few days ago, she'd obviously forgotten what she'd said before. She claimed to have been at the Technologies for Small Businesses Conference. *Wrong!*' He grinned. 'She underestimated my memory. Everything that happened at that time is seared into my brain, Mags. Understandably enough, I think you'd agree? I always suspected she might know something, and her unnecessary lie about the confer-ence supported that conclusion. Okay, so she could have forgotten which conference she was at, but why not just say so if that was the case? Why lie about it? So, I put a tracker on her car. Followed her to Craibstone Wood on one of the bikes from Sunnyside. Confronted her, just as she was putting on her walking boots.' He paused. 'Tried to get her to tell me what had happened that day, but the stupid bitch fought me. Correction – she *tried* to fight me. Before I knew it, she was dead, having told me precisely nothing. But no matter. It's all worked out in the end.'

'What did you do with her?'

'With the body? Slung it in the boot of her car, drove a few miles to the river, chucked her in there. Maybe she'll wash up somewhere, but there won't be anything on the body to indicate murder. Actually, it wasn't murder. I didn't want her dead, did I? Not before she'd told me what I wanted to know, anyway. I hit her too hard, Mags, but that was her own fault for cutting up rough. I don't think the police will suspect suspicious circumstances even if they find her. She could just as easily have tripped on the riverbank, having extended her usual walk by a few miles, and hit her head. Fallen in. But I doubt she'll be found now. Probably halfway to Ireland.' He nodded. 'She helped you get away, didn't she? Stupid bitch.'

'Yvonne was a really good person.' For some reason, Maggie felt she had to say it. 'She didn't deserve that.'

Nick raised his eyebrows.

He crossed the room to Duncan's body. He dropped to his knees, pressing his fingers to first one wound and then the other. Then to Duncan's neck. Then he rolled him onto his back and – *oh Jesus!* – brought his lips down on Duncan's mouth.

He placed his palm on the bloody chest and pushed, like he was performing compressions.

'Oh, dear. A hopeless case.' He stood and looked down at Maggie's phone. He wasn't wearing the gloves any more.

'Right, time to make that call.' He put the phone to his ear, and his face suddenly changed as he put on a look of shock and tears came into his eyes. '*Ambulance!*' he yelled. 'Please, *ambulance!*' And then he was giving it, 'My dad's been stabbed! My stepmother – she's *killed him*! Please, I need an ambulance. I've tried to bring him back, but – but . . . No, I don't think he's breathing. I tried doing first aid on him. Yes. Okay. But his chest – he's been stabbed in the chest . . . No, I think there's blood in his airway –'

And suddenly there was someone else in the room.

Maggie had forgotten her name.

The airhead lassie that was married to Nick. She must have stepped through the smashed door, and now she was taking in the scene, her eyes flicking from Maggie to Duncan to Nick.

'Oh God!' The lassie pushed past Nick; dropped to her knees at Duncan's side; put a hand, without flinching, to his neck.

'Lulu!' Nick's eyes widened, now, in real shock. And then he was speaking into the phone again: 'And we need the police too. I forgot to say, we need the police. I've tied her up, but . . . Yes. Okay, yes, I'll do that. My wife is here. Can I hand you over to her?'

He shoved the phone at Lulu and dropped to Duncan's side.

'He killed him!' Maggie got out. 'He killed Duncan!'

But the lassie, Lulu, was speaking into the phone. 'I'm trained in first aid. I'll do it. I'm going to hand you back to my husband. Nick . . .' She put her fingers into Duncan's mouth. 'Nick, take the phone. Tell me what they're saying.'

'You can help him?' Maggie got out.

Oh, please, let her not be an airhead.

Let her be able to save him.

Nick's hand was trembling convincingly as he took the

phone from Lulu. 'Right,' he said after listening to the person on the other end. 'She's doing that. You're trying to clear the obstruction?'

Lulu nodded.

'Now you have to tip his head back . . . Oh God, oh God. *Dad!*' And now into the phone: 'I've already tried that!' And to Lulu: 'Chest compressions. Thirty compressions and then two rescue breaths. Do you know how to do that?'

But Lulu was already doing it, deftly, her eyes focused on Duncan's face.

'She's doing it,' he said into the phone. 'My wife knows how to do it. But please – they need to hurry! He's not responding! Is he, Lu? Is he responding?'

'No,' she said shortly, not looking away from Duncan.

'This is all my fault, Lulu!' Nick choked. 'Dad sent me a text message saying he'd locked himself in the loo and she'd gone haywire. I didn't think, I just came straight here. I should have replied, I should have told him to stay in the loo! By the time I got here, she had the knife and she was threatening him with it, but when I – when I smashed the door to get in, she stabbed him! She just – she pushed the knife into his stomach, and before I could get to them, she'd done it again. Look, there, in his chest! Oh God, Lulu, *she's killed him for real this time!*'

'I *knew* he was in danger!' Nick sobbed, as Lulu continued with the compressions. 'I could *see* how angry she was! I could *see* she was furious that we were being reconciled. I should never have left him alone with her! Oh God, Lu, *is he dead?*'

Lulu said nothing.

She couldn't think straight. After that frantic cycle through the dark landscape, to be confronted by this, this scene of horror –

All she could focus on was this man under her, this man whose life could depend on her keeping a cool head. She had learned first aid as a teenager and taken refresher courses regularly, but she'd never had to do it for real.

She knew he was dead.

She knew he wasn't responding.

But still, she had to try.

By the time the paramedics arrived, two big, capable men, Lulu was close to collapse. She let Nick put an arm round her and guide her to a chair. 'I'll get you a glass of water.'

She watched as one of the paramedics continued the

compressions while the other checked Duncan for vital signs and then bent over Maggie, untying her wrists and ankles and helping her sit up. Maggie, all the while, watched Duncan.

More men arrived, the police this time, just as the paramedic who had been performing the compressions sat back on his heels and looked at his watch. 'Twelve-forty-three.'

'Oh God, oh God, no!' Nick dropped the glass of water he was carrying and went to Duncan. *'No! Dad!'*

'I'm sorry. He didn't make it,' the other paramedic said gently, a hand on Nick's shoulder. 'We're going to take him in the ambulance.'

'I want to come!'

The other paramedic had been having a whispered conversation with the policemen. Both policemen were in their mid-thirties, she guessed. One had red hair in a short back and sides style and close-set eyes, while the other was a bit of a pin-up with boyish hair and regular features. The red-haired one said, 'I'm sorry, but no one can leave just yet.' And he nodded to the paramedics.

When they had left with Duncan's body, he said, 'I'm PC Collins and this is PC Webb. I must ask you to remain where you are and not touch anything. You're all going to have to come to the station to give statements. Our colleagues are on their way, and when they get here we'll transport you there.'

'She killed him! She's *killed my dad!*' Nick yelled, pointing a trembling finger at Maggie. 'She couldn't stand it that he was finally reaching out to me. And so *she killed him!*'

Lulu stared dully at Nick. She had felt it so deep within her, almost the first time she'd met him: a connection. Something she'd never felt with any other human being. It hadn't just been that they were on the same wavelength, it had been as if their thoughts were perfectly synched, the peaks and troughs of the waves exactly matched.

All that had been nothing but a mirage?

'I didn't,' was all Maggie said.

She looked so small, somehow shrunken from the last time Lulu had seen her. She sat, her back against the sofa, her legs in dark navy jeans stuck out in front of her. She was wearing, incongruously, pink fluffy slippers, which just made her seem all the more vulnerable and pathetic.

The policemen were looking from Nick to Maggie, obviously weighing things up, trying to get their heads round what had happened here.

Which was the perpetrator and which was the innocent bystander?

34

'Check her record!' Nick was going. 'She's been in prison for GBH! Oh God, I knew she was dangerous and I knew she was angry with Dad, I knew she was furious with him, and I *left him here with her alone!*'

'Okay, sir. We'll get all your statements in due course.'

'She poisoned Dad against me. She even tried to set up their disappearance to make it look like I'd killed them! Left her own blood on the floor. Left the cooker on, as if something had suddenly happened. Put a third mug and bowl on the table to place me there. She wanted me *convicted of their murders!* She's a *fucking nutter!*' And suddenly, convincingly, Nick was sobbing. 'You were always jealous of me taking Dad's attention away from you, weren't you, Maggie? We were always so close, and you couldn't stand that. And now, you couldn't bear us being back together. They were having a huge row about it when we left.' He looked across the room at his wife. 'Weren't they?'

The airhead looked blank, and a kick of anger went through Maggie.

Nick had just *killed Duncan*.

And here was his wee airhead wife, along for the ride.

'No,' went Maggie. 'He's twisting everything.'

The good-looking cop spoke for the first time, eyeballing Lulu. 'Do *you* know what happened here?'

His colleague frowned. Likely this was against protocol. Likely they were meant to keep the questions until later, until they were at the station under controlled conditions where their statements could be recorded and each of them questioned separately, so their stories could be compared.

'This is my wife,' went Nick. 'She got here just after Maggie stabbed him – she didn't see anything.'

'Okay,' said the red-haired cop. 'You'll all get the chance to tell us your versions of what happened once we're at the station and –'

'I did see what happened,' Lulu's voice suddenly rang out. 'I got here just in time to see him stab Duncan. Nick. My husband. Maggie was already tied up. It was Nick who killed Duncan.' And she turned to Nick, and Maggie registered, just for a split second, the cold calculation in the lassie's eyes.

It all happened too fast for the cops to do anything.

'What the *fuck*?' Nick roared. 'You fucking *bitch*!'

He swooped on the knife that still lay on the floor where Duncan's body had been. And then he had leapt across the room at Lulu, his arm raised to bring the knife down, but with surprising speed she had dodged him, and he stumbled, and she was across the room, away from him, and at last, at last, *at last*, the policemen had hold of him, were overpowering him, disarming him, yanking his arms behind his back to snap on the cuffs.

At last.

35

LULU - JANUARY 2020

The courtroom of the High Court of Justiciary in Edinburgh smelt of wood polish and carpet cleaner. From the grand, classical exterior, Lulu had expected a grand, classical, lofty courtroom, but it was a relatively small, low-ceilinged space furnished like an office, with blond wood and lots of computers, and a navy-blue carpet and chairs. As she made her way slowly from the door to the witness stand, it struck her that this ordinary setting was all wrong for the 'solemn proceedings', as they called trials in the High Court, being played out in it. For the things Lulu was going to have to say.

The room, as the advocate depute had briefed her, contained the jury – fifteen people, in Scotland – the Lord Commissioner of Justiciary, the advocate depute or prosecutor and his assistant, the defence advocate and her assistant, the clerk and other court staff, and the media and 'rubberneckers', as he'd put it, in the public gallery.

And, of course, the accused.

She could feel Nick's eyes on her, on her swollen belly, as she stepped into the box and turned to face the court, but she didn't look at him. She looked at the public gallery where her parents and brothers were sitting alongside Isla, Maggie and Michael.

They all gave her encouraging smiles.

Mr Oliphant, the advocate depute, took her through the events leading up to Yvonne's disappearance and Duncan's murder, and as she detailed her brief marriage to Nick it was as if she were talking about someone else, a man she had loved who had himself disappeared.

'And now, Ms Tidwell, if you could tell us what happened on 25 June last year.'

As the lie approached, Lulu could feel all the 'tells' assailing her – shortness of breath as the fight or flight response kicked in, making it difficult to speak more than a few words at a time; a desire to put her hand to her mouth in a subconscious attempt to cover up the lie; a need to blink more.

This, though, was one of the advantages of a knowledge of psychology. As she spoke the actual lie, as she told the court how she'd arrived at Rose Cottage and seen her husband stab his father, she made a supreme effort to centre herself, to keep her hands folded in front of her, to regulate her breathing, not to blink too much. At one point she had to catch herself up, stop herself repeating, 'He stabbed him in the stomach.' A huge tell was that liars tended to repeat important phrases in a subconscious effort to ram the lie home. And people listening to them could subconsciously pick up on that.

Thank goodness she didn't need to worry about her story matching whatever Maggie, the previous witness, had said. Quick-thinking Maggie had told the police, when first questioned, that she'd been out of it when Nick had killed Duncan, or at least extremely woozy and not aware of what was happening. And she'd stuck to that ever since. She had

realised, she'd told Lulu later, that her account of the stabbing could well contradict whatever Lulu said. So it was safer
just to say she'd been out of it.

'She's lying!' Nick suddenly shouted from the dock, and
Lulu didn't have to fake the shock that went through her, one
hand going instinctively to her stomach as, at last, their
eyes met.

He had jumped up from his seat and was being restrained
by two burly men, one on either side of him, but he was
looking straight at Lulu.

The silent message he sent her, as their gazes locked, was
unmistakable.

'OH MY GOD, *Lulu*, you were *brilliant!*' Isla ran at Lulu in the
corridor outside the courtroom and caught her up in a hug,
and Lulu closed her eyes and breathed in the essence of
young person, the light scent Isla used, the sweets she'd been
surreptitiously popping in the courtroom, orange blossom
and cherries and summer days in the sun.

'Was I okay?' Lulu muttered.

'You were more than *okay!*' Isla had a soft Welsh accent
that Lulu could listen to forever. And a soft heart to match. It
was almost impossible to think of her as Nick's sister, and
Lulu preferred not to. She preferred to think of Isla purely as
Maggie and Duncan's daughter and the lovely soon-to-be
auntie of her own child who would also, in Lulu's mind, have
nothing to do with Nick but be Duncan's grandchild. 'And
when he shouted at you,' Isla went on, 'and you sort of
flinched and put your hand on your belly, you should have
seen Mr Oliphant's face! He was made up! And the defence
woman, she was spitting feathers!'

Then Mum and Dad and Dennis and John were hugging
her too, and Mum was fussing, guiding her along the corridor

and out into the freezing January air, and chiding her for not being able immediately to find her gloves, as if Lulu were still a child. And Dad took her arm as they made their way down the historic High Street of Edinburgh's Old Town to the café where they'd booked a table for lunch.

Maggie and Michael were coming along behind, deep in conversation, and Isla was running back and forth between the two groups like an eager puppy. The thought reminded Lulu of Milo. She hoped he was okay.

'Does it seem like I'm enjoying this too much?' Isla said, as if reading Lulu's mind, as the two of them stood studying their reflections in the mirrors of the café's loo. Isla looked nothing like Nick, thank God, apart from her height. She was tall, with Maggie's strong nose, but where Maggie was, as she said herself, no oil painting, Isla's features were in proportion, with those huge green eyes and wide cheekbones. She had the striking looks of a model, completely at odds with her bouncy, rather gauche personality. She seemed much younger than twenty-three.

'Oh, I'm going to enjoy it too, now that's out of the way,' said Lulu, using a damp tissue to wipe the make-up from her sweaty face. 'It's been a long time coming.'

Isla sighed. 'But, I mean – this is my brother's trial for murdering my dad and my auntie!'

'Half-brother,' said Lulu.

'I thought it would be really traumatic, you know? Hearing it all over again, what he did to Dad. But I've been playing it over and over in my head for so long, it's like – hey, nothing new. You know? Every single hour of every single day, I'm there, in that cottage – even though I *wasn't* there – seeing Dad . . .' Her mouth wobbled.

Lulu nodded.

Isla took a breath. 'It's like, finally, everyone else is hearing about it, the jury are hearing what he did. The whole world knows now. It's like, I don't know . . . Oh God, I'm not going to say *closure!*'

'But it is. Of course it is. He's being brought to justice. You have to . . .' Lulu stopped and looked at this girl who was rapidly becoming one of her best friends. 'You have to try to consign those images, those thoughts of what happened to your dad, to the past. I – I wouldn't be able to offer you therapy myself – we can't treat family – but I can point you in the direction of a couple of really good people.'

And thoughts of Paul suddenly came into her head.

She'd been having nightmares about Paul, about what must have happened when Nick arrived at his door, having found out his address, presumably, by snooping through the files on Lulu's laptop. She should have known that it was all wrong, the idea that Paul would have killed himself *in front of Milo*. He'd have found another home for the little dog he adored, surely, before doing it, or at the very least have left him with a friend.

The police in London were putting together a case against Nick. He'd been caught on CCTV a couple of streets from Paul's house on the morning of his death. It was hoped that there would be enough evidence for another trial. And they were looking again, too, at the sudden deaths of two of his girlfriends. The police in the Borders were also re-examining Dean Reid's murder in the light of what Andy Jardine had told them about being forced by Nick to provide him with a false alibi.

'Aw, thanks, Lulu!' Isla reached out to touch Lulu's arm. 'You're the best!' But she was looking at Lulu in the way Lulu was beginning to know well.

'Out with it.'

'It's just . . . you know, Mum? I think Mum . . . she had bad experiences with counselling and stuff when she was young, and it's kind of put her off. But if *you* were the one suggesting it and recommending someone . . . I think she needs to talk to someone about Dad. About Nick. About everything. Probably Michael does too. In a way, it's worse for him, isn't it, not even having Auntie Yvonne's body?'

'When Nick's been convicted and sent away, it'll be better for both of them. But yes, I'm sure they would benefit from therapy. The right kind of therapy.'

They returned to the court house to hear the start of the case for the defence. As the doors were opened, the others filed in, but Maggie drew Lulu to one side, beyond a seating area and a big potted fern.

Maggie was neat and smart in a navy skirt and jacket and a white silk blouse. As the last witness for the prosecution, Lulu hadn't been in court to hear Maggie's testimony, but Mum had told her that Maggie had stood up to the defence advocate's cross-examination with quiet dignity. When the advocate had suggested that Maggie, not Nick, had killed Duncan, Maggie had said she might have a chequered past, but thanks to Duncan she had turned her life around and would hope no one would judge a respectable woman in her fifties on what she'd done as a troubled teenager who'd been abused as a child.

Now, Maggie fixed Lulu with a hard stare.

'You didn't know he had done it,' she said in a low voice. 'When you arrived at Rose Cottage. You couldn't have *known* that Nick killed Duncan. He'd set it up that carefully. The ruse with the text message, telling you Duncan had messaged him saying I'd gone psycho – you couldn't have known he was lying. He was dead convincing. And he was your husband, for fuck's sake.'

Lulu considered what to say. 'I was pretty sure.'

'Aye, but even so. You were taking a massive risk, eh, accusing him in front of the police, when *you could have been wrong*? You could have been condemning an innocent man, and not just any innocent man. Your own fucking husband that you *fucking loved*, God help you. There was more to it, aye?'

Maggie was sharp all right.

'It was a test,' Lulu admitted. 'Denouncing him like that was a test. I knew how obsessed he was with Duncan. And he was obsessed with me too, wanting me all to himself like I was his possession. When he found out that Duncan wasn't dead, that you hadn't killed him like he thought – it turned his world upside down. The fact that his beloved dad had abandoned him, rejected him, betrayed him, as he saw it . . . it was completely devastating for him. I thought, if the only other person he loved betrayed him in the same way . . .'

'If you rejected him the way Duncan had done, he wouldn't be able to stop himself going for you?'

'That was the test,' Lulu agreed. 'If he was innocent, if he hadn't killed Duncan, he wouldn't react that way. He'd be shocked and upset, but he wouldn't –'

'Try to kill you.'

'He couldn't control himself.' Lulu shuddered. 'He snapped. I guess he just couldn't understand what he had done to deserve such treatment from the only two people he had ever loved.'

Maggie, she realised, was holding onto her composure by a thread.

'You're a fucking psychologist,' she said tightly. 'Oh, you're full of all the answers now. I'm sure you've analysed it half to death. Just like that daft psychiatrist we took Nick to right before he murdered Dean and tried to murder Isla. *Oh, nothing to worry about, Mr and Mrs Clyde. Nick's only problem, as far as I can see, is the common wee bint he's got for a stepmother.*' Maggie nodded. 'That was the gist of it. I've emailed that bastard Jamie Stirling-Stewart, going on about how I'm going to report him for professional negligence, and

I'll maybe go to the press and all.' She smiled grimly. 'Emailed me right back grovelling – oh aye, full of apologies now, but he didn't think to try and contact me, did he, when Nick was all over the media? Thought he'd got away with it, the fucker.'

Lulu felt a momentary pang of sympathy for the psychiatrist.

Maggie focused her attention back on Lulu. 'How come you didn't rumble him sooner? You were in denial, I suppose, like Duncan was. Love does that to you, eh?' And her face changed. 'Fuck. Sorry.'

'It's okay,' Lulu said wearily. 'That's all gone. It's all gone as if it never was, what I felt for him. That Nick wasn't real. He was playing a part, I think, right from the start. I think he must have seen me in Ithaca and for some reason fixated on me. Apparently, it was a lie, what he told me about stuff going missing from that guest house, about the owners being dodgy. One of my brothers emailed the police there to ask about it. There's never been any trouble there before. We think Nick must have broken into my room and stolen all my stuff. Then he lay in wait and followed me around as I tried to find a police station; followed me to the taverna. Threw himself into the role of my knight in shining armour.'

None of it had been true, she supposed. He didn't have her weird sense of humour. He hadn't made up stories about people when he was a teenager. He probably didn't even like falafels.

'Aye, that sounds like the Nick I know.'

Lulu swallowed. She still found herself thinking *Nick would love this* if something entertainingly surreal happened. She'd never admit it to anyone, but part of her still loved *that* Nick, the mirage, and missed him like crazy. But she had to stop thinking like that. The mirage had been so dangerous in so many ways. 'And the one *I* know, now. Now I'm seeing him clearly. Now I'm seeing –'

'The psychopath,' Maggie supplied.

'Yes. I suppose so. Everything he said, everything he did – I can see behind it, now. Like his obsession with the Romans, who were so civilised and yet so savage. So *inventively* savage. He used to talk about what they did to people in the arena. I think he enjoyed all that.' She swallowed. 'Although – in my defence, he's not a classic psychopath. Karla, one of my old professors at uni, she's been very supportive, but she's also . . . well, to tell the truth, she's alarmingly enthusiastic about the fact that Nick could represent a rare psychopath subtype.' Lulu smiled. 'She can't help herself. She wants to write a paper with me when I'm back in Australia.'

The penthouse apartment had been sold, and Lulu had netted just over three million in the divorce settlement. For the moment, she was renting a cottage near Maggie and Isla in Wales. Better for a dog than London. Lulu had gone straight to the dog shelter after Nick's arrest and got Milo out of there. He had been so pathetically glad to see her, wriggling around her legs like he didn't know what to do with himself. She had picked him up in her arms and wept.

Maggie and Isla had fallen in love with him too, and he was spoilt rotten. He adored their smallholding, particularly the hay barn, where he spent many happy hours snuffling around attempting to look like a proper country dog – but if a mouse or, as on one memorable occasion, a rat happened to show itself, Milo was out of there like greased lightning, much to Isla's amusement.

But best of all were the long winter nights when Milo and Lulu snuggled on the sofa in front of a roaring log-burner in her little cottage, often with Maggie and/or Isla for company – and for a few days before the trial had started, her whole family had descended, squeezing themselves into the room with much hilarity. Mum said the cosy scene had almost converted her to bad British weather.

The plan was for Mum to stay with Lulu after the trial until she'd had the baby, and then Mum, Lulu, baby and Milo would return to Leonora. 'Plenty galahs in Leonora need therapy, love,' as Dad had put it.

Milo would love Braemar Station.

She hoped he was okay now, staying for the duration of the trial with a friend of Maggie's. The friend had an assertive cat which despised poor Milo.

'A rare subtype?' Maggie repeated sceptically.

'Rare because he can form attachments. He genuinely did feel something approaching love – for Duncan, for me. Only, it was warped. It was all about him.'

'Then it wasn't love, was it?' Maggie looked off, and Lulu knew she was thinking about Duncan. 'Real love is all about the other person.'

Lulu nodded slowly. 'When he was so worried for my safety in London, at Sunnyside, he kept saying he couldn't lose me too. You're right. He wasn't thinking of *me*, he wasn't worried for *me*. He was worried for himself and how my death would affect him. The emotion was all about him. Maybe there was no actual empathy involved.' Part of her, the scientific, objective part, felt a little surge of enthusiasm of her own, wondering if Karla had thought of that and hoping she hadn't, hoping this could be her own insight.

'Spot on,' said Maggie. 'What he felt for you, for Duncan – it was all about *him* and getting what he wanted. Duncan spoilt him rotten, so Nick latched onto him – had a warped obsession with him, aye. But is that really *attachment*?'

Lulu hesitated. But Maggie needed to hear this. 'Karla thinks he could represent a particularly dangerous subtype of psychopath, because of the attachment thing. The combination of complete self-centredness and deep emotion...'

Maggie suddenly turned away from Lulu, gripping the strap of her shoulder bag, and Lulu reached out to her; took her into her arms. For a moment, Maggie was stiff in Lulu's embrace, and then she slumped against her.

'You've carried so much,' said Lulu quietly. 'You've been so strong.'

Maggie soon recovered herself, pulling away and adjusting the front of her jacket. 'Aye, well, I've had to be.'

'He's going to prison. Probably for the rest of his life. For multiple counts of murder. He can't hurt any of us now.'

Maggie looked at her. 'Don't kid yourself, Lulu. Wherever he is, even if they lock him up in maximum security and throw away the key, none of us will ever be safe while that man is alive.'

EPILOGUE
NICK - JULY 2020

I t was a good photograph of Lulu, who looked a million dollars even in that simple white shift dress. A good photograph, and a recent one, judging by the size of the baby sitting on her lap. Christopher Duncan Tidwell, she'd called him, without any consultation whatsoever, although this was *his fucking son*.

She'd gone back to her maiden name.

He'd found that out at the trial.

But this was *his son*.

He had the photo pinned to the cork board above his bed, and, in the fifteen minutes before lights out, he had got into the habit of lying here looking at it and running things over in his head.

But the time for planning was past.

He reached up to touch her lovely face.

'See you soon, Lu.'

His son was a fine-looking baby, sturdy and confident, beaming gummily at the camera, which would have been wielded, he supposed, by one of Lulu's Neanderthal family. The two of them were sitting out on the verandah at Braemar

Station with a scruffy small dog at Lulu's feet, and although they were in the shade, the boy had a little sunhat on and the light beyond the verandah was fierce, even though this would be their winter.

Lulu didn't do social media any more, but no one could stay off the internet entirely. One of her many aunties – Auntie Win, a big, loud, ugly woman he remembered all too well from the wedding – had posted the photo on Instagram with the comment, *My gorgeous niece and great-nephew, Christopher Duncan!*

Christopher Duncan Tidwell was a loser's name.

Christopher, for God's sake!

He just didn't get why Lulu had done it. Why she'd betrayed him like that. Perjured herself, even, to put him away.

The bitch.

The absolute *bitch*.

But she could wait. First, there was the little matter of Maggie. Or rather, Isla.

The best punishment he could think of for Maggie, for Lulu, was to lose their children. Just like he'd lost his entire fucking family.

See how they liked it!

He'd got hold of Dad and Maggie's new names right after Lulu had dropped her bombshell, had told him his family were alive and well and staying at a place called Rose Cottage. He'd contacted the agency responsible for letting the place, pretending to be the homeowner, whose name was all over the internet because the silly bastard blogged about what a holiday let guru he was. Nick had made out that he wanted to check the names of the people currently in the cottage as someone had emailed him purporting to be the guests, but he had his doubts.

And it had been child's play to trace Teresa and Isla Black.

While he'd still been on remand, he'd employed a private investigator, a dodgy old guy recommended by a fellow inmate, to find out all about them. It seemed that Isla had left university and was back on the smallholding with Maggie. They had started a joint venture supplying local restaurants with baked goods and organic produce.

Too, too easy.

So.

Do away with Isla.

Then off to Australia. Get his son. Take him to the Bahamas. Nick had secreted a few million in an account there, more than enough to fund a lifetime of ease for himself and his boy. He'd rename him. What, he hadn't decided yet. But not a loser's name like Christopher. Something strong but not naff. A traditional name. Maybe Alexander. Or he could go with the Scottish tradition of using a surname as a first name. He liked Kerr.

They couldn't be Clyde, of course.

LC, the guy in the cell next door who'd become Nick's fixer, just below Nick himself in the D Wing hierarchy, had contacts on the outside who would set him up with a new identity. He would try to keep the name Nick, but he wasn't wedded to it.

He looked at his watch.

Five minutes to lights out.

He shut his eyes. Best to get some kip while he could.

It was going to be a crazy twenty-four hours.

THE KEY TURNED in the lock of the cell door, and LC's low, growly voice said in the dark, 'Let's go.'

How LC had got the keys to his own cell door and to Nick's, Nick didn't know or care. He pulled the holdall from under his bed, which he'd packed surreptitiously, bit by bit, throughout the day. As instructed, he was wearing dark clothing, even down to a pair of black trainers he'd swapped with another guy last week for cigarettes.

'We've got five minutes,' LC hissed. 'Keep close.'

Nick followed him out onto the walkway around what they called – ironically, surely – the atrium, as if it were a feature in a snazzy hotel. For a musclebound guy, LC moved fast, whipping round the corner and down the stairs and through a door that led to a long, dimly lit corridor.

They met no one.

The screws were lazy fat bastards at the best of times, but he imagined that LC had ensured they weren't intercepted by throwing around some of the ten grand Nick had transferred to his bank account.

The laundry was close and stifling, even at this time of night. It stank of cheap washing powder and sweat. The sheets were never quite clean. They all smelt of some hairy bastard's crotch.

LC didn't put on the light. He flicked on a torch, and in its glow Nick saw his face for the first time, the scar on his eyebrow, the snake tattoos on his thick neck. He always felt there was something familiar about LC, but he couldn't place him. He'd probably seen his ugly mug in coverage of the man's trial, although he didn't know what he was in for. In here, you didn't ask that kind of question.

Not that Nick would have had a hope of keeping quiet what he himself had been convicted for, even if he'd wanted to. Trial of the decade, they'd called it. But he had no problem with that. Being a serial killer carried a certain cachet. It would have been different if he'd killed kids, but all his victims had been adults. Dean had been nineteen. Perfectly acceptable.

LC was looking at his watch.

There was a diversion organised for 2:30 am exactly. Nick

glanced at his own watch. Two minutes to go. He had to hand it to LC, he was a fine *aide de camp*.

'Okay,' LC grunted. 'Soon as the alarm goes, I'll open the fire escape and you leg it. There'll be a rope ladder over the wall approximately fifty metres from the east side of C Wing. Over there.' He pointed.

Nick nodded. 'Thanks, LC. Who knows, if this goes smoothly, there might be a little something extra for you in your account.'

LC grunted. ''Preciate it.'

Silence, as Nick watched the minute hand of his watch move around the dial.

'I knew your old man,' LC said suddenly. 'I was one of the young offenders he tried to rehabilitate.'

So that was why he looked familiar.

In the eerie light of the torch, LC grinned reminiscently, revealing a gold-capped tooth. 'He was onto a loser there, right enough.'

'Evidently.' Nick laughed. 'Stupid bastard. I thought your face was vaguely familiar, but I don't remember you. I suppose it was over twenty years ago.'

LC walked to the fire door and eased it open, standing just inside it. The night air rushed in. 'I was Liam then. Changed to LC when I came inside. Sounds harder, you know? Aye, Duncan and Maggie were amazing. I thought the world of them. They were the only folk in my life who ever actually cared about me – them and Pam, Maggie's pal who worked in the coffee shop when she was on maternity with Isla.'

Oh fuck.

'Maggie and Duncan were like the mum and dad I never had.'

Before Nick could step back, LC had grabbed his jumper.

'I let them down, but at least I can do this for them, eh?'

Nick felt a sensation like a punch to his chest, but as he looked down he saw the man's tattooed fist holding a knife. A knife with blood all over the blade. A knife he'd just pulled out of Nick's chest.

'You *piece of shit!*' LC spat in his face.

All the strength suddenly seemed to leave Nick's body.

As he collapsed to the hard concrete floor, LC leant over him. Brought his mouth close to Nick's ear. Spoke three words, clearly and succinctly.

'Maggie says hi.'

FROM JANE

I have always been fascinated by the story of the *Mary Celeste* – the abandoned sailing ship found adrift, with no one on board and no signs of disturbance. Among the people who vanished were the captain, his wife and their small daughter. What happened to them? Why did they abandon a perfectly sound and seaworthy ship? It's still a mystery.

In *The Stepson*, I had lots of fun thinking of reasons for (almost) a whole family to vanish in similarly baffling circumstances. I hope you also had fun working out what had happened and why.

Many thanks are due to Brian Lynch for brainstorming ideas and knocking the plot into shape with his usual good humour and patience, and to the rest of the brilliant team at Inkubator Books for turning the manuscript into a real, actual book and sending it out into the world, a process that never ceases to give me a thrill. Many thanks also to Lesley McLaren and Lucy Lawrie for all their suggestions, which greatly improved the story and characters and made me think of problems that had never occurred to me before, such as how difficult it would be to fall out of a window (thanks, Lesley – a galleried landing is much better!).

Thanks also to my family and friends for continuing to be so encouraging about this strange thing I do, disappearing into imaginary worlds at every opportunity.

Most of all, thank *you* for choosing to spend a few hours with my characters in *The Stepson*. I would love to know what you thought of it. You can contact me via my website at https://www.janerenshaw.co.uk

Finally, reviews are so important to us authors. I would be very grateful if you could spend a moment to write an honest review (no matter how short) on Amazon. They really do help get the word out.

ALSO BY JANE RENSHAW

INKUBATOR TITLES

THE CHILD WHO NEVER WAS

WATCH OVER ME

NO PLACE LIKE HOME

THE STEPSON

JANE'S OTHER TITLES

THE TIME AND PLACE

THE SWEETEST POISON